Why Shoot a Butler?
Georgette Heyer

BANTAM BOOKS
TORONTO · NEW YORK · LONDON

*This low-priced Bantam Book
has been completely reset in a type face
designed for easy reading, and was printed
from new plates. It contains the complete
text of the original hard-cover edition.*
NOT ONE WORD HAS BEEN OMITTED.

WHY SHOOT A BUTLER?

*A Bantam Book / published by arrangement with
Doubleday & Company, Inc.*

PRINTING HISTORY

*Doubleday, Doran edition for The Crime Club, Inc.
published February 1936*

Serialized in England in WOMAN'S PICTORIAL

Bantam edition January 1970
2nd printing .... January 1970
3rd printing .... February 1970
4th printing .... May 1970
5th printing ..... October 1970
6th printing ...... August 1977

ISBN 0-553-10598-1

Published simultaneously in the United States and Canada

*Bantam Books are published by Bantam Books, Inc. Its trade-
mark, consisting of the words "Bantam Books" and the por-
trayal of a bantam, is registered in the United States Patent
Office and in other countries. Marca Registrada. Bantam
Books, Inc., 666 Fifth Avenue, New York, New York 10019.*

PRINTED IN THE UNITED STATES OF AMERICA

TO

One Who Knows Why

FOREWORD

THERE IS, and always has been, a lamentable lack of humorous mystery stories. Undoubtedly this is due to the fact that the injection of humour into the detective story almost inevitably destroys the fundamental elements of this type of fiction: suspense and mystery. To combine successfully mirth, mystery and suspense is one of the most difficult technical feats in writing, and only occasionally does an author appear who possesses the qualities necessary to the accomplishment of this feat.

Georgette Heyer is such a one. Her *Merely Murder* was as hilarious as it was mystifying, and this book is equally excellent. She seems to possess a secret formula not given to the ordinary writers of detective fiction. What the trick is I can only guess, but I suspect that it works as readily as it does because she is intelligent enough to draw on character, rather than on situation, for her humour. However that may be, I am sure that her work is unique and that because of the two aspects of her novels, hilarity and homicide, her work is doubly entertaining.

J. W. P.

CHAPTER I

THE SIGNPOST was unhelpful. Some faint characters on one of its blistered arms informed the seeker after knowledge that Lumsden lay to the west, reached, presumably, at the end of a dubious-looking lane. The other arm indicated the direction of Pittingly, a place Mr. Amberley had never heard of. However, if Lumsden lay to the west, Upper Nettlefold ought to be found somewhere in the direction of the obscure Pittingly. Mr. Amberley switched off his spot-lamp, and swung the car round, reflecting savagely that he should have known better than to have trusted to his cousin Felicity's enthusiastic but incomplete directions. If he had had the sense to follow the usual road he would have been at Greythorne by now. As it was, Felicity's "short way" had already made him late for dinner.

He drove on rather cautiously down a bumpy lane flanked by quickset hedges. Wreaths of autumn mist curled across the road and further exasperated him. He passed a road winding off to the left, but it looked unpromising, and he bore on towards Pittingly.

The lane twisted and turned its way through the Weald. There were apparently no houses on it, nor did Pittingly— a place towards which Mr. Amberley was fast developing an acute dislike—materialize. He glanced at his watch and swore gently. It was already some minutes after eight. He pressed his foot down on the accelerator and the long powerful Bentley shot forward, bounding over the rough surface in a way that was very bad for Mr. Amberley's temper.

Pittingly seemed to be destined to remain a mystery; no sign of any village greeted Mr. Amberley's rather hard grey eyes, but round a sharp bend in the lane a red taillight came into view.

As the Bentley drew closer its headlights, piercing the

mist, picked out a motionless figure standing in the road beside the stationary car. The car, Mr. Amberley observed, was a closed Austin Seven. It was drawn up to the side of the road, its engine switched off, and only its side and taillights burning. He slackened speed and saw that the still figure in the road was not that of a man, as he had at first supposed, but of a female, dressed in a belted raincoat with a felt hat pulled low over her forehead.

Mr. Amberley brought his Bentley to a standstill alongside the little Austin and leaned across the vacant seat beside him. "Is anything wrong?" he said, not without a touch of impatience. Really, if on the top of having lost his way he was going to have to change a wheel or peer into the bowels of the Austin's engine, it would be the crowning annoyance.

The girl—he guessed rather than saw that she was quite young—did not move. She was standing by the off door of the Austin with her hands thrust into the pockets of her raincoat. "No, nothing," she said. Her voice was deep. He got the impression that something was wrong, but he had not the smallest desire to discover the cause of the underlying agitation in her curt words.

"Then can you tell me if I'm on the right road for Greythorne?" he asked.

"I don't know," she said ungraciously.

A somewhat sardonic gleam shot into Mr. Amberley's eyes. "A stranger to these parts yourself, no doubt?"

She moved her head and he saw her face for a moment, a pale oval with a mouth he thought sulky. "Yes, I am. Practically. Anyway, I've never heard of Greythorne. Good night."

This was pointed enough, but Mr. Amberley ignored it. His own manners were, his family informed him, abrupt to the point of rudeness, and the girl's surliness rather pleased him. "Tax your brain a little further," he requested. "Do you know the way to Upper Nettlefold?"

The brim of her hat threw a shadow over her eyes, but he was sure that she glowered at him. "You ought to have taken a turning to the left about a mile back," she informed him.

"Damn!" said Mr. Amberley. "Thanks." He sat back in his seat and took out the clutch.

To turn the car in this narrow lane was not easy. He drove on till he was clear of the Austin and began his manœuvres. After considerable trouble he got the Bentley round, its head lamps illuminating the girl and the Austin in two brilliant shafts of light. As the car swung round she flinched, as though the sudden blaze of light startled her. Mr. Amberley saw her face, chalk-white, for a moment before she averted it.

Instead of straightening up the car he kept it stationary, his foot hard on the clutch, his hand mechanically grasping the gear-lever. The headlights were directed full into the smaller car and showed Mr. Amberley something queer. There was a small hole in the windscreen, with splinters radiating out from it in a star shape. He leaned forward over the wheel, staring. "Who's in that car?" he said sharply.

The girl moved quickly, shutting the interior of the Austin from Mr. Amberley's keen scrutiny. "What has it got to do with you?" she said breathlessly. "I've told you the way to Upper Nettlefold. Why don't you go?"

Mr. Amberley pushed the gear-lever into neutral and put on his brake. He got out of the car and strode towards the girl. Now that he was close to her he saw that she was good-looking, a fact that did not interest him, and exceedingly nervous, a fact that aroused all his suspicions.

"Very silent, your companion?" he said grimly. "Get away from that door."

She stood her ground, but she was obviously frightened. "Will you please go? You have no business to molest me in this fashion!"

His hand shot out and grasped her wrist. He jerked her somewhat roughly away from the door and peered in. A man was sitting in the driver's seat, curiously immobile. His head was sunk on his chest. He did not look up or speak.

The girl's hand shook in Mr. Amberley's hold, which had slowly tightened on it. The figure at the wheel did not move.

"Oh!" said Mr. Amberley. "I see."

"Let me go!" she said fiercely. "I—it—I didn't do it!"

He retained his grasp on her wrist, but he was looking at the dead man. The clothing, a dark lounge suit, was disarranged, as though someone had rifled the pockets; the striped shirt was stained with red, and a dark stain ran down the front of the waistcoat.

Mr. Amberley put out his free hand to touch the slack one inside the car. He did not appear to feel any repulsion. "Not cold," he said. "Well?"

"If you think I did it you're wrong," she said. "I found him like it. I tell you I wasn't even here!"

He ran his hand down over her coat, feeling for a possible weapon. She began to struggle, but found that she was quite powerless in his grip. His hand encountered something hard in the right pocket. Without ceremony he pulled out a small automatic.

She stood still. Hatred vibrated in her voice as she said: "If you take the trouble to inspect it you will find it's fully loaded. The magazine holds seven. It isn't cocked."

"Are you in the habit of carrying loaded guns?" he inquired.

"That's my affair."

"Undoubtedly," he agreed, and lifting the gun sniffed gingerly at the end of the barrel. He let go her wrist and slipped out the magazine. As she had said, it held seven cartridges. Pulling back the breech he satisfied himself that it was empty. Then he snapped the magazine home and handed the gun to the girl.

She took it in a somewhat unsteady clasp. "Thanks. Satisfied I didn't do it?"

"Quite satisfied that you didn't do it with that gun," he replied. "Probably you didn't do the actual shooting, but you know something about it."

"You're wrong. I don't know anything. He was like that when I found him."

"Dead?"

"No—yes, I mean."

"Make up your mind which it is to be," he recommended.

"Damn you, leave me alone!" she flashed. "Can't you see I'm upset and don't know what I'm saying?"

His cool glance swept over her. "Since you put it like that; no, I can't. You seem to me remarkably self-possessed. Come on, out with it! Was the man dead when you found him?"

She did not answer immediately, and it was plain that she was trying to think what was best to say. The fury went out of her face, leaving it cold and rather wary. "No," she said at last; "I thought he was."

"What made you think he wasn't?"

"He said something," she replied sullenly.

"Yes? What did he say?"

"I don't know. I didn't catch it."

"You're a bad liar," he commented. "I suppose it didn't occur to you to render a little first aid?"

"I tried to stop the bleeding." She unclenched her right hand and disclosed a handkerchief saturated with blood. "I saw it was no use. He died almost as soon as I got here."

"And you didn't think well of trying to stop my car to claim assistance?"

She bit her lip, shooting one of her sudden fiery glances at him. "What was the use? You'd only think I'd done it."

"A little cold-blooded, aren't you?" he suggested.

"You can think what you like," she told him. "It makes no difference to me."

"You're mistaken. What I think is likely to make a considerable difference to you. Come here a moment." He grasped her arm above the elbow and drew her towards the smaller car. "Don't stand in the light," he said irritably and once more bent to inspect the quiet form inside. "Did you search his pockets?".

She shuddered. "No."

"Someone did." He reached his hand in at the window and carefully slid it between the dead man's coat and body. "No notecase, no pocketbook." He withdrew his hand and again let the girl go. "Damn!" he said unemotionally and wiped the blood off his fingers.

The girl said: "I—I feel rather sick."

Mr. Amberley raised one eyebrow. "I'm not surprised," he said politely.

She sat down on the running-board of the car and put her head down on her knees. Mr. Amberley stood wiping his fingers on his handkerchief and frowning at her. Presently she sat up. "I'm all right now. What are you going to do?"

"Inform the police."

She looked up at him squarely. "About me?"

"Probably."

Her hands kneaded themselves together. She said bitterly: "If you think I did this why did you give me back my gun? I might easily shoot you too."

"I don't think it. But I should very much like to know what you were doing here at this hour and why you carry a gun."

She was silent. He said, after a moment's pause: "Not exactly communicative, are you?"

"Why should I be? You're not a policeman."

"Just as well for you I'm not. You'd better burn that handkerchief." He turned away towards his own car.

She got up, surprised and uncertain. "Are you—are you letting me go?" she asked, staring after him.

He opened the door of the Bentley. "I'm not a policeman," he reminded her over his shoulder.

"But—but why?" she persisted.

He got into his car and slammed the door. "If you did it," he informed her pleasantly, "you're such a damned little fool the police will precious soon find you out for themselves. Good night."

The car moved forward, was backed again a few feet, straightened, and driven away down the lane the way it had come.

The girl was left standing irresolutely beside the Austin. She watched the Bentley's tail lamp disappear round the bend in the road and blinked rather dazedly.

She felt in her pocket for her torch and drew it out. Switching it on she turned once more to the car. The blood had stopped oozing some time ago and had congealed in the chill evening air. The girl directed her torch at the body and cautiously put her hand in at the open window and felt in the dead man's outer pockets. There was a cheap tobacco pouch in one, and a pipe; some matches in the other. She tried to insinuate her hand into his trousers pockets, but she could not do it without moving the body. She drew back with a shiver and glanced up and down the deserted lane.

The mist, though it was still patchy, was growing thicker. The girl gave her shoulders a shrug and turned away. Her torch, flashing over the ground at her feet, revealed her handkerchief lying where she had dropped it. She picked it up, all wet with blood as it was, and screwed it up in her hand.

The torchlight made the mist look like a blank wall ahead, but served to show where the ditch ran beside the lane. The girl began to walk back along the road in the direction of Pittingly. At the top of a slight rise the fog was no more than a wisp of white smoke, and a gap in the hedge, some few yards farther, was easily distinguishable. There was a stile and a footpath leading across the fields. She swung herself up and over and strode out briskly, eastward. The path led to another stile and on, cutting across a beechwood to more fields, and ahead, the twinkling lights of Upper Nettlefold.

Instead of turning north, through the village, the girl set off down the road to the south, following it for some five hundred yards till a rough lane, hardly better than a cart-track, was reached. A board nailed to a weather-beaten gatepost bore the legend "Ivy Cottage" in somewhat crooked letters, and a little way down the lane a white gate gleamed.

The girl opened it and trod up the roughly flagged path to the door. It was not locked and she went in, shutting it behind her. Immediately before her stairs rose sharply between two walls to the upper floor. On either side was a door, one leading into the kitchen and the other, on the right, into the living room of the cottage.

It stood ajar. The girl pushed it wide and stood on the threshold, leaning against the wall. Her dark scornful eyes rested on the one occupant of the room, a young man sprawling in a chair by the table, blinking owlishly across at her.

She gave a hard little laugh. "Sobered up yet?"

The young man sat up and tried to push his chair back. "I'm all right," he said thickly. "Where—where've you been?"

She came right into the room and pushed the door to behind her. It shut with a bang that made the man start. "My God, you make me sick!" she said bitterly. "Where have I been? You know very well where I've been! You're rotten, Mark! A rotten, drunken swine!"

"Oh, dry up!" he said angrily. He staggered to his feet and brushed past her to the door. She heard him presently in the scullery and guessed that he was dowsing his fuddled head in the sink. Her lip curled. She pulled off her hat and threw it on to a chair and went over to turn down the oil-lamp, which was smoking.

The man came back into the room. He looked ashamed and would not meet her eyes. "I'm sorry, Shirley," he muttered. "Don't know how it happened. I swear I didn't have more than a couple of drinks—well, three at the outside. I didn't even mean to go into the damned pub, but that farmer chap from what's the name of the place —?"

"Oh, what does it matter?" she said impatiently. "You couldn't even keep off the drink for one night. You knew what you'd got to do, too."

"Oh, don't rag me, Shirley!" he said, a kind of weary exasperation in his voice. "All right, all right, I know I'm a swine. You needn't rub it in. Had to meet that fellow, hadn't I? I suppose you went instead."

She took the gun out of her pocket and laid it down and began to unbuckle her coat. "Yes, I went," she said briefly.

"Nothing in it, I suppose? I've always said it was a hoax. Only you would come down to this rotten hole and make me live in a filthy, draughty cottage all to go chasing red herrings——" He broke off, his eyes riveted on her coat. "Gosh, Shirley—what's that?" he asked hoarsely.

She put the coat down. "Blood. I shall have to burn it."

He turned a sickly colour and grasped at the edge of the table. "What—what happened?" he said. "You didn't —you didn't use the gun, did you?"

"I didn't have to. He was dead."

"Dead?" he repeated stupidly. "What do you mean— dead?"

"Shot. So you see it wasn't such a red herring after all."

He sat down, still staring. "Gosh!" he said again. He seemed to make an effort to pull himself together. "Who did it?"

"I don't know. It looks fairly obvious though. His pockets had been searched, so whoever shot him must have known about this meeting. Anyway they didn't get it."

"How do you know?"

"He hadn't got it with him. He just managed to tell me that. Had cold feet, I suppose, and didn't dare carry it on him."

He stretched out his hand across the table and clumsily patted hers. "Sorry, Sis. Loathsome for you. Poor old girl!"

She said hardly: "That's all right. Only it's a nuisance."

"Nuisance! I should say it is. Why, we're no better off than we were before! If the thing really does exist. And if this chap was shot it looks pretty certain that it does."

She threw him an impatient look. "It exists all right. I know where it is too. He told me."

"He told you?" Her brother leaned forward. "Where then?" he said eagerly.

She got up. "Do you think I'd tell you?" she said contemptuously. "And have you blurt it out the next time you're drunk?"

He flushed. "Damn it, it's my affair, isn't it?"

She said fiercely: "Yes, it's your affair, and you leave me to do the work. All right, I'll do it, but you'll keep out of it! See?"

He wilted, but said obstinately: "You're a girl. You can't do it. Gosh, I don't like the sound of this murder."

"I don't suppose you do," she said. "You'd better keep your mouth shut about it." Her face softened. "Oh, Mark, for God's sake, leave the drink alone for a bit!" she said. "We're going to need all our nerve for this job, and what use are you, fuddled six hours out of the twelve?"

"All right," he muttered, looking away from her. "Honestly, it wasn't my fault today. I didn't mean even to go into the pub, but——"

"I know," she said. "You met a chap who wouldn't let you off. I've heard it before."

CHAPTER II

QUITE a short drive brought Frank Amberley into Upper Nettlefold, a small country town some ten miles from Carchester. His original annoyance received a spur from the knowledge that if he had not previously ignored the turning to the left off the Pittingly Road he would not only have arrived at Greythorne in time for a belated dinner, but he would also have escaped running into a nasty and probably troublesome murder case.

"And why the devil did I let her go?" he demanded aloud.

No answer was forthcoming. He scowled. "Dam' fool!" he said.

He really did not know what had prompted him to leave the woman standing there in the road. He was not susceptible, and although her brusque self-possession had amused him he had not been attracted by her. A sulky-looking wench! The sort that would stick at nothing. But she hadn't done that murder, all the same. He ought to have taken her into the police station of course. If she didn't actually shoot the man she knew something about it. No disguising that fact from one who had abundant opportunity of observing crime every working day in the year. At the same time if he had given her up to the police what chance would she have had? The thing looked pretty black. Given a little more data (and he had no doubt there was plenty to be found) he could make a nice damning case for the Crown himself.

But that wasn't his business; his duty had been quite clear. Not that that aspect of the case was likely to worry him. But if he wasn't careful he would find himself in the unenviable position of accessory after the fact. And all because of what? He was damned if he knew.

He ran into Upper Nettlefold and drove to the police

station, an old red brick building in the market square. A young constable was there, the telephone receiver held to his ear, and an expression of weary boredom on his face. He glanced at Mr. Amberley without interest and said into the mouthpiece that nothing had been heard yet, but he was doing all he could about it. After which he listened for a moment, repeated the gist of his former remarks and hung up the receiver.

"Yes, sir?" he said, entering something on the sheet before him.

Mr. Amberley was busy filling a pipe. "Sergeant Gubbins about?" he inquired.

The young constable admitted that Sergeant Gubbins was about.

"I'll see him," said Mr. Amberley, striking a match.

The constable looked at him with disfavour. The hard eyes glanced up over the bowl of the pipe. "Rather quickly," said Mr. Amberley.

"I don't know about that, sir," said the constable stiffly. "I'll speak to the sergeant."

He withdrew, and Mr. Amberley strolled over to the wall to inspect a poster describing the delights in store for all those willing to purchase a ticket for the annual police concert.

The door at the end of the room which had the word PRIVATE painted forbiddingly on the frosted glass opened to admit the egress of a burly individual with very fierce moustache and a red face. "Well, sir, what can I do for you?" said this personage in a voice calculated to strike awe into the hearts of malefactors.

Mr. Amberley turned. " 'Evening, Sergeant," he said.

The sergeant abandoned his severity. "Well, Mr. Amberley, sir!" he said. "I haven't seen you down in these parts, not for six months. I hope I see you well, sir? Anything I can do for you?"

"Oh, no!" said Mr. Amberley. "But I thought you'd like to know there's a dead man on the Pittingly Road."

The constable, who had gone back to his place by the desk, gasped at this, but the sergeant took it in good part.

"You will have your joke, sir," he said indulgently.

"Yes," said Mr. Amberley. "But this isn't my joke. You'd better send someone along. I'm at Greythorne when you want me."

The smile faded. "You're not serious, sir?" said the sergeant.

"Perfectly. Sober, too. A man in an Austin Seven, shot through the chest. Very messy."

"Murder!" said the sergeant. "Good Lord! Here, sir, just a moment! Where did you say you found him?"

Mr. Amberley returned to the desk and demanded a sheet of paper. Supplied with this he drew a rough diagram. "Where that accursed place Pittingly is I don't know, but the car is approximately at this point, about a mile from the turning into this town. I stopped to ask the way to Greythorne and found the fellow was dead. Probably murdered. I'd come with you, but I'm an hour late for dinner already."

"That's all right, sir. You'll be at Greythorne for a day or two, I take it? There'll be an inquest—but I don't have to tell *you* that. Get on to Carchester, Wilkins. You didn't happen to notice anything particular, did you, sir? Didn't pass anyone on the road?"

"No. It's pretty foggy, though. The man wasn't cold when I touched him, if that's any use to you. Good night."

"Good night, sir, and thank you."

The constable held out the telephone receiver, and while the sergeant reported to headquarters he stood rubbing his chin and staring at the door which had swung to behind Mr. Amberley. As the sergeant hung up the receiver he said blankly: "Well, he's a cool customer and no mistake."

"That's Mr. Frank Amberley, Sir Humphrey's nephew," said the sergeant. "He's a very clever young man, that's what he is."

"Walks in here as bold as brass talking about dead men on the road like as if they was as common as dandelions," said the disapproving constable.

"So they are to him," replied the sergeant severely. "If you ever read the papers, my lad, you'd know all about him. He's a barrister. Going a long way, he is, by all accounts."

"Well, he can't go too far for me," said the constable. "I don't like him, Sergeant, and that's a fact."

"You send Harper in to me and stop mooning around the place," commanded the sergeant. "There's plenty don't like Mr. Amberley, but that isn't going to bother him."

Meanwhile Frank Amberley's car had shot off in the direction of the High Street. From Upper Nettlefold he had no doubt of his way and he reached Greythorne, a substantial stone house standing in grounds that ran down to the river Nettle, in little more than ten minutes.

He was met in the hall by his cousin, a mischievous damsel of eighteen, who demanded to know what had happened to him.

He pulled off his coat and cast Miss Matthews a withering glance. "Your short way," he said scathingly.

Felicity giggled. "You are an ass, Frank. Did you get lost?"

"Very." He turned as his aunt came out into the hall. "Sorry, Aunt Marion. Not my fault. Am I too late for dinner?"

Lady Matthews embraced him and said vaguely: "Dear Frank! Dreadfully late, and a cheese soufflé! Darling, tell somebody about Frank. Oh, here is Jenkins! Jenkins, Mr. Amberley has arrived."

She smiled charmingly upon her nephew and drifted away again towards the drawing room. Amberley grinned and called after her: "Aunt Marion, need I change?"

"Change, dear boy? No, of course not. You haven't lost your luggage, have you?"

"No, but it's past nine."

"Dreadful, my dear. We were afraid of an accident."

Felicity tugged at her cousin's sleeve. "Frank, you couldn't have got lost for a whole hour! Own up! You started late!"

"You're a little beast, Felicity. Let me go, I must have a wash."

He came downstairs again five minutes later and was escorted by Felicity to the dining room. While he ate she sat with her elbows on the table, propping her chin in her hands.

"The ball," she announced, "is on Wednesday." Frank groaned. "Did you bring a fancy dress?" Felicity said anxiously.

"I did."

"What is it?" demanded Felicity, agog with female interest.

"Mephistopheles. Suits my style of beauty."

She was doubtful. "I don't really mind about that," she informed him. "You see, I'm going as a Powder-Puff, and you won't suit my style at all."

"God forbid. A Powder-Puff! Look here, what is this ball about, and why, and where?"

Her brown eyes opened to their widest extent. "Good Lord, didn't Mummy tell you in her letter?"

He laughed. "Aunt Marion's letters are exactly like her conversation—the important bits left out."

"Well, it's at Norton Manor. Joan's engaged."

"Joan?"

"You know! Joan Fountain. You must have met her here."

"Fair girl with eyes? Who's the man?"

"Oh, rather an angel. His name's Corkran. He's got pots of money, I believe. Anyway they're engaged, and the ball is sort of in honour of it."

"Half a minute. What's this chap's Christian name?"

"Corkran? Tony. Why?"

Frank raised his brows. "Old Corks! I thought it must be. He was at school with me."

"How delightful for him!" said Miss Matthews politely.

At that moment the door opened and a tall, thin man with white hair came in. Frank got up. " 'Evening, Uncle."

Sir Humphrey shook hands. "Well, Frank? I've only just heard that you'd arrived. What kept you?"

"Felicity, sir. She told me a short way from town. It wasn't."

"So the great Mr. Amberley got lost! The mighty are fallen, Frank."

" 'Fraid so, sir."

"The whole truth is, he didn't start in time," said Felicity indignantly. "And it's no use saying you were busy, Frank, because I know quite well you're—what is it barristers get into in the summer, Daddy? Recess, or something. I say, Daddy, he says he knows Joan's young man."

Sir Humphrey, observing that his nephew had come to the end of his repast, pushed the port decanter towards him. "Indeed? A singularly brainless young man, one would be led to infer, but I believe of excellent family. These fancy-dress festivities, I understood, are to celebrate the engagement. Felicity is very friendly with Miss Fountain."

It was apparent to Mr. Amberley that the friendship did not meet with Sir Humphrey's whole-hearted approval. He searched his brain for data concerning the Fountains and found it void.

Felicity was called away to the telephone. Frank cracked and peeled a nut. "That wasn't entirely true."

"What was not entirely true?" inquired Sir Humphrey, refilling his glass.

"Oh—my losing my way. I did, but not for an hour. I stumbled on a murder."

"God bless my soul!" ejaculated Sir Humphrey, feeling for his pince-nez. He fixed them on his bony nose and regarded his nephew in great astonishment. "Who's been murdered?"

"I've no idea. Middle-aged man respectably dressed. Couldn't place him. Might have been a tradesman. Something like that. He was in an Austin Seven on the Pittingly Road."

"Tut, tut, tut!" said Sir Humphrey, much perturbed. "Shocking! Shocking! No doubt a case of these road bandits."

"It might have been," replied his nephew noncommittally.

"Better say nothing to your aunt and cousin," recommended Sir Humphrey. "Dear me, how very unpleasant!

Murders at our very gates! I do not know what the world is coming to."

He was still tut-tutting when they presently joined Lady Matthews in the drawing room, and when his wife inquired mildly what had happened to disturb him his disclaimers were so earnest that she at once turned to Frank and told him that he had better make a clean breast of it.

Having a more correct opinion of his aunt's nerves than Sir Humphrey had, Frank made no bones about it. "Horrid happenings, Aunt. I've been finding dead bodies. One, to be precise."

Lady Matthews displayed no particular alarm. "Good gracious, Frank; not here, I trust?"

"No, on the Pittingly Road. Someone's been murdered. Uncle thinks probably by bandits."

"Dear me!" said his aunt. "So mediæval. On the Pittingly Road too. Such an improbable place to choose. My dear, did they give you anything to eat?"

"Yes, thanks; excellent dinner."

Sir Humphrey, always a Perfect Husband, patted his wife's hand soothingly. "You must not allow this to worry you, Marion."

"No, my dear, why should I? Very disagreeable for poor Frank though. I hope we haven't got a gang of desperate criminals near us. Terrible if one's own chauffeur turned out to be the leader of a sinister organization."

"Ludlow?" said Sir Humphrey taken aback. "My love, we have had Ludlow in our employment for over ten years! What in the world makes you suppose that he can have anything to do with this shocking affair?"

"I'm sure he hasn't," replied his wife. "I find that nothing of that nature ever really happens to one. But in this book"—she dived her hand among the sofa-cushions and produced a novel in a lurid jacket—"it was the chauffeur. So unnerving."

Sir Humphrey put on his pince-nez again and took the book. "*The Stalking Death*," he read. "My dear, surely this doesn't entertain you?"

"Not very much," she admitted. "The nice man turned

out to be a villain after all. I think that's so unfair when
one had become quite fond of him. Frank, did I tell you
to bring a fancy dress?"

"You did, Aunt. Who are these Fountains? New?"

"Oh no, not new. Surely you remember old Mr. Fountain? Though why you should I can't imagine, for he went
nowhere. He's dead."

"Is that why he went nowhere?" inquired Frank.

"Not at all, dear. How should I know his movements
now? How long has Jasper Fountain been dead,
Humphrey?"

"Two years, or rather longer if my memory serves me."

"I expect it does. I never liked the man but at least one
never saw very much of him, and Felicity did not insist on
becoming intimate with that girl—not that I have anything against her. Far from it; I am sure she is charming,
but I always disliked Basil and I daresay I always shall.
How is your mother, dear boy?"

"All right, and sent her love. Don't side-track, Aunt.
Who is Basil and why don't you like him?"

Lady Matthews looked up at him with her gentle smile.
"Don't you find, Frank, that one never knows why one
dislikes a person?"

Mr. Amberley considered this gravely. "I think I usually do know," he pronounced at length.

"Ah, so masculine," murmured his aunt helplessly. "I
can't explain."

Sir Humphrey, who had retired into the evening paper,
emerged to say: "My dear Marion, don't make a mystery
out of Fountain. There's nothing wrong with the fellow at
all. I can't say I care very much for him, but I am
possibly old-fashioned—dear me, Felicity, pray shut that
door! There's a direct draught."

Felicity obeyed. "Sorry. That was Joan. She's had a
ghoulish day. Whatever do you think, Mummy? Her fancy dress had come, and there was a bill with it, and Basil
saw it and kicked up a frightful row, and said he wouldn't
pay. Anone 'ud think he was going bankrupt. Joan says
he's always groaning about money, which is too absurd
when he must be rolling."

Sir Humphrey looked over the top of his glasses. "You should not encourage your friend to talk disloyally about her brother, Felicity," he said.

"He's only a 'step,'" Felicity said impenitently. "And pretty moth-eaten at that. However, Joan's managed to smooth him down over the frock. I expect he's comforting himself with the thought that he won't have to support her at all much longer."

"Do you mean to tell me that you've been all this time telephoning to one person?" interrupted Frank.

"Yes, of course. Why not? I say, by the way, Joan says she tried to make Basil be Mephistopheles, because of her and Tony being Marguerite and Faust, only he wouldn't. Rather fortunate. I told her I was bringing one who really looks the part. She was thrilled."

"Do you mind elucidating this mystery?" said Frank. "It's beginning to get on my nerves. Who is Basil?"

"Joan's step-brother, idiot."

"I had gathered that. Is he the present owner of the manor?"

"Yes, of course. He inherited everything when old Mr. Fountain popped off."

Sir Humphrey again looked up, mildly pained. "Died, my dear."

"All right, Daddy. Died. He was Mr. Fountain's nephew, and as Mr. Fountain hadn't got any children of his own, he was the heir. Quite simple."

"Oh yes, Jasper Fountain had children of his own," interposed her mother. "That is to say, one. He died about three years ago. I remember seeing the notice in *The Times.*"

Felicity was faintly surprised. "I never heard of any son. Are you sure, Mummy?"

"Perfectly, darling. He was an extremely unsatisfactory young man and went to South America."

"Africa, my dear," corrected Sir Humphrey from behind the paper.

"Was it, Humphrey? Very much the same thing, I feel. There was a very unpleasant scandal. Something to do with cards. But the young man drank, which probably accounted for his erratic habits. His father would never have anything more to do with him. I don't know what became of him, except that he died."

"That finishes him off, then," said Frank. "Does the objectionable Basil have—er—erratic habits?"

"Not that I am aware of, my dear."

Sir Humphrey laid down the paper. "Nowadays the papers contain nothing but sensational descriptions of most unpleasant crimes," he said severely. "Do you young people feel like bridge?"

Upon the following day Felicity, having shopping to do for her mother in Upper Nettlefold, decreed that Frank should accompany her. His suggestion that the expedition might be conducted by car was sternly contradicted. Wolf, said Felicity, must be taken for a walk.

Wolf was Felicity's Alsatian. When fetched from the stables he evinced his satisfaction by bounding round his mistress and barking madly for the first hundred yards of their walk. Exercising him was not, as Frank knew from experience, all joy, as he was not in the least amenable to discipline, had to be caught and held at the approach of any motor vehicle, and had a habit of plunging unadvisedly into quarrels with others of the canine race.

The narrow main street of the town was, as usual upon a weekday, crowded with cars whose owners had parked them there while they shopped. Wolf exchanged objurgations with an Airedale seated in a large touring-car and Felicity, her attention attracted towards the car, announced that it belonged to Tony Corkran. At that moment a slim, fair-haired girl in tweeds came out of the confectioner's with a young man at her heels.

"There is Joan!" Felicity said and darted across the street.

Frank followed, basely deserting Wolf, who had obvious designs on a butcher's shop.

Felicity turned as he came up. "Oh, Frank, whatever do you think? Joan says their butler's been murdered! By the way, this is my cousin, Frank Amberley, Joan. He says he knows you, Mr. Corkran. I say, how thrilling about

Dawson, though! How did it happen? Frightfully ghastly, of course," she added, as an afterthought.

"Your butler?" Frank said, released from Mr. Corkran's hearty handshake. "Oh!"

"Beastly, isn't it?" said Anthony, a young man of engaging ingenuousness. "What I mean to say is—one moment the fellow's murmuring, 'Will you take hock, sir?' and the next he's been bumped off. Bad business, what?" He regarded his erstwhile school-friend with the respect due to Higher Beings. "Of course, I know these little *contretemps* are everyday matters to you brainy johnnies at the Bar. Still—not nice, you know. Definitely a bad show."

"Definitely," Frank agreed. He was frowning slightly. His cousin accused him of lack of proper interest. "No. By no means," he said. "I'm quite unusually interested. How did it happen, Miss Fountain?"

The fair girl said shyly: "Well, we don't know very much yet. It was Dawson's half-day and he seems to have gone off in the Baby Austin. Basil keeps it for the servants because the manor's such a way from the town and there aren't any buses near us. We didn't know a thing about it till a policeman turned up late last night and told Basil they'd found a man dead on the Pittingly Road, and he'd been identified as Dawson. He'd been shot. It's rather awful. Because he'd been at the manor for simply ages, and I can't imagine anyone wanting to shoot him. Basil's dreadfully upset about it."

"An old retainer, in fact?"

"Oh, rather!" said Anthony. "Stately old fossil. Frightfully keen on the done thing. Pretty grim."

Joan gave a little shiver. "It's horrid. I—I hate it having happened. I mean—Dawson wasn't our retainer, really, because we took him on with Collins when Uncle Jasper died, but all the same it's a beastly thing to happen, and it makes it seem pretty heartless to go on with the dance on Wednesday."

"Yes, but my dear old soul, we can't sit and gloom about the place forever," objected her betrothed. "I don't mind telling you that Brother Basil's getting on my nerves already. After all—a poor show, and all that sort of thing, but it's not as though it was his best friend, or what not."

"Darling, it's not that," said Joan patiently. "I keep on trying to explain to you what Basil feels about dead things. He can't bear them. You will insist on thinking he's a callous sort of he-man just because he looks the part, and he isn't. It's one of the things I like about him."

"But dash it all," expostulated Anthony, "he shoots and hunts, doesn't he?"

"Yes, but he doesn't like being in at the death, and I bet you've never seen him pick up the birds that have been shot. Don't say anything about it, because he'd hate anyone to know. He wouldn't even bury Jenny's puppies for me. Wouldn't touch them."

"Well, anyway, I think all this mourning's a bit over-done," said Corkran.

Joan was silent, she looked troubled. Felicity had begun to say: "It isn't particularly enlivening to have one's butler shot——" when she was interrupted by a disturbance in the middle of the road. "Oh, good Lord! Wolf!" she cried.

Wolf, emerging from the butcher's shop, had encountered a bull-terrier. Mutual dislike had straightway sprung up between them, and after the briefest preliminaries battle was joined. As Felicity spoke a girl ran forward and tried to catch the bull-terrier. Mr. Amberley joined the fray and grabbed Wolf by the scruff of his neck. The girl's hands grasped the bull-terrier round the throat. "Hold your dog!" she panted. "I'll have to choke Bill. It's the only way."

Mr. Amberley glanced quickly up at her, but her face was bent over the dogs.

The bull-terrier had acquired a satisfactory grip on Wolf's throat, but his mistress ruthlessly squeezed his windpipe and he had to let go. Mr. Amberley swung Wolf back and held him.

The girl clipped a leash on the bull-terrier's collar and at last looked up. "It was your dog's fault," she began and broke off, staring in a startled way at Mr. Amberley and growing rather pale.

"It usually is," said Frank coolly. "But I don't think your dog's hurt."

Her eyes fell. "No," she said and would have moved away had not Felicity come up.

"I say, I'm most awfully sorry!" Felicity said. "I ought to have had him on the lead. I do hope he hasn't hurt your dog?"

The other girl smiled rather scornfully. "Rather the other way round, I should say."

Felicity was surveying her with friendly interest. "Aren't you the girl that's living at Ivy Cottage?" she inquired.

"My brother and I have taken it furnished."

"Are you going to stay long? You are Shirley Brown, aren't you? I'm Felicity Matthews. This is my cousin, Frank Amberley."

Miss Brown bowed slightly, but she did not look at Mr. Amberley.

"I rather wanted to get to know you," persevered Felicity. "I'm awfully glad we got ourselves introduced. There are practically no young people in this benighted place. Do you know Miss Fountain?"

The girl shook her head. "No, I'm afraid I don't go out much. My—my brother is rather an invalid."

"Oh, bad luck!" sympathized Felicity. "Joan, this is Miss Brown, who is living at Ivy Cottage."

"May I suggest," interposed Frank, "that you are obstructing the traffic?"

Felicity became aware of an indignant motorist who was violently sounding his hooter. She drew the rather unwilling Miss Brown on to the pavement. "Have you heard the news?" she asked. "The Fountains' butler has been murdered! Isn't it awful?"

"No, I hadn't heard. Are you sure he was murdered?"

"He was shot through the chest, you see," said Mr. Amberley gently. "Seated at the wheel of an Austin Seven."

"I see," Shirley said.

Mr. Corkran was puzzled. "Yes, he was. But how the devil did you know all that?"

"I found him," said Mr. Amberley.

He created a sensation; only the dark girl at his side betrayed neither surprise nor incredulity. There was something rather tense in the way she held herself, but her eyes, travelling from Joan's shocked face to Felicity's eager one, were indifferent to the point of boredom.

"I thought," said Mr. Amberley, interrupting the fire of questions, "that you might as well know now as later."

"Oh, did you?" said Felicity witheringly. "Go on, tell us how it happened!"

He threw her a mocking glance. "I'm reserving my evidence for the inquest, loved one."

Shirley Brown stiffened slightly. She said, as though jesting: "The whole truth and nothing but the truth, in fact."

"I see you know all about the procedure," said Mr. Amberley.

She gave him back look for look, but said nothing. The two dogs, who had been snarling softly all the time, created a diversion by attempting to lunge suddenly at each other's throats. Shirley twisted the bull-terrier's leash round her hand and stepped back. "I mustn't wait any longer," she said. "I have some shopping to do. Goodbye."

Joan watched her walk away down the street. "What a queer sort of a girl!" she remarked.

"Oh, I don't know! Rather nice, I thought," said Felicity. "Look here, we can't stand here for ever. I've got to go to Thompson's and Crewett's. Come with me? Frank, for God's sake hold on to Wolf. I shan't be more than five minutes."

Left to their own devices the two men began to stroll down the street together.

"I say, Amberley, there's something damned odd about this murder," Anthony said.

"Well, don't tell it to the whole of the town," recommended the rudest man in London.

"Yes, but joking apart, you know, why should anyone want to take a pot-shot at a butler? Respectable old blighter, been at the manor umpteen years. The thing just isn't done. I mean, I could think of a lot of people who might get shot—gangsters, and cabinet ministers, and all that push—but not butlers. After all, why shoot a butler? Where's the point?"

"I've no idea," said Frank discouragingly.

"There isn't one," Anthony declared. "That's what makes the thing look so fishy. I'll tell you what, Amberley; it's all very fine to read about mysteries, but in real life—no. Cut 'em right out."

"I will."

"Yes," said Anthony, suddenly gloomy. "But if you were staying at the manor you wouldn't be able to. The whole place is stiff with mystery."

"Oh?" said Frank. "Why?"

"Damned if I know. There isn't anything you could put your finger on, so to speak, but it's there all right. For one thing there's Brother Basil." He lowered his voice confidentially. "Between ourselves, he's a bit of a dud. I've got no time for him at all. Bit awkward as things are. If it weren't for Joan I don't mind telling you you wouldn't catch me staying at Norton Manor."

"Because of its mystery or because of its host?"

"Bit of both. Mind you, I don't say there's anything wrong with the house. It's the people in it. Like a lot of cats snooping round in the dark. Look here, don't repeat this, but it's an absolute fact that you can't do a darned thing but what you get the feeling that you are being watched. It's getting a bit on my nerves."

"Are you being watched?"

"I don't know. Shouldn't be surprised. Brother Basil's got a valet who's always popping up out of nowhere. Another one of the leftovers from the old régime. Now if he'd been murdered I shouldn't complain. Nasty piece of work, I think, and so does Joan, but Brother Basil likes the fellow."

"What, by the way, is wrong with Brother Basil?" asked Frank.

"Wrong with him? Oh, I see what you mean. I don't know: sort of fellow who drinks his bath water. Damned bad-tempered—I don't mind telling you Joan has a pretty thin time of it with him. Full of spurious *joie de vivre,* don't you know? One of these hearty blokes. Calls you old boy and slaps you on the back."

Frank jerked his thumb downwards in a certain Roman gesture.

"Quite," agreed Mr. Corkran. "I knew you'd feel the same about it. There's another thing too——"

What this might be was not divulged, for at that moment the two girls joined them. Joan Fountain, who had finished her shopping, was ready to go home. As she shook hands with Amberley she said: "Felicity has promised to come over after dinner. I do hope you'll come too."

"Thanks, I should like to," Amberley said, somewhat to his cousin's surprise.

When Joan and Corkran had driven off, Felicity said that she hoped her cousin didn't mind having to go to the manor. "I practically had to accept," she explained. "Apparently things are pretty dire since the murder. Basil's got nerves or something, but Joan says he's always better when there are visitors. Do you mind awfully?"

"Not awfully," Frank replied.

Felicity glanced shrewdly up at his profile. "I believe you wanted to go."

"I did," said Mr. Amberley.

CHAPTER III

THEY reached Greythorne again to find an inspector from Carchester waiting in the drawing room. He knew Mr. Amberley of old and took no pains to disguise the fact that he did not like him. He put a number of questions to him and sniffed at the answers, which he wrote down in his notebook. Having informed Amberley that he would be required to attend the inquest at eleven o'clock on the following morning he took his leave, saying pointedly that after the inquest he did not expect to be obliged to bother Mr. Amberley further in the matter. There was some justification for his unfriendliness, for he had once worked on a case with Mr. Amberley, who had entered into it almost by accident and stayed to bring about a particularly neat conviction. The inspector had not enjoyed that case; in fact, he had been heard to say that he never wanted to set eyes on Mr. Amberley again.

Out of deference to Sir Humphrey's dislike of such topics the murder was not discussed at Greythorne. Frank played tennis with his cousin during the afternoon and in the evening motored her to Norton Manor, which was situated seven miles to the east of Upper Nettlefold and about three from Greythorne.

The manor was a house dating from the early eighteenth century. It presented a gracious façade of stone and old red brick, and stood in a small park through which the river Nettle wound its way under overhanging willows. Inside, the house had the finely proportioned rooms of its period, but was furnished in a heavy style that spoke ill for the late Mr. Fountain's taste.

Amberley and his cousin were admitted by a tight-lipped man of medium height who was fulfilling the duties of the deceased butler. As she stepped into the hall Felicity said:

"Good evening, Collins," and hearing the name Amberley looked him over quickly.

The valet was in no way remarkable. He had a lean, somewhat unhealthily pale face and kept his eyes discreetly lowered.

Felicity was speaking sympathetically to the man about Dawson's murder. She thought that since he had worked with the butler for several years he must feel his loss considerably and was consequently a little dashed by his calm answer.

"You are very kind, miss," Collins said. "A very tragic affair, as you say. But though naturally I should not wish such a thing to have happened, Dawson and I were never what one could call really friendly."

He moved towards one of the doors that opened on to the hall, and feeling rather snubbed Felicity followed him. She gave him her cousin's name, and for a moment the veiled eyes lifted to Amberley's face. They were cold eyes, expressionless, uncomfortably remorseless. They were swiftly hidden again. The valet opened the door and announced the guests.

Joan and her fiancé and a large man with a handsome, full-blooded countenance, were gathered round the fire. Amberley was introduced to the large man and sustained a crushing hand-clasp. Basil Fountain was boisterously pleased to welcome visitors to the house. He was one of those men who radiated goodwill. Amberley could understand and appreciate his friend Corkran's revulsion. Fountain's personality was indeed hearty, but under it lay a certain irritability which flared up under small provocation. He bustled about, offering drinks, pulling up chairs, chaffing Felicity in the most cheerful way, but when his step-sister did not immediately obey his command to bring her friend near to the fire he spoke roughly, with a flash of temper that was as uncontrollable as it was transient.

He was soon smiling again. He said: "You know Corkran, don't you? He's going to become one of the family, as I've no doubt he told you," and laid an affectionate hand on Anthony's unresponsive shoulder.

He was obviously of a hospitable nature. He pressed

refreshment upon his guests, offered cigars and cigarettes, and brought Felicity a cushion. Not until he was perfectly satisfied that everyone was quite comfortable did he broach the subject which must necessarily be engrossing the greater part of his attention. He turned to Amberley and said simply: "I'm particularly glad you came over with your cousin tonight. I understand it was you who found poor Dawson."

"Yes, I found him, but I'm afraid I can't tell you much about it," Amberley replied.

Fountain clipped the end of his cigar. There was trouble in his face; he looked all at once like a man who cannot shake off the memory of a bad nightmare. "I know," he said. "He was shot, wasn't he? You didn't see anyone or find anything? Any clue, I mean."

"No," Amberley answered. "Nothing."

Joan leaned forward. "I wish you would tell us just what you saw," she said. "The police gave us such a bald account, and we feel in a way responsible, because he was our servant."

"Yes, tell us what you can," said Anthony, "and then no more." He smiled across at Joan. "It's no use worrying so much, darling. Much better not think about it."

Fountain looked at him with quick impatience. "It's not easy to forget the murder of one of your own staff," he said. "You take it very lightly, but he was not your servant. It is a most horrible thing to have happened." He gave a little shiver. "I can't get it out of my mind. The fellow being done to death like that—cold-bloodedly!" He seemed to feel Amberley's gaze upon him and looked up. "You think I'm taking it too hard? Perhaps I am. I don't deny it has upset me." He struck a match and held it to the end of his cigar; Amberley saw the flame quiver. "I can't make out what happened," Fountain said jerkily. "The police spoke of road-bandits. Was he robbed?"

Corkran, one eye on Joan's pale, anxious face, chose to be flippant. "Robbed? Of course he was. I bet a bob you find out that he was making off with the family plate. I say, where is this damned draught coming from?" He looked round and saw that the door was standing ajar. He made as if to get up, but Fountain was before him.

"Don't bother, I'll shut it," he said and walked heavily across the floor towards it. He glanced out into the hall before he shut the door, and Anthony, observing this, said suspiciously that he supposed that fellow Collins was prowling about as usual.

Fountain looked annoyed, but shook his head. "No. But we'd better not talk so loud. Naturally the servants are agog with curiosity." He glanced at Amberley. "Can't blame 'em, can one?"

"I think," said Amberley slowly, "that I might steel myself to the pitch of blaming a servant whom I found listening at keyholes."

"That's Corkran's tale," said Fountain rather angrily. "All moonshine! I don't hold any brief for Collins, but ——" He broke off, and reverting suddenly to his jovial manner began to talk about the coming ball.

The door opened softly and the valet came in carrying a tray of drinks. A chill, a feeling of uneasiness, seemed to enter with him. Fountain's voice sounded forced; Joan's laugh held a nervous ring. The valet moved noiselessly across the pile carpet to a table against the wall and set down the tray. He went out again as softly as he had come in. Amberley noticed that he shut the door with quiet firmness behind him.

He looked across at Fountain and said directly: "You don't like that man?"

The others showed some surprise at this sudden, unconventional question. Fountain stared back at Amberley, the laugh dying on his lips. He shook his head. "No. Not much. Shouldn't keep him, only that my uncle wished it."

"Do you know of any enmity between him and Dawson?"

"No. Don't think they hit it off particularly well, but I never saw anything of it."

"You don't think that—Collins had anything to do with it?" The question came from Joan.

"No, Miss Fountain. I only wanted to know."

"Well, he hadn't," said Fountain. "I happen to know that he was here at the time the murder was committed."

"You're quite sure of that, I suppose?" Amberley said.

Fountain gave a laugh. " 'Fraid so. He does look a typical villain, doesn't he? I say—ought not to joke about it, you know. You were going to tell us just how you found Dawson's body."

Amberley's account, his cousin complained, did not err on the side of sensationalism. It was very brief, even a little bald. He stressed no points and advanced no theories. While he talked he was aware of an atmosphere of almost painful anxiety. It did not come from Felicity, frankly thrilled; nor from Corkran, still flippant; but Joan sat with her eyes fixed on his face, a haunted expression in her own; and Fountain, impatient of Anthony's interruptions, jarred by Felicity's evident enjoyment, listened intently, his cigar held unheeded between his fingers, its long ash fallen on the floor at his feet. That he was honestly upset by the murder nobody looking at him could doubt. He wanted to know everything that Amberley could tell him and again he pressed the question: "Are you sure you passed no one on the road?"

Amberley's story, shorn of all decorative detail, did not take long to recount. A silence followed it which was at length broken by Corkran. He proposed cheerfully that he and Fountain and Amberley should play a three-ball game of golf next afternoon to get rid of the taste of the inquest.

Fountain did not want to play; so much was apparent in his quick headshake. "You two play. I shall have to go to town."

"Will you? What for?" asked his step-sister.

"I must see about engaging a new butler," he answered shortly. "I spoke to Finch's Registry Office on the telephone today. I'm afraid it may be a bit of a job. Servants don't like coming to such an isolated place. And then there's this dreadful business. Puts them off, you know. Bound to."

"Oh, my godfathers, does that mean we've got to have

Collins gliding about the place indefinitely?" groaned Corkran.

"I must get someone. It isn't Collins' work and he doesn't like doing it." Fountain saw that his cigar had gone out and threw it away. He made an effort to shake off his evident depression and got up, suggesting a game of snooker.

He marshalled them all into the billiard room, quite in his usual manner, nor was any further reference made to the murder. Yet for all his laughter, for all Corkran's airy persiflage, Amberley was conscious of that vague sensation of discomfort which seemed to brood over the house and which Anthony had tried ineffectively to describe.

He was not sorry when the evening came to an end, but the visit, little though he might have enjoyed it, had given him something to think about. Silently he cursed himself for his rash, unaccustomed quixotry in shielding by his silence the girl he had found beside the murdered man's car.

It was not she who had fired the shot; of that he was convinced. But her presence had not been accidental, nor had her agitation (he was convinced) been entirely due to finding the butler's body. She had given him the impression that she was suffering less from shock, or from horror, than from bitter disappointment.

It looked like being an interesting case. There was the girl, a lady, who had so evidently gone to meet the butler; there was Fountain, shaken by the news, plainly aghast; there was Joan, frightened, nervous of the house, nervous of the valet; there was Collins himself, impassive yet oddly sinister, listening at doors, as anxious as his master to hear all that Amberley had to tell.

Nothing in that, Amberley reminded himself. Why should they not want to know every detail? Yet he could swear that something lay behind, something obscure that would not readily be disclosed.

He determined to look into the butler's record. He had little expectation that anything would come out at the inquest. Whatever the butler's secret was and whoever held the key to it, were mysteries which would need a deal of solving.

Nor was he mistaken. The inquest next morning provided the sensation hunters who flocked to it with very little to interest them. The doctor and the gun expert were dull witnesses, and the most hopeful witness, Amberley himself, disappointed everyone by giving his evidence in a dry and exceedingly succinct manner. No one came forward with a startling disclosure; no one seemed to know of any secret in Dawson's life, and no one knew of anybody who might be supposed to wish the butler out of the way. The jury returned a verdict of murder against person or persons unknown, and the case ended.

"In fact, sir," said Sergeant Gubbins afterwards, "it's a queer case, and do you know why, Mr. Amberley?"

"I can think of several reasons, but by all means tell me."

"It's because there ain't nothing queer about it, sir," said the sergeant darkly.

Mr. Amberley regarded him enigmatically. "You ought to go a long way, Sergeant—if you're lucky."

"Well, sir, it isn't for me to say so, but I won't say you're wrong," said the sergeant, much gratified.

"But you will have to be very lucky," said Mr. Amberley gently.

The sergeant looked at him suspiciously and pondered the remark for a while in silence. Having considered it carefully he said with some indignation: "It don't surprise *me* to hear you make a lot of enemies, sir. Not that I'd be one to take offence, because I know you will have your joke. But there's a lot of people mightn't like the way you have of saying things. Now if I didn't know you like I do, I wouldn't tell you what I'm going to. But you gave us a tip or two over that robbery case we had when you were down here, and freely I admit it."

"Yes, you made a bit of a mess of that, didn't you?" said Mr. Amberley. "Still got that chuckle-headed inspector at Carchester, I notice."

The sergeant grinned. "He'll be getting promotion soon. Maybe I will too."

"What for?" asked Mr. Amberley, interested.

"Solving this murder case, sir."

"Oh!" said Mr. Amberley. "Well, don't let me waste your time. You run along and solve it."

"That's just it, sir. I thought that you, having a bit of a knack of hitting on things, in a manner of speaking, and making a sort of hobby of it—well, what I thought was, I might do worse than tell you what's puzzling us."

"You might, but if you imagine that I'm setting up as an amateur detective——"

"Oh no, sir, nothing like that. Though when you spotted it was Bilton had those diamonds I must say that I did think to myself that you were fair thrown away in your profession. Of course, you happened to be present when the theft took place, which was an advantage we hadn't got. Still, I will say it was a very neat bit of work, Mr. Amberley, and we were all very grateful to you, because it was touch and go whether we called in the Yard or not."

"Just like this case," nodded Mr. Amberley.

"You've hit it, sir," said the sergeant. "It's the chief constable. He's what you might call—well, a bit timid. Now when I said that there wasn't anything queer about this case, what I meant was, it's all straight on the surface. Nothing known against Dawson, no enemies, no women, been in service at the manor for years, everything above-board. Well, that ain't natural. Take it from me, Mr. Amberley, when a man gets himself murdered there's always something behind, and ten to one he's a wrong 'un. Setting aside women, that is. Now in this case there's only one thing that looks a bit fishy."

"Do you wear glasses?" asked Mr. Amberley suddenly.

"Me, sir? No, I do not."

"You should."

"Not me, Mr. Amberley. I see as well as I did when I was a two-year-old."

"That's what I meant. Go on."

"Blessed if I know what you're driving at, sir," said the sergeant candidly. "Well, this fishy thing is the money Dawson had put by. It all goes to his sister. She's a widow, living in London. He hadn't made a will, so she gets it. And there's a tidy sum by what one can make out."

"I always imagined butlers made a bit on the side."

"Some do and some don't. But I never heard of one who made as much as Dawson did. As far as we can make out he's got a matter of a couple of thousand laid by. Spread about, too. Make anything of that, sir?"

"Spread where?"

"Post Office Savings Bank here, them War Loan Certificates, and a bank at Carchester. Looks funny to me. The inspector doesn't make much of it. Of course, people do get ideas into their heads about spreading their money about, but what I'd like to know is how did he come by so much? Always paying in money he seems to have been."

"How much at a time?"

"Well, not a great deal, sir, but steady. I could let you have the figures."

"Yes. Or rather, no. You'd better not."

"Colonel Watson wouldn't object, sir, if that's what you're thinking. Not as it's you, if you understand me."

Mr. Amberley's saturnine smile appeared. "The question is, Sergeant, am I on your side?"

"Beg pardon, sir?"

"I'm not sure that I am," said Mr. Amberley. "I'll let you know when I've thought it over. Meanwhile, I want some lunch. Good hunting!"

The sergeant was left to stare after him in great perplexity. The chief constable, Colonel Watson, who presently came hurrying out of the courtroom, found him scratching his head meditatively. "Has Mr. Amberley gone, Sergeant?"

The sergeant sprang to attention. "Just this minute gone, sir. He's in one of his funny moods."

"Oh, you've been talking to him, have you? Very irregular, Sergeant, quite out of order. I suppose Mr. Amberley didn't throw any more light than he did in his evidence?"

"No, sir. Mr. Amberley went off highly humorous," said the sergeant heavily.

At Greythorne only Felicity evinced much interest in

the result of the inquest. Sir Humphrey, although a justice of the peace, deprecated the introduction of such subjects into the home circle, and Lady Matthews had already forgotten most of what it was about. But when Amberley met Anthony Corkran at the clubhouse that afternoon he found that worthy agog to talk the matter over. In company with the Fountains he had been present at the inquest, and he expressed himself much dissatisfied with the result.

"Is that the end of it?" he demanded. "D'you mean to tell me there's nothing more going to be done?"

"Oh no, there's a lot more to be done. Find the murderer, for instance. Look here, there are several things I want to ask you, but first I want to play golf. What about it?"

"Absolutely all right with me," Anthony assured him. "Might think out a solution on the round, what?"

The course was a long one with a fair amount of trouble on it. Mr. Corkran warned his friend that it was imperative to keep straight and pulled his first drive into a clump of gorse bushes.

"Thanks, Anthony," said Mr. Amberley. "Example is better than precept—every time."

It was past five when they finished the round, and the light had already grown very bad. They found the clubhouse rather empty, as was usual on a weekday, and they had no difficulty in securing a corner to themselves. Over the first half-pint of beer, Anthony would discuss nothing but his tendency to pull, embellished by illustrative anecdotes of fatal pulls on half the golf courses of England. But when he had taken Amberley from Sandwich by way of Wentworth and Hoylake to St. Andrews he at last ran dry.

Amberley allowed him to brood over the afternoon's round for a few minutes, while he sent for more beer. When this came Anthony roused himself from his absorption and of his own accord abandoned the subject of golf.

"This 'ere murder," he said. "What about it?"

"Not enough. That's the trouble. What is Brother Basil afraid of?"

"Ah, you noticed it, did you? Blessed if I know. Jolly

sort of atmosphere about the place, isn't there? The sooner I get Joan out of it the better."

"When is the wedding, by the way?"

"Next month. As far as I can make out, I look like being a fixture there till then, or practically. I was supposed to be pushing off after these fancy-dress revels—— I say, why do women get all unhinged when it comes to fancy dress? Even Joan's definitely insane on the subject. I ask you, Amberley, *do* I look the sort of silly ass who'd do well as Faust?" Frank shook his head. "Of course I don't. A dance is all right, but why drag in the fancy dress? However, that wasn't what I was going to say. Being a fixture. Well, I always meant to push off on Thursday, but apart from Joan wanting me to stay a bit longer, Brother Basil's all for it."

"Pleasure of your company, or funk?"

"Funk," said Corkran positively. "The man's all chewed up with it, and God knows why. All I know is that he doesn't want to be left alone at the manor. It's since the murder that he's got the jumps to this extent."

"Do you know anything about him?"

"No, not much. Nothing much to know. Good family, public school man, and all that sort of thing. Always been fairly well-off, I gather, on account of old Fountain making him his heir. Naturally I've gleaned a bit from Joan, in the way of conversation. As far as I can make out Brother Basil's led a comfortable sort of life, no worries, or debts, or riotous living. Ordinary bonhomous sort of chap. Simple Pleasures and Athletic Ideal, you know. Shoots, hunts a bit, quite a stylish bat, I believe. He's keen on all outdoor sports. Devilish healthy. Had me out before breakfast to bathe when I stayed with him down at Littlehaven. He's got a bungalow there—rather decent, except for the damned boat."

"What damned boat?"

"Motorboat. According to Basil you can cross the Channel in it without being seasick. Well, I didn't cross the Channel, so perhaps that accounted for it."

Amberley laughed. "Not a good sailor, in fact."

"The world's worst," said Corkran. "Anyone can have

the super motorboat as far as I'm concerned. Joan, too.
She bars it completely, which feeds Brother Basil stiff. He
and she don't hit it off particularly well, you know.
Though according to her things were fairly all right till the
old man died. She swears it's something to do with the
manor. Of course, the truth is she doesn't like the place,
so she's got it into her head there's something wrong with
it. Then, on top of that, there's Collins."

"Yes, I'm rather interested in Collins," said Amberley.
"Were he and Dawson the only survivors from the old
régime?"

"Oh Lord, no! Practically the whole staff's the same.
There's a housekeeper who's been there since the year dot,
and the cook, and a couple of gardeners, and a whole
bevy of skivvies—I don't know about them, by the way.
They may have changed since old Fountain kicked the
bucket. But the hardy perennials all stayed put. You see,
Brother Basil was no stranger to 'em. Old Jasper seems to
have been very fond of him; always having him down to
stay. So they all knew him and seem to have liked him. I
tell you, there's no data at all."

"I begin to think there's something in what the sergeant
said," remarked Amberley. "Queer case. Nice little holiday problem."

"Well, if you want a Watson, don't forget me, will
you?" said Corkran. "And talking of Watson, do you
remember Freddy Holmes? Chap with freckles in the
Army Class?"

"In Merritt's House? Yes, what about him?"

"I'll tell you," said Corkran, drawing his chair closer.

The conversation ceased from that moment to have any
bearing on the murder, but became frankly an interchange
of school reminiscences. It lasted for an hour and might
have lasted for three had not Corkran chanced to catch
sight of the clock. He then fled, having promised to fetch
his betrothed from a tea party at least half an hour earlier.

Amberley followed in a more leisurely fashion and
drove his Bentley into Upper Nettlefold to buy tobacco on
his way home. When he came out of the shop he found
that his car was not unattended. A dark, wild-looking boy

in grey flannel trousers, a polo sweater and a tweed coat was leaning against it, solemnly staring at the switches on the dashboard. He wore no hat, and a lock of black hair strayed artlessly across his forehead.

Amberley paused outside the shop and began slowly to fill a pipe, his eyes resting thoughtfully on the dark young man.

The youth continued to lean heavily.

"Anything I can do for you?" Amberley inquired.

The dishevelled head was turned. "Nobody," said the youth simply, "need do any—anything for me."

"That's good. Mind if I remove the car?"

The youth disregarded this. "D'you know what I've been doing?"

"Yes," said Amberley frankly.

"I've been—I—have—been having—tea with—with a fellow," announced the youth.

"Strong tea. I should go home now if I were you."

"Thash—what I was going to do," said the youth. "He's a fellow I met—th'other day. He's a *nice* fellow. I don' care what anyone says, he's a nishe—a nice fellow. Shirley—Shirley doesn't like him. What I shay—say—is—bloody snob'ry. Thash what I say."

Mr. Amberley's expression changed from contemptuous amusement to sudden interest. "Shirley," he repeated.

"Thash right," nodded the youth. He looked hazily at Amberley, yet with a certain cunning in his face. "She's my sister."

"If you get into my car I'll return you to her," said Amberley.

The youth's eyes narrowed. "Who are you?" he demanded. "I'm not going to—to tell you anything. See?"

"All right," Amberley said peaceably and managed to thrust him into the car.

He was not an easy passenger. While he babbled aimlessly all went well, but when he had switched off the engine for the second time Amberley came near to losing his temper.

Mark cringed a little before the wrath in his face and wanted to get out. He seemed to become obsessed all at once with the idea that he was being kidnapped. It was with considerable difficulty that Amberley succeeded in allaying his fears, and then he began to talk about the murder. Very little of what he said made sense, nor did Amberley press him to be more explicit. He said several times that no one was going to make a cat's-paw of him, maundered a little of hidden dangers and of dark plots, and asserted loudly that whoever else got murdered it would not be himself. As Amberley swung the car into the lane that led to Ivy Cottage he suddenly grasped his sleeve and said earnestly: "I didn't think there was anything in it. Shirley thought so, but I didn't. A hoax. Thash what I thought. But it isn't. I see it isn't now. I've got to be careful. Not speak to anyone. Not give anything away."

"I shouldn't," said Amberley, drawing up at the gate of the cottage. He got out of the car and went up the flagged path to the front door. He knocked, heard a dog bark, and in a few minutes was confronting Shirley Brown.

She was evidently startled to see him, but she tried to conceal it. "May I ask what you want?" she said brusquely.

Mr. Amberley wasted no time on delicate euphemisms. "I want to get rid of a damned nuisance," he said. "I've brought your brother home. He's extraordinarily drunk."

"Oh, my God, again!" she said wearily. "All right, I'll come." She glanced up at him. "Decent of you to bother. Thanks."

"Stay where you are," said Amberley. "I'll fetch him." He went back to the car and opened the door. "Your sister's waiting for you."

Mark allowed himself to be assisted out of the car. "I didn't say anything I shouldn't, did I?" he said anxiously. "You'll tell her I didn't."

"All right." Amberley guided his erratic steps up the path.

Shirley looked him over. "Oh! You'd better go and sleep it off," she said. She took his arm and nodded to Amberley. "Thanks. Good-bye."

"I'm coming in," said Amberley.

"No, thanks. I can manage him."

"Nevertheless, I am coming in," he repeated. He put her aside without ceremony, and guided Mark into the house and up the narrow stairs. "Which room?" he said over his shoulder.

She was standing at the foot of the stairs frowning up at him. "On the left."

When he came down again some minutes later she was still standing where he had left her. She said: "I daresay it's very kind of you to take so much trouble, but I wish you'd go."

"I'm sure you do. Where did you learn your pretty manners?"

"Where you learnt yours!" she shot back at him.

"Do you know, I think I'm treating you with a remarkable amount of forbearance," he said. "Did anyone ever slap you really hard when you were a child?"

An unwilling smile crept into her eyes. "Often. Thank you *so* much for bringing my brother home. I'm most *awfully* grateful, and I do *wish* I could ask you to stop, only *unfortunately* I'm rather busy just now. How's that?"

"I prefer the original version. You might ask me into your sitting room."

"No doubt, but I'm not going to."

"Then I won't wait for the invitation," he said, and walked in.

She followed him, half angry, half amused. "Look here, I admit I owe you a debt of gratitude for not making trouble the other night, but that doesn't give you the right to force your presence on me. Please go. Why are you so anxious to pursue our acquaintance?"

He looked sardonically across at her. "I'm not in the least anxious to pursue it. But I'm interested in that murder."

"Of which I know nothing."

He said unpleasantly: "Lie to me by all means, Miss Brown, but choose a better lie than that. If you've any sense you'll stop being mysterious and tell me just what you're playing at."

"Really?" She raised her brows. "Why?"

"Because your extreme reluctance to behave in a normal manner is fast convincing me that you're up to some mischief. I don't like lawbreakers, and I have every intention of finding out what your game is."

"You'll be very clever if you do," she said.

"You are likely to discover, my misguided young friend, that I am considerably cleverer than anyone you've yet had to deal with."

"Thanks for the warning. But I have no game and I am not at all mysterious."

"You forget I've spent half an hour in your brother's instructive company."

Her calm left her; she cried hotly: "So you pumped a drunken boy, did you? A rotten, low-down trick!"

"That's better," he said. "Now we're getting at something."

"What did he say to you?" she demanded.

"Nothing of which I could make sense," he said. "Surprising as it may seem, I refrained from pumping a drunken boy. I am also refraining from pretending, in order to make you talk, a knowledge I don't possess."

She glanced up at him in a puzzled way. "Yes. Do you mind telling me why?"

"Natural decency," said Mr. Amberley.

"Mark talks a lot of nonsense when he's drunk," she said. She seemed to consider him. "I wonder what you think I am?" she said with a crooked smile.

"Do you? I'll tell you, if you like. An objectionable little fool."

"Thanks. Not a murderess, by any chance?"

"If I thought that you would not be standing here now, Miss Shirley Brown. You are obviously playing some game which is probably silly and almost certainly dangerous. If you let that brother of yours out alone you'll very soon find yourself in a police cell. As an accomplice he's rotten."

"Possibly," she said, "but I don't want another. I believe in playing a lone hand."

"Very well," he replied. "Then I'll say—*au revoir!*"

"Dear me, am I going to see some more of you?" she inquired.

"You are going to see much more of me than you want to," said Mr. Amberley grimly.

"I've done that already," she informed him in a voice of great sweetness.

He had reached the door, but he turned. "Then we are mutual sufferers," he said, and went out.

She gave a sudden laugh and ran after him as far as the front door. "You're a beast," she called; "but I rather like you, I think."

Mr. Amberley looked back over his shoulder. "I wish I could return the compliment," he answered, "but honesty compels me to say that I do not like you at all. So long!"

CHAPTER IV

"ODD how a mere strip of black velvet alters people," remarked Corkran, surveying the shifting crowd critically. "I've made three bloomers already."

Amberley was dangling his mask by the strings. "You can usually tell by the voice."

"You can't always. Oh, hell!"

"What's the matter now?"

"This blasted sword again," said Faust disgustedly. He hitched it round. "Can't dance with it, can't move a step without jabbing somebody in the shins with it. I'm going to park it somewhere soon and trust to luck that Joan doesn't spot it."

Joan, a dazzlingly fair Marguerite, passed at that moment in the arms of an Arab sheikh. She caught sight of the two in the doorway and slid out of the dance, drawing her partner with her. "Haven't you got a partner for this one?" she asked in concern. "Point me out somebody you'd like to be introduced to."

"My dear old soul, I can't dance with this sword on," protested Corkran. "I've made myself fairly unpopular as it is."

"That," said the sheikh, "is putting it mildly. I've got about an inch of skin missing from my calf."

"Oh, dear," said Joan, looking distressed. "Can't you manage to keep it out of people's way, darling?"

"I can," said Faust. "I can go and take the blighter off."

"But you look so awfully nice with it on," she sighed. "You ought to lay your hand on the hilt, like that."

"In the best circles," interposed Amberley, "it was never considered really good form to dance with a sword at one's side."

44

"Wasn't it?" said Joan doubtfully. "But I've seen pictures——"

"That's good enough for me," announced Faust, and prepared to depart.

As he turned the end of the scabbard dug into a complete stranger who looked furious and said icily that it was quite all right. "That makes the third time I've caught that bloke with it," whispered Faust, not without satisfaction.

"Perhaps you had better do without it," Joan said reluctantly. She turned her attention to Amberley. "You mustn't take off your mask till midnight, you know," she reproved him.

He put it on again. "Why are masks *de rigueur,* Marguerite?" he inquired.

"You mean we ought just to have had dominoes with them? I know, but I specially wanted a fancy-dress ball, and masks are such fun that I thought we might have them too."

"Your brother doesn't wear one, I notice," remarked the sheikh, nodding to where Fountain, an imposing Cardinal Wolsey, stood talking to Mme de Pompadour.

"No, because he's the host. Shall I find you a partner, Mephistopheles?"

Amberley was watching a girl at the other side of the ballroom. "Will you introduce me to the contadina?" he asked.

Joan glanced in the girl's direction. "Yes, of course, but I don't know who she is."

"Kitty Crosby, isn't it?" said the sheikh.

"I thought Kitty was coming as a gipsy."

"Oh, was she? It might be Miss Halifax. No, I don't think it is, though."

Joan looked up at Amberley. "That's the fun of it. Do you know, I didn't recognize one of my oldest friends? Come on, I'll introduce you."

She led him to where the contadina was standing. "May I introduce Mephistopheles?" she said, smiling.

The contadina's eyes gleamed through the slits of her mask. She bowed and cast a fleeting glance up at the scarlet-clad figure before her.

"Shall we dance?" said Mr. Amberley.

"I should like to," she replied.

He drew her out into the room and took her in his arms. She danced well, but showed no desire to talk. Mr. Amberley guided her through the maze of shifting couples and said presently: "I wonder whether you are Miss Halifax or Miss Crosby?"

The red lips curved. "Ah!" said the contadina.

"Or neither?" pursued Mr. Amberley.

The hand in his moved slightly. "You will see at the unmasking, Mephistopheles."

"I wonder?" said Mr. Amberley. He was aware of her gaze searching his face and smiled down at her. "A bit of a mob, isn't it?" he said. "Do you think the Fountains can really know everyone here tonight?"

"Oh, but surely!"

"In these days of gate-crashing . . ." murmured Mr. Amberley.

"I don't think that is done in the country," she said.

"I expect you know much more about it than I do," he agreed politely.

The music came to an end. Mr. Amberley did not join in the clapping, but led his partner to the door. "You must let me get you something to drink," he said. He nodded towards a sofa in an alcove of the hall. "Will you wait for me there?"

The contadina appeared to consider. Then she shrugged. "Very well."

He found her seated on the sofa when he returned with two glasses. "You haven't run away," he observed, and handed her one of the glasses.

"Why should I?" she said coolly.

"I thought you might have grown impatient. There's a bit of a barge round the refreshments." He sat down beside her. "You remind me so much of someone I've met," he said thoughtfully. "Now who can it be?"

She sipped her hock-cup. "Funny," she said. "I don't seem to know you at all. You don't live here, do you?"

"Oh no!" he replied. "I'm merely a bird of passage. I'm staying with the Matthews'."

"Yes? For long?"

"No, just till I've cleared up a little matter that's interesting me."

She inclined her head. "I see. It sounds most intriquing."

He looked down at her. "Somehow I don't think you can be the girl I had in mind."

"No? Who is she?"

"Oh, nobody you would be likely to know. Rather a callow young thing."

She stiffened. "Really, I can't pretend to be flattered."

"But didn't I say I felt sure you couldn't be her?" he said. "Let's talk of something else. Are you fond of shooting?"

"I have never done any," she replied in a voice of dangerous calm.

"No? It's an odd thing, but nine women out of ten would rather have nothing to do with firearms." He offered her his open cigarette case. "You occasionally find an exception to the rule. I met a girl the other day who carried a businesslike automatic about with her. Fully loaded."

She took a cigarette from his case; her hand was quite steady. "In these days it's probably wise to carry a gun after dark," she said.

He paused in the act of striking a match. "Did I say it was after dark?" he asked, surprised.

"I assumed that it must be," she replied rather sharply. "Wasn't it?"

He held the match to the end of her cigarette. "As a matter of fact it was," he admitted.

She exhaled a long spiral of smoke and turned her head slightly so that she could survey him. "I'm trying to place you," she said. "I have a feeling you are probably a newspaper reporter."

She saw the flash of his teeth as he smiled. "Aren't you going to tell me why you think that?" he suggested.

She shook her head. "I shouldn't like to be rude," she said sweetly. "Are you a reporter?"

"No, fair lady. I'm a barrister."

He guessed that she was frowning.

"Oh!" she said. "A barrister."

"In the criminal court," nodded Amberley.

She got up abruptly. "That must be most interesting. I must go back to the ballroom; I'm engaged for this dance." She paused and he saw her lips curl scornfully. "May I compliment you on your costume? It suits you to perfection."

Mr. Amberley's shoulders shook slightly. He watched her walk away across the hall and wandered off in search of his cousin.

He had seen her go upstairs with an infatuated youth not long before. Mr. Amberley had a poor opinion of the youth, and saw nothing against interrupting the tête-à-tête and claiming Felicity for the dance which was undoubtedly his. He picked his way between the couples scattered on the staircase and reached the upper hall. It was as spacious as the one below, and had been provided with chairs and screens placed discreetly to form small sitting-out places. At one end was the broad staircase lit by a great window with many lights; at the other a graceful archway gave onto a wider passage that ran at right angles to it. Having reason to believe that his cousin was to be found in the picture gallery, which someone had said lay at the back of the house, Amberley went to the archway and glanced up and down the passage.

One end to the right of the arch was lit up; the other lay in shadow, as though to indicate that that portion of the house was not being used tonight. Amberley guessed that it led to the servants' quarters and the back stairs, and turned right.

The floor was carpeted in pile that deadened the sound of footsteps. Various doors, one labelled Ladies' Cloakroom, opened onto the passage at wide intervals; between them stood some obviously show pieces of furniture, very different from the massive mahogany that ruined the sitting room downstairs. Apparently the late Mr. Fountain had preferred the solid productions of his own period to these more graceful furnishings of an earlier age. Nor, it seemed, had his heir cared to banish the Victorian chairs and tables and cabinets in favour of these banished works of art.

Pictures in heavy gilt frames hung on the white walls. Mr. Amberley, something of a connoisseur, glanced up at them as he passed and presently came to a halt under a fine Reynolds. He was still standing thoughtfully surveying the picture when his host came out of the gallery at the end of the passage.

Fountain was in great spirits tonight; his enjoyment of the ball was unaffected and immense. He had been circulating freely among his guests, an excellent host, anxious to make the party a success and contributing largely to the general gaiety by his own evident geniality and pleasure.

When he saw Amberley he at once came up to him and clapped him on the shoulder. "This won't do, this won't do, Mephistopheles," he said chaffingly. "Not dancing? Don't tell me you haven't got a partner!"

"I have. I was going in search of her when I stopped to look at your pictures. I envy you your collection."

"Do you?" said Fountain. "Not much in my line, I'm afraid. I've got some jolly fine sporting prints though, if you like them. In my study."

"I prefer this," answered Amberley, still looking up at the Reynolds. "Who was she?"

"My dear fellow, I haven't the foggiest idea! Some great-grandmother, I expect. Got the family beetle brows, hasn't she? Not a bad-looking wench. You ought to get on to my housekeeper. She knows much more about all these hoary ancestors than I do."

Amberley turned away from the portrait and remarked that the ball was a great success.

Fountain looked pleased. "I think it's going quite well, don't you? Awfully silly, really, but I find I'm not too old to enjoy this sort of thing. Once I can get a lot of cheery people round me in a jolly party with a good band and dancing and all the rest of it, I forget all my worries. Daresay you'll laugh, but this is the kind of thing I like. Always did."

"Have you many worries?" said Amberley lightly. "It doesn't look like it."

A cloud descended on Fountain's brow. "I suppose we all have our private troubles," he answered. "There's a good deal of worry attached to a place like this, you know."

"I suppose so. You don't like the house, I gather?"

"No," Fountain said with odd vehemence. "I hate it. I used to think I liked it. Always rather looked forward to living here eventually. But sometimes I wish to God I was back in my town flat, without all the—worries of an estate to bother me."

"Yes, I can quite understand that. But I expect there are compensations."

A grim little smile twisted Fountain's mouth. "Oh yes. There are substantial compensations," he said. "Fact is, I wasn't cut out to be a country squire. Look here, quite sure you don't want me to introduce you to some charmer? No? Well, I must get back to the ballroom. Hope you find your truant." He went on down the passage and Amberley proceeded in a leisurely way to the picture gallery, where he succeeded in retrieving Felicity.

The unmasking was to take place in the ballroom at midnight, immediately before supper. Quite twenty minutes before twelve people had begun to congregate in the hall and ballroom, deserting the inglenooks upstairs for the fun of the unmasking. The noise of laughter and of chatter, mingled with strains of the latest quickstep, floated upstairs, contrasting queerly with the brooding stillness there.

There was a movement in the long passage; a door was opened softly and a girl came out and stood for a moment looking down into the shadows at the far end of the corridor. There was no one in sight, no sound of voices in the picture gallery where the lights still burned; even the medley of sound coming from below was hushed at this end of the house.

The Italian contadina stole along the passage slowly, looking for something. The painted eyes above her looked down as though watching what she would do. She reached the archway and glanced through it into the hall. It was empty. She seemed to hesitate, and still with that feeling that unknown eyes watched her, glanced nervously over her shoulder. There was no one there. She went on, but paused by a court-cupboard and put out her hand as though to touch it. Then she drew it back; it was not a court-cupboard that she was looking for.

Almost at the end of the corridor a slim shaft of light coming from an open door was cast on the opposite wall and caught the corner of a walnut tallboy. The girl saw and went forward.

The open door disclosed the well of the back stairs. She peeped through, but the place seemed deserted. One more look she sent over her shoulder, then glided towards the tallboy and softly pulled out the bottom drawer of its upper half. The drawer ran easily and made no sound, but the brass handles clinked as she released them and the tiny noise made her start guiltily.

The drawer was empty; the girl put one hand in, feeling with trembling fingers along the back.

Something impelled her to look up; the breath caught in her throat, and her groping hand was checked. A shadow had appeared in the panel of light on the wall, the shadow of a man's head.

The girl's eyes remained riveted on it while seconds passed. No sound had betrayed his approach, but someone was behind her, watching.

She slid the drawer home inch by inch; her throat felt parched, her knees shook.

A smooth voice that yet held a note of menace spoke: "Were you looking for something, miss?"

She turned; under the mask she was deadly pale. The valet stood in the doorway behind her, motionless.

She said with what assurance she could muster: "How you startled me! I have been admiring some of this wonderful old furniture. I wonder if you can tell me if this is a William and Mary piece?"

His eyes travelled slowly to the tallboy and back again to her face. His tight mouth relaxed into a smile that was curiously unpleasant. It seemed to triumph, to gloat; the girl felt her skin prick, but stood still, waiting.

"The tallboy," said Collins softly.

She swallowed. "Yes. Do you know its date?"

He put out his hand and passed it over the polished surface caressingly. His smile grew. "No, miss," he said politely. "I fear I do not. You are very interested in it, are you, miss?"

"I'm interested—yes. I must ask Mr. Fountain about it."

There was a footstep on the stone stairs; a woman's voice called: "Mr. Collins! Is that you up there? Mr. Collins, will you come? They'll be in to supper in a minute; the champagne ought to go on the ice."

He turned his head; the smile had faded. "I'll be down in a minute, Alice." He looked at the girl beside him with narrowed, calculating eyes. "I think you had better go downstairs, miss," he said. "This way, if you please."

He went before her down the passage; she had no choice but to follow him. He led her to the front stairs and stood aside for her to go down them. She hesitated, desperately seeking an excuse to keep him with her.

A big, scarlet-clad figure stood talking to a Mary Queen of Scots upon the half-landing. He looked round and saw the valet. The girl's heart gave a frightened leap, for the scarlet figure was that of her host and the hour of unmasking must be very near at hand. She slipped past him and went down to the hall.

"Oh, there you are, Collins! I want you," Fountain said.

An ugly look came into the valet's face and was swiftly gone again. He said: "Yes, sir," and followed his master downstairs.

The contadina's eyes stole to the big grandfather clock. In less than five minutes midnight would strike. Unconsciously her hands clasped and unclasped in the folds of her dress. Fountain had gone across the hall to the dining room with Collins; they were standing in the doorway, and Fountain seemed to be giving the valet some instructions. The man was watching her, she knew, though he did not appear to be looking in her direction. Two other people had joined Fountain; the valet bowed and went into the dining room.

At once the contadina began to edge her way through the crowd in the hall to the staircase. There was probably a second door into the dining room, which gave access to the back part of the house where the kitchens were situated, but the girl dared not let slip her opportunity.

A Harlequin with whom she had danced earlier in the evening detained her as she tried to slip past him. He showed a tendency to keep her beside him, pointing laughingly to the clock. One minute to twelve; she made an excuse that she had left a ring in the cloakroom and escaped him. She reached the top of the stairs as the first chime began and ran towards the archway.

The passage was silent and deserted; at the top of the back stairs the door still stood ajar. She reached it, cast a quick glance through, and with a shuddering sigh of relief pulled it to. The shaft of light disappeared, the latch clicked. The girl went to the tallboy and pulled open the drawer she had tried before. Straining her ears to catch the sound of a footstep approaching up the stairs, her hands went feverishly about their work, pressing, scratching along the back of the drawer. Something moved there; the false back came away, revealing a space behind. The girl thrust her hand in, feeling for some object. There was nothing there.

For a moment she stood quite still, her hand in the drawer. Then slowly she drew it out and replaced the false back. There was a bitter twist to her mouth. She pushed the drawer home.

"Admiring the furniture?" said a drawling voice.

She started uncontrollably and swung round. Leaning against the archway that led to the hall was Mephistopheles, without his mask.

The dry sob that broke from her was one of startled nerves. "You!" she panted. "You followed me up here!"

"Why not?" he said.

She could not answer; she stood staring at him, backed against the tallboy.

"Do you usually inspect the furniture in the houses you visit?" inquired Mr. Amberley in a conversational voice.

She made an effort to pull herself together. "I'm interested in period pieces."

"Are you indeed?" He strolled forward and saw her stiffen. "I'm quite uninstructed in these matters. But I'm most curious to know what you find to interest you *inside* the tallboy."

She said, trying to speak naturally: "Of course—I should not have opened the drawer. I only wanted to see whether—it ran easily. I haven't stolen anything, if that's what you think. There—isn't anything to steal."

"You don't have much luck, do you?" he said.

A footstep sounded in the hall; Fountain's boisterous voice said: "Half a moment, you people; I'm going to rout out the picture gallery. Aha, Miss Elliott, so I did spot you! It was the dimple that gave you away. Couldn't disguise that, you know!"

The contadina stood like a statue, but through the mask her eyes were fixed on Amberley's face in a rather desperate entreaty.

Fountain came through the archway into the passage humming a dance tune. He had almost turned right, in the direction of the gallery, when he caught sight of the couple at the other end of the passage. He stopped. "Hullo!" he said, surprised. "What are you two up to?"

Amberley looked down at the girl for a moment, then he turned. "Hullo!" he answered. "We're admiring the tallboy. Do you know the date of it?"

"Lord, what a chap you are for antiques!" said Fountain, going towards them. "No, I haven't the foggiest. But it's a show piece all right. Rotten things, tallboys, I think. If you put things in the top drawers you have to have a pair of steps to get 'em out again. But you can't put me off with furniture, my boy! No, no, it's midnight, and masks off! Now who's this pretty lady?"

He was standing before the contadina, burly and jovial, a hand advanced to take off her mask. Mr. Amberley caught his wrist and held it. "Oh no!" he said. "My privilege. You're very much *de trop*."

Fountain burst out laughing. "*De trop*, am I? All right,

all right, I won't spoil sport! Tallboys indeed! You tell that to the marines."

Someone called: "Basil! *Do* come here!" from the direction of the stairs, and Fountain began to walk away, saying over his shoulder:

"Mind you claim the penalty for being masked after midnight, Amberley!"

In another moment he was gone. The contadina's muscles relaxed. She said: "Why did you do that? Why didn't you let him unmask me?"

"You ought to be grateful to me for not letting him," said Mr. Amberley.

"I am grateful. But why did you do it? I know very well you don't trust me."

"Not an inch," said Mr. Amberley. "But I'm handling you myself."

"If you think I'm a thief—oh, and a murderess too!—why don't you give me up to the police?" she said bitterly.

"Well," said Mr. Amberley, "having given way to a somewhat foolish impulse and refrained from mentioning your presence on the scene of the murder to the police, I can't very well come out with it now. And who am I to question your interest in antiques?"

She put up her hand and ripped her mask off; her face was flushed, her eyes stormy. "I hate you!" she shot out. "You didn't shield me out of—out of—consideration! It was because you want to solve what you choose to think is a mystery by yourself!"

"Quite right," agreed Mr. Amberley. "Though somewhat involved."

She looked as though she would have liked to hit him. "Then let me tell you I'd rather you went downstairs now and let the Fountains know I'm a—a gate-crasher and a thief than—than have you following me and spying what I do!"

"I haven't the smallest doubt of that," he replied. "After all, what would happen if I gave you away to the Fountains? You would merely be shown the door. That wouldn't help me in the least."

She prepared to leave him, but paused to say: "All right!

But if you think you're going to find out anything about me you're wrong."

"Would you like to take a bet on it?" he inquired.

But she had gone. Mr. Amberley gave a laugh under his breath, stooped to pick up the handkerchief she had dropped, and began to stroll away towards the hall.

CHAPTER V

MR. AMBERLEY, with a sloth his cousin found disgusting, spent most of the next morning in a somnolent state in the garden. A burst of hot sunshine induced Felicity, always optimistic, to put up the hammock. Mr. Amberley observed this, and approved. Felicity found him stretched in it an hour after breakfast, tried to turn him out, failed, and went off very scornfully to play hard-court tennis.

But Mr. Amberley was not destined to be left for long in peace. Shortly after twelve o'clock his aunt came out and poked him with her sunshade. He opened his eyes, surveyed her in silent indignation, and closed them again.

"Dear Frank—so sylvan. But you must wake up. The most tiresome thing."

Without opening his eyes Mr. Amberley murmured a sentence he knew by heart. "Bridges haven't sent the fish, and unless I will be an angel and run into Upper Nettlefold for it there won't be any lunch."

"No, nothing like that. At least, I trust not. That man who annoys your uncle."

"Which one?" inquired Mr. Amberley.

"Colonel Watson. In the drawing room. *Must* I invite him to lunch?"

Mr. Amberley was at last roused. He sat up and swung his long legs out of the hammock. "I forgive you, Aunt Marion," he said. "It was very nice of you to come and warn me. I shall take my book into the woodshed. On no account ask him to lunch."

Lady Matthews smiled. "I do sympathize, my dear. Of course I do. But not a warning. He has been talking to your uncle for half an hour. The gold standard, you know. So incomprehensible and unsuitable. He came on business. Something very legal, but he wouldn't go. If he had only told Humphrey that he wanted to see you! We have only just discovered it. Not that he said so. It was sheer intuition on my part. Do come, my dear. Be very rude, and then he will not want to stay to lunch."

"All right, I will be. *Very* rude," said Mr. Amberley, and descended from the hammock.

"So sweet of you, Frank, but perhaps better not," said his aunt dubiously.

The chief constable's manner when Mr. Amberley lounged in through the long window in the drawing room was an admirable mixture of casual surprise and friendly gratification. "Ah, hullo, Amberley!" he said, getting up and shaking hands. "So you are still here! This is a pleasant surprise. How are you?"

"Sunk in apathy," said Mr. Amberley. "Just about half awake. Certainly not more."

This seemed to provide the colonel with the opening he wanted. He laughed and said: "Sunk in apathy! Surely that can't mean bored?"

"Not yet," said Mr. Amberley.

His uncle gave a sudden snort of laughter which he managed to turn into a cough.

"You want something to occupy your mind," said the colonel in a jocular way. "Perhaps you'd like to try your hand at our little murder case!"

Mr. Amberley saw fit to treat this as a joke. Colonel Watson abandoned the facetious vein. "Seriously, my dear fellow, I should be delighted if you cared to give us a hand with it. It's a most interesting problem. Quite in your line."

"Very kind of you, sir, but you don't want an amateur dabbling in these professional matters."

The colonel realized that he did not like Mr. Amberley. Looking back, he could not remember that he ever had liked him. Those hard eyes had a way of staring contemptuously through one, and that ironic smile was the most irritating thing he had ever seen. The fact was the fellow was too damned conceited. Obviously he wasn't going to beg, as a favour, to be allowed to have a hand in the solving of this worrying murder. The colonel dallied for a moment with the idea of taking him at his word and leaving him out of the thing altogether. It would afford him distinct gratification just to turn the conversation on to quite trivial matters, chat for a little and then go, leaving this insufferable young man to wish he had not been so off-hand.

The idea was very tempting, but the colonel put it aside. He was rather dismally aware that he was not a particularly clever man, but he hoped that he was clever enough not to cut off his nose just to spite his face. It was all very well for the inspector to say that they would clear the whole mystery up as soon as certain data came to hand, but Colonel Watson had no great opinion of the inspector's ability to probe any mystery. A good routine-man, yes, and a capable man, but it was no use blinking facts; this sort of thing was not in his line. Of course he didn't want to call in Scotland Yard. The colonel could quite sympathize with him over that; he didn't want to call in Scotland Yard himself. He hated those highly efficient persons who came from the Yard, and complained that they should have been called in sooner, before the trail was cold; and took the whole matter out of one's hands. Really, when one considered it, they were worse than Frank Amberley. He was much ruder than they were, because they took the trouble to disguise their scorn of the previous conduct of the case, and he never had any hesitation in condemning what he chose to think blamable. But at least he could not relegate them all to the status of lower schoolboys, and to do him justice he hadn't, over that Bilton affair, wanted to take all the credit of success to himself.

He ought not to consult a layman. It was irregular, and he did not like irregularity. He ought to have swallowed his pride and called in the Yard at once. He had allowed himself to be overruled by the inspector, and now he dreaded having to apply to the Yard, for they would have considerable justification for complaining of a cold trail. There would be a great deal of unpleasantness about it. On the whole it would be much better to let young Amberley—well, he wasn't so very young, perhaps. Must be about thirty-five, he supposed. Still, too young to sneer at his elders. Never mind about that; no denying the fellow was remarkably astute. Yes, better to let young Amberley see what he could do. He was naturally pretty well known at the Yard, too, so it wasn't like calling in a stranger. If the Yard got to hear about it they wouldn't object. And really the way he had handled that Bilton case was masterly.

The inspector, of course, would be furious. He had never got over that young devil sending him off twenty miles on a wild-goose chase and saying afterwards by way of explanation that he had put him on to a false trail because he couldn't do any harm there.

A smile flitted across the colonel's worried countenance. He could still see the inspector's face; he wouldn't have missed that incident for worlds. Serve the inspector right! He was a self-important ass. And if he didn't like Amberley being let into it he could damned well lump it. The colonel had a shrewd suspicion that the tiresome young man was nosing about a bit for his own amusement. Well, if he wanted to dabble in detection he had better do it on behalf of the police.

He looked up and was annoyed to find that Mr. Amberley, still leaning against the window frame, was watching him with that ironical smile he so much disliked. Damn the fellow! Do him good to have a setback once in a while.

"Look here, Amberley!" he said abruptly, "I wish you would give me a hand over this case."

"I know you do," replied Mr. Amberley, still smiling.

"Frank, behave yourself!" said his uncle.

"Oh, I know his little way, Matthews!" said the colonel. "I've worked with him before. Now, own up, Amberley, you want to have a finger in this pie!"

"All right," said Frank. "But it's in."

"I thought as much. Now you know we can't have outsiders interfering, my dear fellow. No need for me to tell you that."

"Not a bit. I won't interfere."

"No, no, you misunderstand me! That wasn't what I meant."

"I know exactly what you meant, Colonel. You want me to act for the police. Very, very irregular."

"Possibly! Possibly! But you have worked with us before, after all. This case ought to interest you. It's one of the most incomprehensible I have ever struck."

"Ah!" said Mr. Amberley. He reached out his hand towards an open box of cigarettes and took one, and stood tapping it on his thumbnail. "I don't think I want to work with the police," he said.

From the other end of the room Sir Humphrey spoke. "Then pray don't, Frank. I very much dislike this bringing of unsavoury cases into one's home. I see enough in my official capacity without——"

"Quite, Uncle," Mr. Amberley said abstractedly. He put the cigarette between his lips and felt in his pocket for matches.

"Do you mean you take no interest in the case?" asked Colonel Watson, at a loss.

Amberley struck a match and watched the flame creep up the stick. At the last moment he lit the cigarette and flicked the match into the empty fireplace. "I'm taking a lot of interest in it," he said. "And I don't want to waste my time pointing out obvious facts to Inspector Fraser."

"My dear sir, I can assure you——"

"On the other hand," continued Amberley thoughtfully, "if I don't do something about it he's almost certain to queer the whole pitch."

The colonel pricked up his ears. "That sounds as though you're on the track of something," he said.

"Does it?"

"Come, come, Amberley, you must be open with me!"

"When I've got something definite to tell you, you shall have it," said Amberley. "At the moment I haven't. Meanwhile I suppose I'd better know what line the police are taking."

"It's hard to know which line to take," said the colonel, frowning worriedly. "There is no data, you see. Nothing to go on."

Up went Mr. Amberley's black brows, but he said nothing.

"We have a man shot on a deserted road. No sign of struggle. No apparent motive, unless it be robbery. The locality seems to rule out the bandit theory, though one can't, of course, entirely set that aside."

"Do you think you could try?" asked Amberley wearily. "I've no objection to Fraser looking about for a likely bandit; it ought to occupy his time very nicely. But I'm getting a little tired of hearing that singularly foolish theory. Dawson was not murdered by road-bandits."

"That is my own belief," said the colonel, keeping his end up. "The locality alone——"

"Yes, I've grasped that, Colonel. What you don't appear to have grasped is the considerable amount of data at your disposal."

"I think I have all the facts," said the colonel stiffly.

"I know you have," said Mr. Amberley. "I gave 'em to you in my original statement. They were refreshingly significant."

"As for instance—?"

Mr. Amberley sat down on the edge of the table in the window. "I'll recapitulate, Colonel. By the way, it was a premeditated murder, you know."

The colonel jumped.

"I know nothing of the sort, I can assure you. I admit the possibility, but I should require very conclusive proof before I made such a positive statement."

"Just so," said Mr. Amberley. "You would be very wise. And now I'll give you the proof. You have the corpse of a murdered man discovered in a car on a lonely road. First significant fact."

"The lonely road? I understand that you did not think that significant."

"On the contrary, highly significant. You, Colonel, treat it as a merely negative link in the chain. The second significant fact is the position of the car."

The colonel repeated rather blankly: "Of the car? ... Well?"

"Certainly of the car. It was drawn up at the side of the

road, with the engine switched off and only the side lamps burning. Why?"

The colonel made an airy gesture. "There might be several reasons. If the man was held up——"

"He would not have drawn right into the side. The car was definitely parked."

"Well, then, say he had engine trouble."

"Which he thought to overcome by an act of faith, presumably."

"I don't follow you."

"He made no attempt to get out of the car. It was a damp night, the road was muddy. The man's shoes were perfectly dry."

"True." The colonel nodded and fingered his moustache. "Then we're left—in default of other evidence— with the theory that he went to meet someone. But surely an odd place and an odd hour to choose?"

"It depends which way you look at it," said Amberley. "If he had any reason to wish to keep that meeting secret, not such an odd place or hour."

"Yes. Yes, there is something in that," admitted the colonel. "But we must not lose sight of the fact that the man was in no sense a suspicious character. He had been at the manor for many years, he was well known in the district; a decent, quiet servant, with no entanglements, not even a flirtation to his record. And this furtive assignation, you know, undoubtedly points to a woman in the case."

"I should not say 'undoubtedly,' " Mr. Amberley said.

"Perhaps not. No, perhaps not. But go on, my dear fellow. Your third fact?"

"My third fact—also significant—is that Dawson was taken quite unawares and was shot before he knew that he was in any danger."

"Yes, I can see your reasoning. You are going on his position at the time of the murder. You assume that the person or persons whom he had gone to meet were lying in wait for him?"

"As a matter of fact, I don't. If the person he was going to meet had any reason for wishing him dead it is unlikely that Dawson would not have known it. In which case he would have been on his guard. Which he was not. Taking into consideration the hour, the place and the manner of the murder, I suggest that someone who had a very good reason for not wishing the assignation to take place discovered that it had been made and followed Dawson to the spot, and there shot him."

"How?" demanded the colonel. "You forget the man was in a car. He must have heard another car had there been one."

"I should imagine that he not only heard it, but also saw it," said Amberley. "Though I incline to the belief that the murderer was on a motor bicycle."

"Oh, you do, do you? And why?"

"Merely because if you are right in assuming that he lay in wait for Dawson a motor bicycle could have been hidden in the hedge, or possibly run into the field behind. There was a gate. But you may have your car if you like. The main point is that the murderer shot Dawson either from a place of concealment (which probably means that the actual place of meeting was known to him), or from some vehicle driven towards Dawson's car."

The colonel thought it over. "Yes. Quite possible, but not conclusive, Amberley. Not conclusive, you know. Say that I concede it for the purposes of discussion. With whom was the assignation made?"

"I suggest, Colonel, that you depute my friend Fraser to find that out. He won't succeed, of course, but it will keep him occupied for a bit."

"Really, really, Amberley!" expostulated the colonel half-heartedly. "If you haven't any theories to fit that, then tell me what you suppose the motive to be that prompted the murderer to stop the meeting at all costs? Or can't you advance an opinion on that either?"

"Oh, I can tell you that," replied Amberley. "The motive was robbery, of course."

"Robbery? My dear fellow, what are you talking about? A moment ago you refused to listen to that theory!"

"Oh, no, I didn't," said Amberley calmly. "I only begged you to rid your mind of the bandit notion. I see you haven't succeeded. I wish you'd try. It's beginning to bore me."

The colonel bit back something he wanted very much to say. "Perhaps you will consider this little point: If, as you assert, the murder was deliberately planned, I take it we may assume that the assassin knew Dawson and was aware, in point of fact, of his station in life and of his probable resources? Very well. Will you have the goodness to inform me what the unknown assassin can have supposed Dawson to be carrying that was of sufficient value to induce him to commit a murder?"

Amberley regarded him in some amusement. "What a lot you think I know!" he remarked. "When you have discovered the answer to that riddle you will in all probability have discovered your murderer. I advise you to consider carefully two points. One, the fact that the dead man's pockets had been rifled, that there was neither notecase nor pocketbook found on him, but that in one trouser pocket was loose silver amounting to fifteen shillings, and a gold watch and chain in his waistcoat. Two, that during the past couple of years Dawson had been receiving money over and above the salary Fountain paid him. Which reminds me that I should like to know a little more about those various accounts of his."

"The inspector is making inquiries. It goes without saying that we fastened on to that at once. I'm to understand that in your opinion it was not money that the murderer wanted?"

"No, it was not money, Colonel."

The colonel rose reluctantly. "Well, it's all very interesting, but there isn't much to go on," he complained. "I seem to be just where I was. Haven't you any practical suggestion to make?"

"Not at present," said Mr. Amberley. "There is one thing I want investigated—but I think I'll do it myself. I'll let you know the result."

"Well, I shall rely on hearing from you as soon as possible," said the colonel. "In the meantime you must understand that we shall pursue investigations as we think best."

"Do," said Mr. Amberley cordially. "Carry on as you're doing now; you won't do any harm."

The colonel shook hands with Sir Humphrey and said over his shoulder with some hauteur: "We hope to do considerable good."

"Well, that's possible too," said Mr. Amberley. He held out his hand. "Good-bye. And I shouldn't worry, Colonel. Quite simple really, you know."

Sir Humphrey saw his guest off the premises and returned to the drawing room. "Frank, it is apparent to anyone who knows you that you are in possession of facts which you did not see fit to divulge to our friend Watson," he said severely.

"Lots of 'em," agreed Frank.

"Do you know," said Sir Humphrey, "that it is the duty of every honest citizen——"

Amberley held up his hand. "I do, sir. But I've been asked to solve this little problem."

"I should not have thought," said his uncle, "that putting the police in full possession of all the facts—and, I may add, of whatever suspicions you may be nourishing—was incompatible with solving the mystery."

"No?" said Frank. "Well, perhaps you haven't worked with Messrs Watson, Fraser and Company. I think you'd better leave it to me, Uncle."

"I have every intention of so doing," replied Sir Humphrey with dignity. "I have not the slightest desire to meddle in these very distasteful affairs."

CHAPTER VI

FELICITY was left in undisputed possession of the hammock all the afternoon. Amberley had succeeded so well in shaking off the sloth she had condemned that he left for London in his Bentley immediately the chief constable had gone. Lady Matthews was distressed and murmured: "*Beignets de sole*," but not even this gastronomic bait could induce her nephew to postpone his trip until after lunch. Lunch at Greythorne was apt to be a prolonged affair, and even in a fast car the journey to town took over an hour.

He reached London before two o'clock and drove at once to his flat in the Temple. His man, Peterson, was in charge there and displayed no surprise at seeing him. He remained for half an hour and among other things found time to eat a hastily prepared lunch. He then drove to the *Times* office, where he spent a tedious but ultimately satisfactory hour with a stack of back numbers. His researches carried him several years into the past, and he somewhat savagely cursed the inaccuracy of females on the all-important subject of dates. But he ultimately discovered the information he sought and left the *Times* office for a general post office. There he wrote out a long cable in code and dispatched it. His last objective was a firm of private inquiry agents. His business there did not take him long, and by half-past four the Bentley was heading south, down the Kingston By-Pass.

Amberley followed Felicity's short cut to Greythorne, this time successfully, and reached the house just after half-past five.

He found his cousin and Anthony Corkran having a late tea in the library and learned that Corkran had driven over in the early afternoon to get him to play golf. Not finding him he had persuaded Felicity to play instead. They had just returned from the links.

Felicity rang for a third cup and saucer, and poured out tea for Amberley. It appeared that Joan was suffering from a severe headache and had gone to bed immediately after lunch, leaving her swain disconsolate.

Amberley was politely sympathetic. Corkran said gloomily: "Mind you, I don't blame her. Brother Basil has to be seen to be believed today. He's spent a jolly morning finding fault with everything that's been done for the past six months. Oh, he's in a sweet mood, I can assure you."

"Why?" said Amberley.

Corkran held his cup out for some more tea. "Somebody's handed him a dollop of bad news. Up till then everything was going fine. All full of bonhomie and good cheer. He even ate a couple of fried eggs for breakfast, which personally I found a pretty grim sight after champagne at four in the morning."

"Who brought this bad news?"

"A man with one eye and a wooden leg," said Corkran promptly. "He bore the appearance of a seafaring man and—hold on a minute—yes, there was something vaguely sinister about him. We—we heard the thud of his wooden stump as it drew nearer across the hall."

A book hurtled towards him and was neatly fielded. "Rank bad shot," he commented, and put it down.

"Shut up, don't rag!" said Felicity. "That's one of the library books. Go on, Tony, who did bring the news?"

"I see that you've guessed it," Corkran said. "What I said about the sailor—no, sorry! seafaring man—was untrue. It was really brought by a man who gave two resounding knocks upon the door and delivered it up in absolute silence. He did no wait, but went off as silently as he had come——"

"You get a very late first post," remarked Amberley. "I hate to interrupt this enthralling recital, but do you happen to know what the news was?"

"Oh, listen to this, everybody!" said Corkran. "The great detective scents a clue! Do not miss tomorrow's fine instalment. No, Mr. Holmes, I do not. But upon my return to the ancestral home I will lure Brother Basil away by a cunning ruse and burst open the safe. If he's got one. If not I'll just go through all the correspondence in his desk and trust to luck. Among the most sought-after guests for this season's house parties is Mr. Anthony Corkran, whose ready tact and savoir-faire make him so universally popular."

"You are an ass," said Felicity. "I'm sorry it's upset Joan, though. Perhaps Basil's lost a lot of money on the stock exchange."

"No. Wrong. That I do know."

Amberley was looking at him. "What else do you know, Corks? Mind divulging it?"

Anthony looked doubtful. "Well—not strictly the clean potato, is it? What I mean is—guest in the man's house, you know. The Public School Spirit, and Playing for the Side, and all that wash. That's how Brother Basil talks, by the way. He does really."

"How do you know it was bad news at all?" asked Felicity.

"Well, when a chap opens a letter, reads it and turns a sort of pea-green, and sits staring at the fatal document like one struck with the palsy, the astute spectator at once divines the cause. Besides, I asked him."

"Did he say it was?"

Anthony thought for a moment. "Yes, and no. When he got green about the gills, I said I hoped he hadn't had bad news. I don't mind telling you that he looked pretty tucked up. Well, he gave a sort of start and folded up the letter, and said in a forced kind of way that it wasn't exactly bad, but rather disturbing. It certainly disturbed him all right. And the funny thing, is——" He stopped, and a frown descended upon his cherubic countenance. He looked at Amberley, evidently considering something, and said abruptly: "Look here, I will tell you. I really don't much mind about the *esprit de corps* muck. He may be my blinking host, but the way he treats Joan gets me bang in the gizzard. The letter that shocked him so came from a private detective agency. I happen to know, because he sat with it in his hand, staring at it, and when I looked up, the heading across the top of the sheet caught my eye."

"I see," said Amberley slowly. "And it upset him. H'm!"

"Don't tell us what you've thought of, will you?" said Felicity scathingly.

"No, my sweet, I won't."

"Well, you may think it helps towards solving the mystery," said Anthony, "but as far as I can see it merely adds to it. The thing is getting like pea-soup. If you're trying to implicate Brother Basil I admit it's a kindly thought, but it won't work. I should simply have to come forward and say he was in my company at the time the murder was committed."

"As a matter of fact," said Amberley, "I wasn't thinking of the murder."

Next morning he learned that Basil Fountain seemed to have more or less recovered from the shock of the news he had received, but that there had been some sort of row with Collins. For this piece of information Amberley was indebted to Joan Fountain, who walked over to Greythorne with Corkran partly to exercise a couple of terriers and partly to bring Felicity a book she had promised to lend her. Joan looked pale after the previous day's indisposition, and it seemed to Amberley that her smile was a little mechanical. Usually reserved, she had lowered her barriers slightly and made only a small attempt to check Felicity's freely expressed opinion of her stepbrother.

It was plain that she clung rather pathetically to Corkran's reassuring presence. For her, the root of all evil lay in the manor, nor did she disguise the fact that from the first she had had an uncontrollable aversion from it. It spelled discomfort, prying eyes, mystery, and her brother's worst moods. She did not try to explain what she felt, or to apologize for her unreason. She thought every house had an atmosphere peculiar, each one, to itself. At Greythorne, for instance, was only happiness and warm kindliness. But the manor brooded over past sins and past tragedies. It was secret, and so still that depression met one at its very door.

Into these psychic realms neither Corkran nor Amberley could follow her, yet each of them had felt the tension that preyed so much on her spirits. In Corkran's opinion it was not the house which was at fault, but its inmates, by which he meant the master and the valet. Joan shook her head; perhaps she and Basil had never had much in common, but until they came to the manor there had never been such friction as now existed. The manor had had its effect on him as well as on her. As for the valet—— She gave a shiver and was silent.

Upon hearing the row in full swing in Fountain's study that morning Anthony had cherished hopes of the valet's departure. What had passed between them was not known, but Joan thought Collins was objecting to his extra duties. They had heard Fountain's voice raised angrily, and later they had seen Collins come out of the study with his mouth shut in a hard, thin line, but although Fountain had said that the valet was becoming insufferable, and by God, he had a good mind to sack him, nothing had been done. Instead, Fountain had gone up to town to interview a prospective butler.

It was proving as difficult as he had feared to fill Dawson's place. The only candidates who had so far applied for the post were quite ineligible, while the few suitable men whose names had been sent to Fountain by Finch's Registry Office did not care to come to a house which was situated seven miles from the nearest town and nearly two from the main road. However, the registry office had rung up at tea-time the previous day to inform Fountain that a fresh applicant had appeared, who did not seem to mind the manor's out-of-the-way position. He had gone up to interview the man, and if he, like the rest, was no good, he was going to insert an advertisement in the *Morning Post*.

It seemed a good moment, to Joan, since Fountain would not be at home, to invite Felicity and Amberley to tea at the manor. Felicity accepted, but Mr. Amberley had a previous engagement. Pressed, he was irritatingly evasive. Felicity excused him to her friend on the score that he was probably going to hunt for clues.

Joan had not known that he was taking anything more than an ordinary interest in the murder case. She seemed pleased and asked shyly whether he thought he would be able to solve the problem.

"I think so," he answered with unusual gentleness.

"I'm glad," she said simply. "I know it is worrying Basil. It's upset him very much. It almost seems to haunt him."

When Amberley set out shortly before four in the afternoon to keep his "previous engagement," he took the road into Upper Nettlefold and bore straight through the town in the direction of Ivy Cottage.

The road was a continuation of the High Street, which ran southwards out of the town past a row of new cottages. The houses soon came to an end. The road bent to the west and ran along for a few hundred yards beside the river Nettle. Then the river took a curve to the left and the lane leading to Ivy Cottage came into sight, cutting up beside some undulating pasture-land.

Mr. Amberley had just reached the foot of the lane and had slowed down for the turn when he heard himself hailed. He stopped, and saw the burly form of Sergeant Gubbins mounted on a bicycle and pedalling strenuously towards him.

Amberley drew into the side of the road and switched off his engine. "Well, Sergeant?" he said.

The sergeant got off his bicycle, puffing, and remarked that it was a warm day. Mr. Amberley agreed.

The sergeant shook his head a little sadly. "I hoped you might run into the station this morning, sir. I saw the chief constable yesterday."

"Coincidence," said Mr. Amberley. "So did I."

The sergeant fixed him with a reproachful eye. "When he told me what had been said up at Greythorne—well, what I feel is, it ain't like you, Mr. Amberley."

"What isn't?"

"The way you're treating this case. Not like you at all, it isn't. Because me knowing you as I do I've got a feeling you're keeping things up your sleeve. Now that's a thing I wouldn't have believed of you, sir. Then there's what you said to me the other day, after the inquest. Not that I set any store by that at the time, me knowing that you're apt to get humorous in your way of talking. But when the colonel happened to mention your saying to him how you didn't know that you wanted to work for the police that made me very surprised. Because putting two and two together, and calling to mind that very same remark which you passed to me, it does seem to look as though you meant it, which is a thing I wouldn't have believed."

"Sorry," said Mr. Amberley.

The sergeant said severely: "Of course I know you go against the law a lot in the way of business——"

"What?"

"Getting off them as ought to be at Dartmoor," said the sergeant. "Often and often you've done that, but as I say, that's in the way of business and fair enough. But it's putting ideas into your head, sir, that's what it is."

"Look here!" said Mr. Amberley. "Just what are you driving at?"

"You're not acting straight by us, begging your pardon, sir," said the sergeant doggedly. "Keeping things back. You haven't given us anything to go on, and it's as plain as a pikestaff you've got your suspicions."

"Is it? I'm sorry to hear it. Don't hustle me, Sergeant."

The sergeant eyed him speculatively and perceived suddenly that Mr. Amberley's attention had wandered. He was looking past the sergeant to the gate of Ivy Cottage, which was just visible up the lane. The sergeant was about to turn round to see what was interesting him so much when he was stopped.

"Don't turn round, Sergeant," Amberley said quietly.

The sergeant was immediately possessed by an almost uncontrollable desire just to glance over his shoulder, but he managed to check it. "What have you seen, sir?"

Amberley was no longer looking up the lane. A minute ago the wicket-gate had opened, a man had slipped out, and cast rather a furtive look to left and right. When he saw the car at the bottom of the lane, with its owner apparently deep in conversation with Sergeant Gubbins, he had turned abruptly and walked away, up the lane.

"Very interesting," said Mr. Amberley slowly. "And what, Sergeant, do we make of that?"

The sergeant swelled with indignation. "A fat lot of chance I have of making anything of it, haven't I, sir? 'Don't turn round,' you say, and then ask me what I make of it!"

Mr. Amberley was stroking his chin meditatively. "It looks as though I'm not so far out," he said.

"Does it, sir?" said the sergeant in considerable dudgeon. "Well, isn't that nice? P'raps if I'm patient you'll see fit to tell me what you've seen."

"A man, Sergeant. Just a man."

"You do sometimes," agreed the sergeant, heavily sarcastic. "I can see a couple now. Young Thomas and Mr. Fairleigh they are. You wait, sir, and you'll see them too."

"An ordinary, respectable personage," mused Mr. Amberley. "Yet he wasn't pleased to see us here. Where does that lane lead to, Gubbins?"

"Fawcett's farm," said the sergeant shortly.

"Nothing else?"

"It stops there."

"Ah!" said Mr. Amberley. "Do you think our friend Collins can really have business at Fawcett's farm?"

The sergeant was interested. "Collins? Was it him, sir?"

"It was, Sergeant. He's been calling at Ivy Cottage."

"That's funny," said the sergeant. "What would he want there? Gone off to Fawcett's, has he? Then he'll cut across the fields. There's a right-of-way. Now I come to think of it, we don't know much about these Browns. The young fellow's in the Blue Dragon most nights. Drinks himself silly, that's what he does. But what does he want with a valet?"

"I wonder," said Mr. Amberley.

"Yes, sir, I've no doubt you do, and if I was sure you didn't do more than wonder—— What might you have been meaning when you said what you did just now, about it looking as though you weren't so far out?"

"I see it's no use trying to conceal anything from you, Sergeant," said Mr. Amberley, shaking his head.

"Well, I hope I've got my share of brains, sir," replied the sergeant, slightly mollified. "I don't say I set out to be one of these people who think they know everything and, consequent, talk so clever there's no understanding what they're driving at half the time—*if* anything, which some people might doubt."

Mr. Amberley grinned. "Such as?"

"Just someone I happened to have in my mind," said the sergeant carelessly.

"Oh, I see. I thought you were talking about me for a moment."

The sergeant strove with himself. "Now look here, sir!" he said. "I can't stand in the road bandying words with you all day while you have your little bit of fun with me. I've got my work to do. I *was* going to mention to you that I don't like the look of that Collins, and never have, but what's the good? It wouldn't interest you."

"Not in the least," said Mr. Amberley frankly, "but it would interest me very much to know why he goes calling at Ivy Cottage."

"Well, that's something we *can* find out," said the sergeant, his spirits rising. "I don't say that I see what it's got to do with the crime, but if you want to know there'd be more sense in me investigating it than joining a lot of goggling fools in turning over dead leaves for a cartridge-case. Which is what the inspector set some of the men on to do. And they haven't found it yet, nor they aren't likely to, though Constable Parkins found a kettle with a hole in it and the half of an old boot in the ditch."

"Did they find any trace of a bicycle having been pushed into the field behind the hedge?" Anthony inquired.

"No, sir, not so far as I know."

"Did they look in the field?"

"Oh yes, sir, they looked all right, but I wouldn't say but what they were a bit distracted like, on account of a lot of young bullocks Mr. Fawcett's got in that field. They were a bit playful, I understand."

"Splendid! Did they play with Inspector Fraser?"

The sergeant put up a large hand to cover his mouth. "Well, sir, I did hear as how the inspector didn't stop long enough to give them the chance, so to speak."

Mr. Amberley laughed and switched on his engine again. "Not fond of animals, perhaps. Now, Sergeant, you mustn't keep me gossiping with you. I've got something better to do, you know."

"Me? Me keep you——? Well, I'm——"

"And I'd rather you didn't investigate Collins' visit to Ivy Cottage, if it's all the same to you. I'll do that myself."

The car began to move forward; the sergeant walked beside it for a few steps. "That's all very well, sir, but when do we get something to go on?"

"All in good time," promised Mr. Amberley; "I haven't got much myself yet. I'll tell you this, though; unless I'm much mistaken you'll find that the murder of Dawson is the least interesting part of the whole problem. So long."

The sergeant fell back and stood watching the car go up the lane to Ivy Cottage. He shook his head darkly, turned his bicycle round, and resumed his interrupted progress into Upper Nettlefold.

Amberley left his car outside the little white gate and went up the path to the front door. The window of the living room was open, and through it he heard Mark Brown's voice say petulantly: "You made a bloody mess of the whole thing. You ought to have let me do it. I bet I wouldn't have let anyone steal a march on me. You let him get the thing and then you send for him to come up here. The hell of a lot of use that is! Supposing anyone had seen him?"

Amberley knocked loudly on the door, and the voice ceased abruptly. After a moment the door was opened by Mark Brown, and the bull-terrier bounded out apparently delighted to welcome the guest.

Amberley said easily: "Good afternoon. I came to return a piece of lost property to your sister."

Mark recognized him and flushed. "Oh, it's you, is it? Come in, won't you? I say—I'm afraid I was a bit screwed the other day. Awfully decent of you to have brought me home."

Amberley brushed that aside. When he liked he could be very pleasant, and apparently he liked now. He had Mark at his ease in two minutes, and Mark, losing some of his suspicion, invited him to come in to see his sister.

He came in, escorted by the bull-terrier, and preceded Mark into the little sitting room, where Shirley Brown was standing behind the table. She gave no sign of being pleased to see him, but watched him intently under her frowning brows.

Mr. Amberley was not in the least dismayed. "How do you do?" he said. "Did you get home all right the other evening?"

"If I hadn't I should hardly be here now," she replied.

"Oh, shut up, Shirley!" interposed her brother, pulling a chair forward. "Won't you sit down, Mr. Amberley, isn't it? Didn't you say you had something belonging to my sister?"

A startled look leaped into her eyes. She said quickly: "Something of mine?"

"Something you left behind you at the manor," said Amberley.

There was a moment's tense silence; the brother's and sister's eyes met for an instant.

"Oh?" said Mark with forced carelessness. "What was that?"

"Just something Miss Brown dropped," said Amberley and brought out a crumpled handkerchief from his pocket. "Here it is."

The tenseness passed. Shirley took the handkerchief. "How very kind of you to go to so much trouble," she said ironically.

"Not at all," said Amberley courteously.

She stared at him in mingled surprise and hostility. Her brother, more hospitable than she, filled an awkward gap by asking Amberley if he would not stay to tea.

Amberley accepted, and meeting Shirley's indignant gaze smiled blandly at her. She swallowed something in her throat and stalked out of the room into the kitchen.

Mark began to apologize for the sparse surroundings. They had taken the cottage for a month, he said. They both worked in town—here his eyes shifted from Amberley's for a moment—and were on holiday. Shirley was Anne March's secretary. He expected that Amberley knew the name. She was a novelist and wrote pretty good tripe. Asked where he himself worked he answered uncommunicatively that it was in a bank. From his somewhat shamefaced manner and from the knowledge that bank clerks were not in the habit of enjoying a whole month's holiday, Amberley guessed that this job had come to an abrupt end. He was not surprised, but with rare tact led the talk away from such uncomfortable topics.

When Shirley reappeared with the tea-tray he was admiring a kaross of King Jackal skins which had been flung over the horsehair sofa. He said that a friend of his had brought one home from Durban. Mark replied that the shops there had lots of them; they were bought mostly by tourists.

Shirley interrupted this amiable interchange by demanding curtly whether her guest took milk and sugar. He transferred his attention to her, and to her annoyance insisted on discussing the ball at the manor. Her monosyllabic replies did not seem to abash him in the least. She knew by the twinkle in his eye that he was amused by her evident annoyance, and she tried to conceal it.

When tea was over she suggested to Mark that he might clear it away, and no sooner had he left the room than she attacked Amberley openly. "Well? What is it?" she asked.

"What is what?" he inquired.

"Why did you come? You don't suppose I believe that it was to bring me my handkerchief, do you? If you do, you must think I'm a fool!"

"I do," he said. A rather disarming smile went with the words and provoked an answering gleam from her.

She suppressed it rigorously. "Nor can I suppose that you came for the pleasure of my—*callow*—company."

He laughed. "At least you have a good memory," he said.

"I think," she said forcefully, "that you are the rudest man I have ever had the misfortune to meet."

"Really? And I should think you're a competent judge too."

She gave a sudden laugh and got up. "You're impossible," she said, and held out her hand.

It was an act of dismissal, but though Amberley rose he did not shake hands. Her hand fell; the laugh faded from her eyes; she said abruptly: "Mr. Amberley."

"Well?"

"I seem to you a suspicious character. I must seem so; I quite realize that. But if I am, why don't you leave the police to deal with me?"

He shook his head. "I'm afraid you overrate our inspector's intelligence. He'd probably have had you hanged."

"You're acting for the police, aren't you? You needn't trouble to deny it; I know you are. And you still think I had something to do with that murder. Well——"

He interrupted. "And had you nothing to do with it, Miss Brown?"

She stared at him, the colour ebbing from her cheeks. "What do you mean?"

"What I say. You went to meet Dawson that night."

"No!"

"Don't lie. He had something that you wanted. And because of that he was murdered. You were too late on the scene, Miss Brown."

"It's not true!" she said huskily. "You've no proof!"

"I shall have," he promised, and picked up his hat. "No, you needn't put on that remarkably wooden expression. I'm not going to ask you to tell me anything. The one piece of information I came for I've got. The rest I'll have soon enough—without the assistance you're so loath to give me."

"What information? What do you imagine you've discovered?"

"You can think that out for yourself," said Mr. Amberley. "Thank you so much for giving me tea. Good-bye!"

CHAPTER VII

MR. AMBERLEY'S hopes of a quiet evening were dashed by a telephone call that came for him in the middle of dinner. Sir Humphrey passed a severe stricture upon people who invariably rang up during a meal because they were "sure of finding one in," and inquired testily of his butler who it was and why he could not give a message.

Upon hearing that his call came from Basil Fountain, Mr. Amberley, who had heartily endorsed his uncle's views, said that he would answer it. He returned to the dining room a few moments later and replied in answer to Felicity's inquiry that Fountain wanted him to motor over to the manor after dinner.

"Whatever for?" said Felicity.

"Apparently," said Amberley, helping himself to salad, "he has remembered a valuable piece of evidence."

"Did he ask me to come too?"

"He did not."

"Swab!" said Felicity, without heat.

When Amberley arrived at Norton Manor it was about half-past nine and a beautifully clear night. The manor was bathed in moonlight, with sharp black shadows thrown out along the ground. The house looked unfriendly, for the curtains were closely drawn and no welcoming light shone from any window.

Amberley was admitted by Collins and conducted to the library at the side of the house. He found his host alone, awaiting him.

Fountain apologized for dragging him out at this hour, but said in excuse that he had only heard from the chief constable that afternoon that he had taken the case on. It appeared that there was something he thought Amberley ought to know about the deceased butler.

He broke off as Collins came back into the room with

80

the coffee-tray and waited while the valet offered this to Amberley. But he did not, for once, seem to mind Collins's hearing what he had to say, for he added, as he lifted the big globe-like liqueur glass from the tray: "I've been speaking to Collins about what I'm going to tell you, but unfortunately he can't help us much. I rather hoped he might have known more than I do. But he tells me Dawson seldom mentioned his affairs in the servants' hall."

Amberley glanced towards the valet's impassive countenance. "Did he give you the impression that he had anything to hide?"

Collins answered in his smooth, expressionless voice: "No, sir. But I fear I did not consider the matter. We were not very friendly."

"When you say that you were not very friendly do you mean that you disliked one another?"

"Oh dear me, no, sir, nothing of that kind," replied Collins. "If there had ever been unpleasantness I could not have remained in service at the manor."

Amberley transferred his gaze to the fireplace. After a moment Collins said politely: "Will there be anything further, sir?"

"No, that's all," said Fountain. He waited till the man had gone and then remarked that he had managed to find a butler to take Dawson's place.

"Really? I heard you had gone to town to interview one. Satisfactory?"

"Seems all right," said Fountain. "He had a very good reference, though I'd have preferred to have had a word over the phone with his late employers. Unfortunately the man's gone to America. He gave Baker—that's the butler —a chit, but one never knows with these references that servants hand you themselves. However, he was willing to come at once, so I decided to give him a trial. Been out of work for a month or two on account of his health. Hope he won't turn out to be a crook." He held out an open box of cigars, but remembering that his guest did not smoke them, looked round for the cigarettes.

Amberley shook his head, and produced a pipe and

began to fill it. "What was it you were going to tell me?" he asked.

The story was rather an odd one. The incident had occurred two years before, when Fountain succeeded his uncle. He had known when he took over the house and the existing staff that the servants had each one whole day off a month, in addition to their various half-days. The arrangement had seemed to him a fair one; in any case he did not wish to make any changes in the rules of the house. Dawson alone of them all was favoured with late leave, which meant that he was not bound to be in by ten o'clock at night on these occasions. This was because he was supposed always to visit his sister, who lived at Brixton, a difficult place to reach from Upper Nettlefold. Fountain had never questioned it until, happening to be dining in town on one of Dawson's off-days, whom should he have seen three tables away but Dawson himself, in company with another man.

Mr. Amberley raised his brows, but made no comment.

The restaurant was the Magnificent—a tawdry, gilded place, certainly, but not exactly cheap. Probably Amberley knew it?

Amberley nodded and put his pipe between his teeth and felt in his pocket for matches.

Well, he had been surprised, but since it was really no business of his what Dawson did in his off-time he had pretended not to notice the man. But on the following morning Dawson had broached the matter of his own accord. He said that he knew his master must have wondered to see him dining at the Magnificent, and he wished to explain how it had come about. The explanation had appeared to Fountain quite satisfactory; so much so that the incident had been banished from his mind only to be recalled when, worrying his brain over the man's murder, he had set himself to think over everything he had ever known of Dawson.

He had been dining with an American, a man whom he had known many years before in New York, when he himself was in service there. Fountain rather thought that he had been a footman in some millionaire's house, but he was not sure; it was a long time ago. All he did know was that Jasper Fountain had picked him up in America and had brought him back to England as his butler. In any case the American with whom he had been dining that night had, according to Dawson's tale, made his pile and come to England on a visit. He had found his old friend's address and invited him to meet him in town one evening. The impression Fountain had had when Dawson told him this was that the man had wanted to dazzle the butler by a display of opulence. Anyway he had not thought any more about it until, as he said, he had tried to run over in his mind all that he knew of Dawson. And in doing that naturally the first thing that attracted one's attention was Dawson's mysterious nest-egg. No one had yet succeeded in tracing this to its source. A suggestion made by himself that Dawson had bet a bit on the turf was quashed by the housekeeper, who asserted that the butler had disapproved of all forms of gambling.

Then it was that he had remembered that night at the Magnificent. He had not doubted Dawson's explanation at the time, but in the light of the facts that had been disclosed it had occurred to him to wonder whether the original story had been true. Could it be, in fact, that the American was not an old friend, but someone over whom Dawson possessed a hold?

"Blackmail? I suppose it might easily be so. Had you any idea that Dawson was that type of man?"

"No, none. But how did he come by that money? Rotten to throw mud at a dead man, but the more I think of it the more it seems to fit in. Two years ago, you see; just about the time when Dawson opened his account at Carchester. What do you think?"

"Undoubtedly interesting," said Amberley. "Can you give me the date?"

"I'm awfully sorry, but I can't," Fountain said ruefully. "I know it was when I first came here, so it must have been sometime in the autumn, I suppose. Anyway I thought I'd better mention it."

"Quite right. It will have to be gone into. Inspector Fraser endeavouring to trace an unknown American—or possibly not an American at all—who dined at a public restaurant two years ago on a date you have forgotten, ought to be an engaging spectacle."

Fountain laughed. "Put like that it does sound fairly hopeless. Hullo—who on earth can that be?"

Somewhere in the distance a bell was clanging. Whoever had pulled it evidently meant to be sure of making himself heard. Through the stillness of the house the bell went on ringing for several moments, with that hollow sound of iron striking iron.

"Front door," said Fountain. "All the others are electric bells. I only hope to God it's not that damned inspector. He keeps on coming here with fatuous questions to ask the staff. They don't like it, I can assure you."

Amberley glanced at the clock. "I don't think the inspector would come at this hour unless it were for something particularly vital," he said.

A silence followed the last desultory clang of the bell. Then they heard the front door being opened and a confused murmur of voices, which grew louder.

Fountain raised his brows in a bewildered, slightly amused way. "What in the world——" he began, and stopped short, listening.

One voice was raised insistently, but they could not distinguish the words. Then came the sound of a scuffle and a desperate cry of "Help!"

Fountain leaped to his feet. "Good God, that's Collins!" he exclaimed and hurried to the door.

The cry rang out again. "Help! Help!"

Fountain wrenched the door open and strode out into the hall. The front door was open, and on the doorstep two men were swaying together in a desperate struggle. One was the valet; the other was Mark Brown.

The light in the porch shone on the barrel of an automatic in Mark's hand. Collins was trying to get possession of it; as he went to his assistance Amberley caught a glimpse of his face, livid, the lips drawn back in a kind of snarl, the eyes alive all at once with rage and hatred.

Before either Fountain or Amberley could reach the front door Mark had wrenched free from the valet's desperate grasp. "Damn your soul to hell; you won't, eh?" he shouted. "Then take that!"

There was a deafening report, but Mark lurched as he fired and the bullet went wide. There was a crash and the tinkling of broken glass as it went through a cabinet at the end of the hall and buried itself in the wall behind.

Before he could fire again Amberley was on to him and had caught his pistol arm and wrenched it round. Mark cried out with the sudden pain and the gun dropped to the ground.

Fountain caught his other arm and held it. Amberley released his grip and bent and picked up the gun, slipping it into his own pocket.

At that moment the billiard-room door was burst open and Anthony came out, with Joan at his heels. "Hullo-ullo-ullo!" he said cheerfully. "Someone starting a rough house?"

"It's all right; there's no harm done," Amberley replied.

Fountain was staring at his captive. "Who the devil are you?" he demanded wrathfully. "What do you think you're doing?"

The shock of his wrenched arm seemed to have sobered Mark a little. He shot a vengeful look up at Fountain. "Let me go!" he muttered. "I'm not going to tell you anything. Let me go!"

Fountain continued to hold him by one arm. "Get on to the police, Collins," he ordered.

The bloodshot eyes gleamed. "You'd better not," Mark said in a threatening voice. "You'll be sorry if you do. Damned sorry, I can tell you. Nobody's going to interfere with me!"

"Squiffy," said Corkran. "Drunk as a lord. Who is he?"

It was Collins who answered. "I rather fancy it is the young gentleman from Ivy Cottage," he said. He had recovered all his habitual composure; there was not a trace of emotion in his face or in his level voice.

"What?" Fountain stared down at Mark.

"Pal of yours, Collins?" inquired Corkran.

"Hardly, sir. I fear the young gentleman is, as you say, not entirely sober."

"You ought to cure yourself of this habit you've got of exaggerating," said Corkran. "Whom did he take a pot-shot at?"

"At me, sir, but I do not think that he is responsible for his actions."

"Whatever makes you think that?" inquired Corkran innocently.

Fountain was still looking at Mark. "A gentleman, is he? You're quite right, Tony; he's drunk." He jerked Mark farther into the hall and pushed the door to with his free hand. He released the boy and stood frowning down at him. "Now look here, young man," he said, "what the hell do you mean by coming to my house and firing at my servant? Do you know I can have you put into prison for it?"

Mark was rubbing his bruised arm. "All right, put me in prison!" he said recklessly. "*I'm* not afraid! I'll make you sorry you dared to interfere with me. That's what I'll do!"

Fountain made a gesture of disgust. "I ought to give him in charge, of course, but he's far too drunk to know what he's doing."

"That's all jolly fine," objected Anthony, "but what brought him up here trying to murder Collins? Just natural high spirits?"

"I didn't want to murder him!" Mark said, looking frightened. "I didn't mean to fire."

Mr. Amberley, who had stood silently watching, spoke at last. "You had better apologize to Mr. Fountain," he said. "You've made a fool of yourself."

Fountain glanced quickly towards him. "Do you know him, Amberley?"

"Slightly. This condition is more or less habitual to him."

"Good Lord! Well, I don't want to be hard on the boy. What do you think I ought to do? Give him in charge or let him go?"

"Personally, I should let him go," said Amberley. "But it's a matter for you to decide."

"Well, I don't know. After all, he might have killed Collins."

The valet gave a little cough. "I'm sure I do not wish to get the young gentleman into trouble, sir. When he comes to himself he will realize that he has been behaving foolishly."

Mark, looking uncertainly from him to Fountain, said: "I didn't mean to do it. I made a—a mistake. I'm sorry."

"Let it be a lesson to you in the future to keep off spirits," said Fountain severely. He stepped back and opened the door. "Now get out!"

Without a word Mark turned and shambled out.

"Well!" exploded Corkran as Fountain shut the door again. "Of all the dam' silly things to do! How do you know it wasn't he who shot old Dawson?"

"Shot Dawson?" repeated Fountain blankly. "Why the devil should he?"

"If it comes to that, why the devil should he shoot Collins?" demanded Corkran. He watched the valet disappear through the swing door at the end of the hall. "I don't say I altogether blame him, but——"

"Tony, don't be so awful!" begged Joan. She was still trembling from the shock of the sudden gun-shot. "Mr. Amberley, you don't think he's the murderer, do you?"

"No, I think it extremely unlikely," he replied.

"All right, say he didn't." Anthony was standing obstinately by his guns. "Why did he come snooping up here? Don't say because he was tight, because I shall be sick if I hear that again. If I went bursting into a strange house and tried to shoot up the place and then said I was tight by way of excuse, would you be satisfied with that? Like hell you would! That chap wanted to shoot up someone to start with. Then he had four or five drinks and thought: By Jove, I'll go straight off and do it. Don't tell me that just because a fellow's three sheets in the wind it's the natural reaction for him to get hold of a gun, stagger off several miles to a house he's never been near before, and turn it into a shooting gallery. It's childish."

"Perfectly true," said Amberley. "If I found you forcing your way into a strange house I should think the worst. But you are not an unbalanced person. This youth is."

"What-ho!" said Anthony, gratified. "The old brainbox full of grey matter, eh?"

"I didn't say that," Amberley answered. "There's a difference between the unbalanced and the merely feeble-minded."

Anthony cast a speculative look round him, in search of a likely missile. Joan interposed hastily. "Oh, don't scrap!" she begged. "Is that really what you think, Mr. Amberley?"

There was a twinkle at the back of Amberley's eyes. "You see, I was at school with him," he said gravely.

"A little more of this, dear old boyhood's friend, and I don't help you to solve the great Nettlefold mystery."

"That 'ud be a blow for the unknown assassin," remarked Amberley. "Seriously, Miss Fountain, my own impression is that young Brown has—or thinks he has—a grudge against someone. Once he's a bit drunk he hasn't a particularly clear idea what it is or whom it's against. For all I know he may have a general hate against capitalism, which is why he raided this place. In any case, I don't honestly think you need be frightened of him." He glanced at his wrist watch. "I must be going. I hope you don't have any more unhinged visitors tonight."

Mr. Corkran saw his chance and pounced on it. "No, two in one evening is a bit steep," he said with immense relish.

Mr. Amberley did not choose the Greythorne Road when he left the manor, but instead turned right, towards Upper Nettlefold. He had not gone very far when his headlights threw into bold relief the figure of a pedestrian wandering somewhat dejectedly along the side of the road. Amberley drew abreast of the figure and pulled up. He leaned across and opened the door of the car and issued a brief command to Mark Brown to get in.

Mark refused petulantly and began to walk on, but when the command was repeated in a distinctly savage tone he gave in weakly and obeyed.

Mr. Amberley seemed disinclined for conversation. Beyond remarking that Mark had made a complete ass of himself he said nothing during the journey to Ivy Cottage. Mark kept up a kind of explanatory mumble, but what little of it reached Amberley's ears above the noise of the engine was neither interesting nor sensible. After a while Mark seemed to realize that no attention was being paid to his involved explanation and relapsed into a sulky silence.

When the car drew up outside Ivy Cottage Mark got out and stalked ahead of Amberley up the garden path. His air of defiant nonchalance was rather spoiled by the uncertainty of his gait.

As he reached it the door of the cottage was flung open and a beam of warm lamplight shone forth. Shirley's voice sounded, sharp with anxiety: "Is that you, Mark?" Then she saw the second, larger figure. "Who's that?" she said quickly.

Amberley strolled into the light. "Don't be alarmed," he said.

She stared at him, but he thought he saw a certain amount of relief on her face. "I suppose I might have guessed," she said. "What has happened?"

Mark, who had been fidgeting restlessly, answered belligerently: "He'll tell you fast enough. And you needn't think I want to hear your remarks about it, because I don't. I'm going to bed."

He tried to thrust his way past her into the house, but she caught his arm. "Where have you been? I went down to the Blue Dragon. They said you'd gone."

He shook off her hand. "Well, perhaps that'll teach you not to follow me about," he said, and flung into the house.

Shirley turned to Amberley. "Will you come in?" she said listlessly.

He followed her into the living room. Seen in the pale lamplight her face looked tired and wan. She made a little gesture towards a chair. "I suppose you brought him home," she said. "It seems to be your mission in life. What has he been doing?"

"Merely trying to get himself arrested." He drew the automatic out of his pocket and laid it down on the table.

"May I suggest that you keep this where he won't in future find it?"

Her pallor grew. "I know. I missed it. I didn't know he'd discovered where I keep it. Where did he go?"

"You know, don't you?" said Amberley softly.

Her eyes lifted to his face; she did not answer.

"He went to Norton Manor."

She said steadily: "When he's drunk he behaves like a madman. What did he do?"

"Nothing much beyond attempting to shoot Fountain's valet."

"Oh, my God," she said bitterly.

"It is sickening, isn't it?" agreed Amberley. "After all the trouble you've taken, too."

"What did they do? What was said?"

"They decided that he was too drunk to know what he was doing and kicked him out."

"Did the valet get hurt?"

"Oh no; no one was hurt."

She was silent, frowning. After a pause she spoke again. "They let him go. Then——" She broke off and began to drum on the table with her fingers.

"Exactly," said Amberley. "It looks as though he's given the show away, doesn't it?"

She looked searchingly at him. "I don't know what you mean."

His voice took on a kinder inflection. "Why don't you make up your mind to trust me?" he said.

She shrugged. "I know of no reason why I should, Mr. Amberley. I know nothing about you except that you are mixed up with the police. And since the police can't help me——"

"I know. But I can."

Her eyes were full of distrust. She pushed the heavy hair back from her forehead. "Please don't bother me any more about it," she said wearily. "I don't wish to argue and I haven't any idea what you're talking about."

His face hardened. "In fact, you prefer to play a lone hand?"

"Infinitely."

He picked up his hat. "You're being unwise. Things are likely to become very dangerous for you, Miss Shirley Brown."

"Dear me, is that a threat?" she asked jibingly.

"Why should I threaten? I'm warning you. Good night."

He was frowning as he drove back to Greythorne, and he was short with Felicity, who wanted to know why he had been such a time. On the following morning he went off immediately after breakfast and drove to Carchester, to the police station. He was conducted at once to Inspector Fraser's sanctum. The inspector greeted him with veiled hostility and said that he had expected to get a visit from him before this.

Mr. Amberley was in an uncompromising mood, and returned an answer so brusque that the inspector reddened with anger. Without giving Fraser time to recover he demanded an account of the police investigations up to date.

The inspector, knowing on whose side the chief constable was likely to be, thought it politic to obey. He took Mr. Amberley through a long list of perfect alibis first. Everyone at the manor had one, even the female staff. By the time that Amberley had heard that the head-keeper had been in Upper Nettleford, that the head-gardener had visited the chauffeur, that the valet had been pressing a suit for Mr. Fountain, that the under-gardener had been with his young lady, he was frankly yawning. When the inspector proposed to continue through a list of cottagers living near the scene of the murder, he cut the recital short and said that he had not come to Carchester to be told who had not committed the murder.

The inspector made an enigmatic reference to amateur detectives and passed on to the search for the cartridge-case. This had not been discovered, nor had any trace of bicycle wheels in the fields behind the hedge been found. The source of Dawson's income was equally wrapped in mystery. In fact, as Mr. Amberley had no hesitation in pointing out, the police had discovered nothing at all.

While the inspector digested this Amberley briefly

recounted the story Fountain had told him the night before.

The inspector was interested. When Amberley had finished he rubbed his hands together and said: "Now we are getting to something. A pity Mr. Fountain didn't remember it sooner. To the trained mind, Mr. Amberley, what you've just told me is highly significant."

"Highly," agreed Amberley. "I wish you joy of it. In the meantime I want a man put on to watch Mark Brown."

The inspector stared at him for a moment. Then his features relaxed into an expression of tolerant amusement. "Mark Brown, eh, sir? Now, now, Mr. Amberley, I'm afraid you've been reading these popular thrillers. I know the style of thing. The mysterious young man who comes down to stay for no reason. But it won't do, you know. The police aren't quite asleep."

"Not all of them," said Mr. Amberley sweetly. "By the way, have you grasped it yet? I want a man put on to watch Mark Brown."

"That's all very well, Mr. Amberley, but we've been into his record. There's nothing to it. You're on to a false trail. He lives in Earl's Court in a small flat with his sister which they've let for a month. She works as secretary to Anne March."

"I want Mark Brown watched."

"I take my orders from the chief constable, Mr. Amberley."

"Very proper. Do you mind if I use your telephone?"

"Of course, if you've got any real reason for having him watched, that makes a difference," said the inspector, beginning to hedge. "What have you found out about him?"

"So far, nothing. I shall be able to answer that question more fully in—say, a couple of days' time."

"Suspicions, eh, sir? The police want more than that to go on, I'm afraid."

"Which is why I don't propose to burden you with them."

The inspector fingered his chin, glancing sideways at

Amberley. "Perhaps you'd better tell me what you have in your mind, Mr. Amberley," he said at last. "I may as well hear it. Do you suspect him of having committed the murder?"

"I should think it extremely improbable that he had anything to do with it."

The inspector flushed. "I don't know what you're getting at, sir, but if Brown isn't implicated in the murder he doesn't interest me."

"That I can readily believe. You never could see farther than the end of your own nose, could you? The murder, as I have said before, is likely to prove the least interesting feature of the whole case."

"Indeed, sir? Funny, isn't it? *I* was under the impression that the murder is the whole case."

"Try and disabuse your mind of that erroneous idea. Unless I am very much mistaken I am on to something far bigger and more fantastic than you've any of you imagined."

The inspector sat up at that. "Are you trying to hoax me, Mr. Amberley?" he demanded. "What is all this about?"

Amberley got up. "There is no point in my telling you, Inspector," he said. "It is a case where the police can't possibly act."

"H'm! Maybe the police could have a shot at it for all that."

"That is precisely what I am afraid of," returned Amberley. "I don't want the only piece of evidence that exists destroyed, you see."

"Look here, sir, you must have something to go on, or I suppose you'd hardly talk like this!"

Amberley smiled. "I have, Inspector. I've got one vital clue." He paused and his smile grew more sardonic. "Which," he added, "in its present condition is entirely valueless."

"I don't pretend to understand you, Mr. Amberley. What you say sounds to me like gibberish."

"I expect it does," agreed Amberley. "You'll have to trust me all the same. Now, are you going to detail a man to keep an eye on Brown, or do you wish me to get on to the chief constable first?"

"I suppose we can have him watched if you make a point of it," the inspector said ungraciously.

Amberley nodded. "Any one of your promising young men will do. The more obvious the better. But watch him damned closely, Inspector. I'll see you again in a day or two. My respects to Colonel Watson. Good morning."

He drove back to Upper Nettlefold and stopped at the station to buy a paper. The ten-thirty from London came in while he was standing by the bookstall, and he turned, idly surveying the passengers who alighted.

From the rear portion of the train a thin, middle-aged man got out with two suitcases. He was quietly and respectably dressed and looked like a superior servant. He saw Mr. Amberley at once, and while he sought in his waistcoat pocket for his ticket, covertly regarded him.

Amberley's eyes, wandering along the platform, came to rest on him and grew intent. The man picked up his suitcases again and walked down the platform towards the barrier. As he came abreast of Amberley, he shot a quick, furtive look up at him. But Mr. Amberley had spread open the paper, and his face could not be seen.

CHAPTER VIII

FOUNTAIN'S new butler seemed, when Amberley saw him, to be settling down quite well at the manor. He was a rather deprecating man with shy, brown eyes and a bald top to his head. Anthony Corkran said that he was all right in his way, but a bit too assiduous. You were always tripping over the man. He supposed one couldn't blame him for making himself pleasant to the other servants, but he showed rather too many signs of growing thick with Collins for Anthony's taste.

It may have been this piece of information, so carelessly dropped, that made Amberley favour the newcomer with a long, hard stare when he first saw him. Baker gave a polite smile and turned away towards the drawing room door to announce Amberley.

He was checked. "The name is Amberley," Frank said gently.

Baker shot him a quick look and said apologetically: "Yes, sir. Thank you."

"Which I do not think you could have known," said Amberley, still more gently.

"No, sir. I was forgetting."

Mr. Amberley followed him in a leisurely fashion to the drawing room.

Fountain, unlike Corkran, was quite enthusiastic over his new butler. The man knew his work, seemed very willing and, what was more, hit it off with the others. He was perhaps a little stupid, but one could not have everything. Even Collins seemed to be getting on quite well with him, and it was not everyone with whom Collins got on, he could assure Amberley.

He left the subject of the butler to inquire whether Amberley had come for any particular purpose. It did not seem as though he had. He put one or two not very important questions to Fountain and prepared to depart. Fountain asked him whether he was any nearer to solving the problem, and was answered by a noncommittal shrug.

"I've got Fraser to put a man on to watch Mark Brown," Amberley said.

Fountain's expression of interest and respect changed ludicrously. It was plain that he did not think much of this new departure.

Mr. Amberley gave a crooked smile. "Shattering your faith in me, Fountain?"

Fountain disclaimed hurriedly. He supposed Amberley had his reasons, but—well, wasn't it a slight waste of time? He could not seriously suppose that Brown had had anything to do with Dawson's murder. He must say it did seem to him a bit of a forlorn hope.

Mr. Amberley smiled again and remarked that he was not the first person who had been disappointed by this, his own first move in the game.

He left Fountain looking after him rather dubiously and motored in to Upper Nettlefold to see his friend Sergeant Gubbins.

Fraser and Fountain might be disappointed, but the sergeant welcome him with open arms and said that he had known all along that he could trust him.

"Why," he said, becoming reminiscent, "I've known you now, sir, a matter of three years and more. Twice I've cautioned you for dangerous driving, and three times I've had you up for parking your car where you hadn't ought to, and once I've worked on a case with you. So if I don't know you, I'd like to know who does. No, all along—and in spite of appearances—I've said: 'You can always trust Mr. Amberley.'"

"Sergeant, you almost unman me," said Amberley. "And what is it all about?"

The sergeant looked very knowing. "Mark Brown, eh, sir? Now that's where you and I know a thing or two. The inspector's not at all pleased about it; not at all, he isn't. He had a lot to say about amateurs meddling in police matters which I wouldn't care to repeat. But he didn't see Albert Collins come out of Ivy Cottage." He paused and scratched his head. "Now I come to think of it, no more did I," he said. "However, you did, and that's good enough for me."

Mr. Amberley asked whether he had told the inspector that and the sergeant deliberately winked. "No, sir, I did not. Didn't happen to think of it," he said offhandedly.

Amberley smiled. "Convenient memory. Don't tell him."

"Not me, sir. Of course," he added, fixing Amberley with a stern blue eye, "if I'd actually seen it that would be a very different affair. But there's no reason why I should report a lot of hearsay to the inspector."

"None at all," Amberley agreed. "Meanwhile, is the boy being watched?"

"He's being watched all right, sir," said the sergeant. "But if you were to ask me, I should have to say that you might as well put on an elephant to watch him as young Tucker; it wouldn't be any more noticeable."

"I don't mind that," Amberley said. "As long as someone's trailing him, that's all I wanted to know."

The sergeant coughed. "Of course you have your reasons, sir?" he said tentatively.

"No," said Amberley frankly. "I've only my suspicions —which may yet prove to be far-fetched. Watching Brown is a precaution and possibly an over-precaution."

"It sounds to me as though it's going to be a funny sort of a case, sir."

"I think it is, Sergeant. Very funny," said Mr. Amberley.

"And what I *don't* see," pursued the sergeant, "is what a young drunk has got to do with it. Because that's what he is, sir. A proper young drunk. Scandalous I call it, at his age. Evening after evening it's the same tale. Down he comes to the Blue Dragon, drinks himself silly, and has to be put outside at closing-time. I'm sorry for the young lady, but what I say is, why don't she have him put into one of these homes you read about where they set out to cure people of wanting liquor? Not but what that does seem a crool sort of thing to do, but there you are! What can you do for such a young boozer? Because it's no good her thinking she can manage him. Mrs. Jones, who does for them at the cottage, says that when he gets the craving it 'ud take a regiment of soldiers to keep him in."

"Goes to the Blue Dragon every night, does he?" said Amberley thoughtfully.

"Regular as clockwork. It's common knowledge, and even old Wagge, who's been in the lock-up for drunk and disorderly I don't know how many times, gets shocked to see a kid of his age making so free with the bottle."

"Does he talk?"

"Not as I've heard. I believe if anybody asks him a civil question for the sake of making a bit of conversation, he acts silly, and says it's no good anyone trying to get anything out of him. I've known a lot of drunks that only had to have four or five before they'd start behaving as though they'd got a whole lot of wonderful secrets which everybody was trying to get out of them."

"Oh, he says that, does he?"

"Not in so many words, he doesn't. No, he just sits and drinks, and if ever he gets talking it's the usual sort of rubbish. But he soon gets past that stage, does young Brown. Well, if he didn't Mr. Hawkins would put him outside. He gets very quiet and sits staring in front of him in a very ugly way. Very ugly indeed, so I've heard. I don't say he wouldn't like to go and murder someone when he's drunk, but I should be very surprised if ever he done it. Very surprised, I should be. Because how he manages to get himself home without being run over, let alone shooting anyone, fairly beats me. And when he's sober he's not the sort of chap who's got the guts—if you'll pardon the expression, Mr. Amberley—to do a murder. Leastways, not to my mind. However, I daresay you know your own business best, sir, and in any case it won't do any harm to have him watched."

"I'm rather hoping it'll prevent harm," said Mr. Amberley, and took his leave.

He went out to his car and drove off across the Market Square. But he was not destined to return immediately to Greythorne. From the pavement Shirley Brown hailed him. He drew up alongside her obligingly. She said in a voice quivering with indignation that she wanted to speak to him. He replied with some humour that that was a pleasant surprise.

She paid no heed to this remark. Wrath blazed in her dark eyes; she even stammered a little as she spoke. He had dared to set a plain-clothes man on to watch her brother! She told him it was no use denying it; he merely laughed. She accused him of double-dealing, for had not he asked her to trust him, while all the time he meant to spy on Mark? With a sudden change of front she poured scorn on the constable who was shadowing Mark; it was obvious to the meanest intelligence that the man was a policeman. The whole thing was an outrage, and she never wished to see Amberley again as long as she lived. With that she swung on her heel and strode off, furious because she knew that he was laughing at her.

Next day Mr. Amberley sustained a second visit from the chief constable, who was plainly restive. He had expected something to happen; he thought he had better look Amberley up. Amberley, who was oddly irritable, said tartly that the colonel might be thankful that nothing had happened; and when the colonel, looking exceedingly nervous, ventured to ask what he meant, he gripped his pipe between his teeth, thrust his hands in the pockets of his grey flannel trousers, and continued to wander round the room without vouchsafing any answer. Pressed more closely, he said that until he received the answer to a cable he had dispatched he could give the colonel no information.

The answer arrived that evening just before ten. The butler brought it into the drawing room where Amberley was sitting, listening to Sir Humphrey on the subject of preserving. Sir Humphrey, quite uninterested in local murders, was justly incensed by the presence of poachers in the district. He told Amberley what his keeper had said and what old Clitheroe-Williams thought ought to be done, and how he himself had heard a shot at five o'clock the other morning, and Amberley gave abstracted answers and did a complicated Patience. Sir Humphrey had just announced his intention of speaking to that fellow Fountain about his head-keeper, who was an incompetent ass if ever there was one and lazy to boot, when the cable was brought in.

Amberley swept the playing cards into a heap, and getting up without waiting to hear the end of Sir Humphrey's monologue, went off to decode it in private.

Felicity, agog with curiosity, made an excuse to follow him presently to the study and begged to know whether the cable had something to do with Dawson's murder. Without looking up Amberley replied that it had not.

Felicity was disappointed. "You seem fairly pleased with it anyway," she said.

"I'm always pleased to find my theories are correct," said Amberley. He got up and glanced at his wrist watch. "I shall have to leave you, loved one. Back soon."

He went round to the garage and got his car out, and for the second time that day drove into Upper Nettlefold and to the police station. The sergeant was just coming off duty when he arrived, but he readily accompanied Amberley back into the station and led him into his little office.

"It's about Mark Brown," Amberley said, without waste of words. "The inspector is inclined to pooh-pooh the necessity of watching him, and it occurs to me that that attitude may have communicated itself to Constable Tucker. Get this, Sergeant! It's absolutely vital that Brown should not be allowed out of the police's sight. Detail a man to relieve Tucker tonight; I'll take the responsibility."

The sergeant responded nobly. "I haven't got anyone free, sir, but if you want it done I'll do it myself, that's what I'll do. Yes, what do you want?"

The constable who was on duty had come in in a hurry. "It's Tucker, Sergeant. At least, it ain't him exactly, but there's an urgent message. He wants you to go at once. It is on the Collinghurst Road."

"Well, what is it?" said the sergeant. "Come on, let's have it!"

"That young fellow he was watching, Sergeant. He's gorn and fallen in the river."

"Well, you needn't make such a to-do about that," said the sergeant testily. "Anyone might have known that was bound to happen one of these days. More fool Tucker to let him."

The constable said simply: "He's dead, Sergeant."

"Dead?" The sergeant's jaw dropped; he looked blankly across at Mr. Amberley.

Amberley, who had turned quickly at the constable's entrance, stood perfectly still for a moment. Then he drew out his cigarette case and took a cigarette from it with extreme deliberation. His eyes met the sergeant's; he shut the case with a snap and felt in his pocket for matches.

The sergeant sat gazing at him somewhat numbly. Mr. Amberley lit his cigarette and flicked the dead match into the grate. He inhaled a long breath of smoke and glanced at the constable. "Who sent the message?"

"I dunno his name, sir. He was a gentleman, all right. He said he had passed in his car and Tucker asked him to drive to the nearest house and get through to us."

"I see. I'll run you out there, Sergeant."

The sergeant roused himself. "Yes, sir. Harmer, get hold of Mason and Philpots, and tell them to bring the hand-ambulance along." The constable went out. The sergeant got up, looking at Amberley. "Lor', sir—was that why you wanted him watched?" he said. "Was this what you was expecting?"

"It was what I was afraid of. Damn that fool Tucker!"

The sergeant dropped his voice lower. "Is it murder, Mr. Amberley?"

Amberley gave a grim smile. "Getting quite acute, aren't you? You'll find the coroner's jury will return a verdict of accidental death. Are you ready to start?"

Not until he was seated beside Amberley in the car did the sergeant speak again. Then he said: "If it was murder are you going to let it go at that, sir?"

"Did I say it was murder?" said Amberley.

The big Bentley tore through the town but slowed as it drew clear of the last straggling houses. The ground dipped here, and they ran into a thick mist which grew denser as the road approached the river.

"Steady, sir!" besought the sergeant. "Get a lot of fog here at this time of the year. It's the clay."

"Yes. You could almost bank on running into fog, couldn't you?"

A little farther along the road they saw a figure loom up through the mist, waving. Amberley ran the car into the side of the road and stopped. The mist was floating in wreaths across the glare of the headlights; through it they could see the blurred outline of a second man and of a figure lying face downwards on the ground.

The sergeant got out of the car as quickly as his bulk would permit. "Is that you, Tucker? How did this happen?"

Mr. Amberley suddenly put up his hand to his spotlamp and switched it on. Its beam swung to the left and rested on the second man. It was Collins, dripping wet, and in his shirt sleeves. "How very interesting!" said Mr. Amberley, and got out of the car.

The sergeant strode up to Collins. "And what might you be doing here, my man?" he inquired.

The valet's face was grey; sweat stood on his forehead; he seemed exhausted.

"It was him got Brown out," Tucker said reluctantly. "When I—when I come up, he was trying to bring him round. We've been working on him solid, but it's no good, Sergeant. He's dead."

"Yes, and that's something you'll explain back at the station," said the sergeant. He looked at Collins. "As for you, you'll come along too, and explain *your*self. Keep your eye on him, Tucker." He turned away and went to join Amberley, who was on his knees beside Mark's body.

The boy's head was turned to one side, and his arms were stretched out.

Amberley spoke without looking up. "A light, Sergeant."

The sergeant produced a torch from his pocket. Amberley took it and turned it full on to Mark's head, searching closely. "Help me to turn him over, will you?"

They shifted the limp body on to its back; Mark's eyes were closed, and his jaw sagged slightly. Amberley pushed the wet hair gently off his brow and brought the torch nearer. After a moment he switched the light off and rose.

"Not a sign of a blow. Accidental death, Sergeant."

"What, with that Collins standing here?" muttered the sergeant. "We'll see about that!"

"I'm afraid we shall," said Amberley. He walked back to the car. "You'd better get inside and put that rug round you, Collins." He got into the car himself as he spoke, and sat down at the wheel, looking frowningly ahead of him.

The sergeant wanted to know whether Collins had been cautioned, and upon hearing that he had not, promptly cautioned him himself. The valet said nothing.

The sergeant spread Tucker's discarded coat over Mark's body and stood beside it, waiting for the ambulance to come up. Tucker began to stammer out an explantion and was sternly checked. "We'll hear all about that up at the station," said the sergeant.

It was very cold on the road, and the mist spread a depressing dampness. The valet was shivering in the back of the car, his pale eyes fixed on the dead man. He raised them to the sergeant's face for a moment. "And," said the sergeant afterwards to Mr. Amberley, "say what you like, if ever a man looked like murder it was him. Dived in to rescue him, did he? Dived in to push him under, more likely. I tell you, sir, when I caught his eye he was looking like a fiend. And I'm not exaggerating neither."

The hand-ambulance came up at last, and Mark's body was lifted on to it and covered with a rug. The two policemen who had brought it set off with it towards the mortuary, and the sergeant climbed into Amberley's car again.

The drive back to the police station was accomplished in silence. When they arrived Collins was sent off under escort to get a change of clothing, and Tucker and Amberley went off with the sergeant into his office.

Tucker's account of the accident was necessarily incomplete, as he had not been near enough to witness it. In obedience to his instructions he had followed Mark to the Blue Dragon earlier in the evening and had hung about outside for some time. He had looked in after a while and observed that Mark was, as usual, sitting at a table in the corner in a kind of huddle, too drunk to get up to any mischief. He had understood from the inspector that Mr. Amberley suspected Brown of meaning to do something that would have some connection with Dawson's murder; he had not thought that in that fuddled state the boy could need much watching. Besides, he never came out till closing-time. He had only gone a few steps up the road to get himself a cup of hot tea, and he had not imagined any harm would come of sitting for a bit in the warm and having a chat with the man who kept the eating-house. He had returned to his post only a few minutes after closing-time to find that Mark had already set out for home. He followed, not that he had seen much sense in it, but those had been his orders. Brown must have left the Blue Dragon before it closed, for although he had walked along at a brisk pace he had not caught up with him. It was just as he had approached the bend in the road that brought it alongside the river that he had heard someone shouting for help. He had broken into a run and arrived on the scene of the accident just in time to see Collins, obviously in an exhausted condition, drag Brown's body up the bank, turn it onto its face, and start to apply artificial respiration. He had joined him at once; they had worked like niggers to bring the young man back to life. He himself had felt sure after ten minutes that it was too late, but Collins cursed him and made him go on. Collins had kept on panting that the boy hadn't been under long enough to be drowned, that they must bring him back to life. But they had not succeeded in getting so much as a flicker out of Mark.

It was Tucker who had stopped the first car that passed them. He had not liked to leave Collins with the body and he had told the owner of the car, who was Mr. Jarrold, from Collinghurst, to ring up the police station and deliver a message.

Tucker told his story straightforwardly, but took care not to look at Mr. Amberley. It was plain that he expected censure, for he said several times that the inspector had never told him that Brown was not to be let out of his sight.

"You're a fool," said the sergeant, and rang for Collins to be brought in.

The valet had been fitted out with a suit of clothes only a little too large for him, and given a hot tot. The grey shade had left his face, and his eyes, which the sergeant had thought murderous, were as cold and as expressionless as ever.

He recounted his share in the night's happenings quite composedly. He had been some little way behind Brown, whom he had just been able to see lurching along through the mist. The young gentleman seemed very intoxicated; several times he had stumbled and he had not been able to keep a straight course. So erratic had been his footsteps that Collins had hurried to come up with him, fearing that some car, its driver unable to see clearly in the fog, might run him over. It had been equally hard for him to see clearly, though he had had his torch in his hand. They must have noticed that the fog was particularly thick down there in the hollow where the road ran immediately beside the river. He thought the boy must have wandered off it and stumbled over the edge of the bank. He had seen him disappear and heard him cry out as he fell. There had been a splash, and he had at once run to the spot where he had last seen the young gentleman. He had shouted to him, but there was no answer; not a sound. Knowing in what condition the gentleman was, he had feared that he would not be able to swim to shore. He had thought it his duty to go in after him and he had done so, only stopping to take off his coat and boots. He had dived in and swum about for what seemed hours. He thought the gentleman must have sunk at once; if he struggled at all it could not have been for long, since there was nothing but silence when he, Collins, entered the water. He had almost despaired of bringing him up when he had grasped something in the water and knew it for a hand. He was not a great swimmer, but he had managed to get the body to the bank and to drag it up on to the road again. He had shouted several times for help, as he himself was exhausted and had hardly enough strength to apply artificial respiration. He had done the best he could until Tucker came up; he thought that Tucker would bear him out over that.

The sergeant listened to this tale in sceptical silence. At the end he said: "That's how it happened, is it? And what might you have been doing on the Collinghurst Road at that hour of night?"

The answer astonished him. "I was following the young gentleman," said Collins.

The sergeant, who had been sure of it, was nonplussed. "Oh you were, were you?" he said rather feebly. "And why?"

Collins glanced fleetingly at Amberley. "I have been endeavouring to get into touch with the young gentleman since a very unpleasant little affair took place at the manor three evenings ago. I think Mr. Amberley will know to what I refer."

"Never you mind what Mr. Amberley knows," said the sergeant. "What was this unpleasant affair?"

Collins moistened his lips. "Well, Sergeant, Mr. Brown being under the influence of spirits, came up to the manor and upon my opening the door to him, addressed me in a threatening way which I could not at all account for. He seemed to mistake me for someone else."

"He did, eh? And what made you think that?"

"I could not suppose, Sergeant, that the young gentleman had really any grudge against me."

"You didn't know him at all, did you?"

A slight crease appeared between Amberley's brows. There had been enough meaning in the sergeant's voice to put Collins on his guard.

"I could hardly say that I *knew* him, Sergeant," said the valet suavely. "I hope I know my place. But I had met Mr. Brown in Upper Nettlefold one afternoon when he was not quite himself. Upon that occasion he was extremely friendly. Indeed, so very friendly that he attempted to make me a present of his cigarette case. I believe that alcohol does take gentlemen like that sometimes. Mr. Brown seemed to be under the impression upon that occasion that I was a friend of his. Nothing would do but that I should take his cigarette case. Naturally I returned it as soon as possible."

"You sent it back to him?"

"No, Sergeant, I took it to Ivy Cottage myself and gave it to Mr. Brown," said Collins tranquilly.

The sergeant shot an eloquent look at Amberley.

"Mr. Brown," continued Collins, "was quite sober at the time and behaved just as a gentleman should."

"It sounds to me like a funny story," said the sergeant. "But go on! Why did he go up to see you at the manor?"

"I have no idea, Sergeant. It has been troubling me a good deal, if I may say so. The young gentleman attempted to shoot me, as you, sir"—he bowed to Amberley—"will no doubt remember. Mr. Fountain, not wishing to be hard on Mr. Brown, who was not himself, let him go. But he used certain expressions towards me which I was quite at a loss to understand. In fact he threatened to shoot me at the first opportunity."

"Which was why you went dogging his footsteps, I suppose," said the sergeant, sarcastically.

"Exactly so, Sergeant." Nothing could shake the valet's calm self-possession. "It was a very unpleasant feeling to know there was a young gentleman suffering from such a dangerous delusion. It seemed to me that I could not do better than to try to meet Mr. Brown and endeavour to discover what it was he fancied he had against me. Of course, it is not always convenient for me to get off duty, but this evening, Mr. Fountain being in London and not expected back until late, I was able to leave the manor. Knowing Mr. Brown's—habits—I took the liberty of waiting for him at the Blue Dragon. Not wishing to have any sort of a scene in public, it was my intention to follow him home and there ask him what I might have done to offend him. Then everything happened as I have informed you, Sergeant."

The sergeant was palpably disgusted with this story, which he did not in the least believe. But there did not seem at the moment to be any way of proving its falsity, nor could he very well charge Collins with having pushed

Mark Brown in the river. Tucker's evidence showed that
Collins had not only plunged in to rescue Mark, but that
he had also refused to give up trying to resuscitate him
when the policeman had pronounced the task to be
hopeless. He looked for guidance towards Mr. Amberley,
but Amberley was speaking to the valet. He wanted to
know whether any car had passed him when he was
following Mark, or any pedestrian. Collins answered
unhesitatingly that he had seen no one until Mr. Jarrold
had come by and been hailed by Tucker.

Mr. Amberley seemed to be satisfied and walked away
to the fireplace and began to fill a pipe.

"I suppose you can go," said the sergeant reluctantly.
"Mind, I don't say I like the sound of this story of yours,
because I don't. If you could bring witnesses to prove it
all happened like you said that would be different. But all
you've told me rests on your word alone, and the only
person who could say different is drowned."

The valet said slowly: "I feel sure, Sergeant, that Miss
Brown will bear me out that her brother had no reason to
want to murder me. Apart from the occasions I have
mentioned I never to my knowledge set eyes on the young
gentleman."

"You may be sure we shall have a word with Miss
Brown, my man," promised the sergeant.

"Yes, Sergeant. I should be very glad if you would,"
said Collins meekly.

"And don't forget you'll be wanted at the inquest," said
the sergeant, and made a gesture of dismissal.

The valet went out escorted by Constable Tucker, and
the sergeant sat back in his chair and looked at Mr.
Amberley.

"Well, sir? What do you make of that?" he inquired.

"I told you you'd get a verdict of accidental death,
Sergeant."

"You aren't going to tell me you believe that pack of
lies, sir?"

"Oh no," said Amberley. "But how very hard they are
to refute! Effusive friendliness on Brown's part to begin
with. Highly probable, Sergeant. A drunken man once

tried to press a fiver on to me. The visit to Ivy Cottage
most reasonably explained; you know, he is remarkably
quick-brained, is Mr. Albert Collins; it is a pleasure to
deal with him. The reason for following Brown tonight. A
little less credible, perhaps, but still quite plausible. I'm
afraid you won't be able to saddle him with Brown's
death, Sergeant."

"Maybe I will, maybe I won't," said the sergeant. "But
if ever I see a wrong 'un Albert Collins is one."

"I think you are probably right," said Mr. Amberley,
picking up his hat. "I am now going to relieve you of a
distasteful job. You needn't notify Miss Brown of what
has happened."

The sergeant looked pleased. "I'd take it very kindly if
you'll really do that, Mr. Amberley, sir. And you might
see what she has to say about this little fairy tale we've
been listening to. You might do it better than what I can."

"I shouldn't wonder," said Mr. Amberley.

CHAPTER IX

SHIRLEY had not gone to bed when Mr. Amberley arrived at Ivy Cottage. She was waiting for her brother to come home, and when she flung open the front door Amberley saw from her pale, anxious face that she was worried by Mark's lateness.

She recoiled when she saw who it was. Her instinct was to slam the door in his face, but she curbed it and remarked that she supposed he had once more brought Mark home.

"No," Amberley said gravely. "I'm afraid I haven't. Will you let me come in for a moment?"

His unusual gentleness warned her that something was amiss. Her eyes questioned him dumbly.

"I haven't come to make myself a nuisance to you," he said with a slight smile. "I've got a piece of bad news to deliver."

Her hand shook on the door. "Something has happened to Mark!" she whispered.

"Yes," he replied briefly.

She stood back, allowing him to enter. "Please tell me. Is he dead?"

He drew her into the living room and stood looking rather sternly down at her. "Yes, he's dead. Will you tell me why you so instantly leaped to that conclusion?"

She put her hands up to her face, pressing the palms against her temples. "You said you had not come—to worry me—with questions. When he's late like this—I always imagine things. How did it happen?"

"He was on his way home, drunk, of course—and he apparently stumbled over the edge of the bank into the river."

Her hands fell to her sides. He saw her draw a quick breath. Her eyes, fixed on his face, held a look of terror.

He realized suddenly that he had never before seen her afraid. For the first time she struck him as being pathetic, with her gallant pretence of calm and those great, searching eyes trying to read what he was thinking.

"I'm sorry to have to break it to you like this," he said.

"It doesn't matter," she jerked out, holding her head up. "Thank you for coming. Do you—happen to know—anything more?"

"Very little. The fool whom I put on to keep an eye on him let him out of his sight. I owe you an apology."

One of her hands went out gropingly towards the table and grasped the edge of it. "You put that man there—to watch him—because you thought—he might fall into the river?"

"Not quite that. I thought that after his exceedingly rash visit to the manor an attempt on his life might possibly be made."

"You're clever," she said in a low voice. "I—misjudged you." She paused. "Was he—pushed into the river?"

"I can only give you the facts and leave you to draw your own conclusions," he replied. "There is one witness only. Collins."

She started. "Ah!"

"Precisely. When Constable Tucker came up to the scene of the—accident—he found Collins dragging your brother's body up the bank. Between them they applied artificial respiration until the sergeant and I came."

She repeated, as though imperfectly understanding: "Collins tried to save him?"

"Apparently. That surprises you?"

She seemed a little dazed. "I can't quite—— Collins was—— Oh, my God, I ought never to have let him come here!"

"Collins?" said Mr. Amberley smoothly.

She did not pay much attention. "My brother. Only I never dreamed——" She broke off and pulled a chair out from the table and sat down a little limply. Mr. Amberley leaned his broad shoulders against the wall and stood watching her. She made no pretence of being heartbroken; he had seen enough of Mark to be sure she could not be. But the news had shocked her badly. It had frightened her too. She did not know which way to turn. He saw her give a little shiver and grip her fingers together nervously in her lap.

He said presently: "When Collins visited you here the other day, what did he come for?"

Her wandering thoughts were brought back with a jerk. "Did he say—he had visited this place?" she fenced.

"I saw him," replied Amberley.

"You must have been mistaken."

"But I was not. Now Collins has given me his version of why he came, and I should very much like yours."

He watched her knuckles gleam white. "I am not going to answer you," she said. "If he came—it was quite an innocent visit—and has nothing to do with you."

"I see. And when the sergeant comes to ask you whether your brother had any reason for wishing to shoot Collins, what are you going to say?"

"None," she answered with an effort. "None—whatsoever."

Amberley ceased to lounge against the wall and came across the room to her and sat down on the edge of the table. She looked up at him half-defiant, half-afraid. He laid his hand over both her tightly clasped ones and held them. "Don't you think it's time you told me all about it?" he said. "Come! I'm not such a bad person to confide in, you know."

To his surprise one of her hands twisted under his and clasped it for a moment. "I know," she said unexpectedly. "But I can't. It's no use asking me. I *daren't* tell you anything. Mark's dead, but I'm not finished yet. I—I don't give in easily."

"You daren't tell me," he repeated. He sat looking down at her somewhat enigmatically. "I'm going to make you," he said. "No, not now, but soon. My—er—*amour propre* is wounded. You shall confide in me. Of your own free will, too." He got up and glanced at his watch. "Now I am going to suggest to you that you come back with me to Greythorne. My aunt will be charmed to have you, and you cannot possibly remain here alone."

She flushed and said gratefully: "Thank you. You're being kinder than perhaps I deserve. But I can't come and stay at Greythorne. I—I shall leave this place and go to the Trust House in Upper Nettlefold. Please don't press me. I'm quite safe with my dog and my gun. I—I don't get drunk, you see."

"The Trust House? You mean the Boar's Head, in the Market Square? I'd much rather have you under my eye at Greythorne."

She smiled faintly. "I don't want to be under your eye, thanks."

"I know you don't. Will you come to Greythorne for tonight and move to the Boar's Head tomorrow?"

"No, thank you. I shall stay here tonight. Really, I shall be all right." She rose and held out her hand. "I—I'm sorry I've been rude to you. Thanks for all you've done for me. Will you would you mind going now?"

He arrived back at Greythorne just as his aunt and cousin were going upstairs to bed. Felicity asked him casually whether anything had happened and was considerably startled by his answer. He said briefly that Mark Brown had been killed.

Lady Matthews, who had reached the half-landing, remarked that it sounded very exciting, but who was Mark Brown? She had never heard of him.

Felicity explained hurriedly and demanded to know who had done it.

"He fell into the river and was drowned. No one did it," replied Amberley.

Felicity was immediately concerned for Shirley, left alone at Ivy Cottage, and Lady Matthews, having by this time grasped the fact that Shirley was the nice girl who had picked up her parcel for her at Hodgson's yesterday, announced that the poor child must not be allowed to stay at that horrid little cottage.

Amberley admitted that he had already issued an invitation to her which she had refused. Lady Matthews said: "Ah yes, dear. No doubt. I must have a coat. Such a shame to drag you out again, but impossible to have Ludlow out so late. The small spare room, Felicity darling. Better tell your father. So unfortunate, for he is put-out already."

It appeared that Lady Matthews had formed the intention of rescuing Shirley Brown herself.

When the Bentley once more stood outside the little white gate Lady Matthews got out and gently refused her nephew's escort. Amberley warned her that Shirley Brown was a somewhat obstinate young woman.

"Poor child!" murmured his aunt charitably.

She was not very long in the cottage, but when she came out again she was accompanied, somewhat to Amberley's astonishment, by Shirley, who carried a small suitcase and was closely followed by the faithful Bill. Shirley seemed curiously meek and she did not look at Amberley. The two ladies got into the back of the car; Bill and the suitcase shared the seat next the driver's. Bill, grateful for the ride, alternately put his head over the side to enjoy the wind in his face, and licked Mr. Amberley's lean cheek.

"It is to be hoped," remarked Mr. Amberley, removing a large paw from his wrist, "that Wolf is shut up."

Bill flattened his ears politely, but he did not share in the hope. A cheerful little fight would, in his opinion, round off the day nicely.

He got it. The chauffeur was bringing Wolf in from his last run as the car drew up at the door, and Wolf bounded up to greet these late homecomers. Bill did not wait to have the car door opened. Before Amberley could stop him he leaped over it. He was aware that he stood upon Wolf's own stamping-ground; if he had not previously encountered the Alsatian, etiquette would have compelled him to forbear battle. But he was one who hated to leave a job unfinished.

The commotion brought Sir Humphrey out upon the scene. He arrived in time to witness the removal of Wolf, raging impotently in the grip of the chauffeur. He ordained that that damned dog was to be shut up and demanded of his wife where she proposed to put the other brute.

Shirley, holding tightly to Bill's collar, said stiffly that she was sorry, and Sir Humphrey, recalled to his duties as host, put the whole blame onto Wolf.

Shirley, still more stiffly, said that she would like to keep Bill with her.

Sir Humphrey's views on the subject of large dogs in houses were widely known. He was about to make his guest privy to them when his wife said: "Of course, my dear. So much safer. We'll go up. Someone must find him a rug. Frank, you are so clever at finding things. Do find a rug. Probably in the oak chest."

She bore Shirley upstairs, leaving her husband silenced but indignant. When she presently came down again he professed himself much displeased with the whole affair. Everyone was in the wrong, principally Frank, who persisted in meddling in what did not concern him. This was what came of it. Dogs in bedrooms. No one had seen fit to consult him before this young woman was brought to the house. Had anyone done so he would have deprecated the plan most strongly. They knew nothing about the girl, and although he was naturally sorry for her, he could not see why his wife should consider it incumbent upon her to interfere.

Lady Matthews, quite unruffled by this severe vote of censure, patted his hand and said: "Dreadful, my dear. But impossible to let her stay alone in that cottage all night."

"I fail to see that it is in any way our affair," said Sir Humphrey, slightly mollified.

"Not in the least, darling. But no friends of her own, you see. So awkward. And quite a nice girl, I feel sure. She reminds me of someone, though I don't know whom."

"I have yet to meet anyone who did not remind you of someone, Marion," said Sir Humphrey. "I shall go to bed, and I trust you told her not to allow that dog to get on the furniture."

In the morning he had recovered his urbanity and had thawed enough to invite Shirley to remain at Greythorne until after the inquest, when he supposed she would be returning to London. He even said that the bull-terrier seemed to be a very well-behaved dog and bestowed a piece of kidney on him, which Bill accepted without hesitation.

Shirley refused the invitation. There were dark shadows under her eyes telling of a sleepless night, and she was very quiet. Lady Matthews did not urge her to stay and prevented Sir Humphrey from pressing the matter. "So much better to let people do what they want to," she said. "Somebody shall ring up and engage a room for you at the Boar's Head, my dear."

They had only just left the breakfast table when Jenkins came in to say that Mr. Fountain was in the library and would like to speak to Mr. Amberley.

This intelligence slightly impaired Sir Humphrey's good humour. He spoke severely of persons who called at uncouth hours and suddenly remembered a dire thing that was to happen today. There was going to be a dinner party. "And considering that both the Fountains and that foolish young man who is staying with them are coming here tonight, I fail entirely to see why a call at ten in the morning can be necessary," he said.

His disillusioned gaze dwelt accusingly on his nephew. Frank said with a grin: "I know, Uncle, I know. All my fault. Even the dinner party."

Without giving his uncle time to retort he went off to receive Fountain.

Fountain was standing by the window in the library, looking out. He turned as Amberley came in and walked towards him, holding out his hand. There was an expression of deep concern on his face. He said without any preamble: "I came round to see you about this tragic business of last night. I only heard when I got back from town."

"Yes?" said Amberley. "You mean Mark Brown falling into the river? Apparently half the village expected something of the sort to happen."

"But you were having him followed, weren't you?"

"I was. Not quite closely enough, as it turned out."

Fountain looked curiously at him. "Well, now that the poor chap's dead I do wish you'd tell me why you wanted him watched. I never could understand that. Did you think he had anything to do with Dawson's murder?"

"When a man—even a drunken man—forces his way

into a strange house and lets off a gun I always think it wise to keep an eye on him," said Amberley.

"I see." Fountain laughed a little. "I wondered whether you'd hit on some dark plot!" He became grave again and said: "Look here, what I really came round for was to ask you about Collins' share in the business. The fellow is naturally a bit worried, because he's got it into his head the police suspect him of having pushed Brown in."

"Oh, I don't think so!" Amberley replied.

"Well, I'm glad of that, for the idea's absurd. Why should he push the boy in? He tells me that he went in after him to get him out. I suppose that's true?"

"I wasn't there," said Amberley. "It looked true enough—at face value."

Fountain knit his brows. "I wish you'd be open with me," he said, a touch of annoyance in his voice. "Collins is in my employment, and I think I've a right to know. Hang it all, first my butler's shot, and then my valet is suspected of having pushed a complete stranger into the river. Isn't it true that he tried to rescue him? Of course, I know you never can believe all servants say, but he'd hardly make up such a tale, would he?"

"Hardly," said Amberley. "No one denies that he brought the body to land and applied artificial respiration."

"Well, I'm glad to hear it," said Fountain with relief. "I've had quite enough mysterious crimes to do with my household, I can tell you. It's damned unpleasant. The next thing I shall know is that the whole staff will leave in a body. What gave Collins the idea that the police suspected him? It seems to me so silly. He can't possibly have had any motive for killing Brown, can he?"

"Not to my knowledge," Amberley replied. "Possibly the police felt that his presence on the scene was insufficiently explained."

This aspect of the case did not seem to have occurred to Fountain. He said: "Yes, now I come to think of it, why was he there? I forgot to ask him that."

Amberley recounted, without comment, Collins's story. Fountain listened to it with a frown in his eyes and remarked at the end that it sounded so futile that it was probably true. He was not surprised the police thought it fishy. "Personally," he said, "I shouldn't be surprised if there was more to it. You know what servants are. Always keeping something back. Not that I think there was anything between him and Brown. What I do think is that he probably fell foul of Brown at the Blue Dragon one night and doesn't like to say so. And when Brown came up to the manor to do him in, he got the wind up and set about making his peace with the fellow."

"Yes," said Amberley thoughtfully. "Not a bad solution."

Fountain looked pleased. "Well, it seems more likely to me," he said. "But why the police should think he pushed Brown in, when they found him pulling him out, is more than I can fathom."

Amberley regarded his fingernails. "Well," he said slowly, "a man might do both, you know. If he was clever enough to think of it."

"Good Lord!" said Fountain in a blank voice. "What a singularly ghastly idea! No, really, Amberley, that's too much! Upon my soul, you're enough to make one's blood run cold!"

Amberley raised his brows. "Sorry to offend your susceptibilities. But that's undoubtedly how I should have planned the affair."

"Perfectly horrible!" said Fountain. He glanced at the clock. "I'd better be off. What's happening to the sister, by the way? Joan says there is one. Pretty awful for the poor girl."

"Yes," said Amberley. "At the moment she's staying here. My aunt fetched her last night."

"What a good soul Lady Matthews is!" said Fountain. "I call that being a real Samaritan. I suppose she'll have to stay till after the inquest, will she?"

"She can't go back to London till then. My aunt would like to keep her here, but unfortunately she won't stay. An independent female. We shall see you all at dinner tonight, shan't we?"

"Yes, rather. Looking forward to it very much," said Fountain, and took his leave.

CHAPTER X

IT WAS MR. AMBERLEY who booked a room for Shirley at the Boar's Head, and it was Mr. Amberley who volunteered to transport her there. She was fighting very shy of him and would have preferred the services of Ludlow, but in the presence of Lady Matthews and Felicity she could hardly say so outright. She had arrived at a very fair estimate of Mr. Amberley's character, and she felt that a delicate hint would have no effect on him at all.

She was persuaded to lunch at Greythorne and left immediately afterwards. When she thanked Lady Matthews for her kindness she seemed to Amberley like a transformed creature. He heard warmth in her voice for the first time, and saw her fine eyes bright with unshed tears.

But when she got into the car beside him up went her barriers again, and she answered him in her usual monosyllabic style.

It pleased him to make idle conversation, such conversation as he might make to a casual acquaintance. She was rather at a loss, but suspicious, which amused him.

He drove her first to the cottage, so that she could collect her belongings. Mark's possessions would have to be packed up later; at present she shrank from the task.

She had supposed that Amberley would wait for her in the car, but he came up to the cottage with her and told her to go and pack her trunk while he tidied things downstairs. She blinked at him; in this domestic rôle he seemed like a stranger.

Since she had left the cottage at a moment's notice there was a good deal to be done; she was upstairs for nearly half an hour, and when she came down she found that Amberley had been as good as his word. There was very little for her to do either in the living room or the kitchen.

He had even cleared the larder by the simple expedient of casting all the perishable foodstuffs in it over the hedge into the field beyond, where a party of white ducks was rapidly disposing of them.

Shirley put the chain up on the back door, shot the bolts home and turned the key in the lock. Mr. Amberley went upstairs to fetch her trunk and bore it out to the car. Shirley took a last look round and came out, locking the front door behind her. She joined Amberley in the car. He started the engine and began to back down the lane to the main road. Suddenly he stopped and said: "Damn!"

"What is it?" she asked.

He began to feel in his pockets. "I believe I've left my pouch in the cottage. Yes, I must have."

She prepared to get out. "Where did you leave it?"

"Not quite sure. No, don't you bother; I'll get it. It's probably in the kitchen. I lit a pipe there. Let me have the key, will you? I won't be a minute."

She opened her bag and gave him the front-door key. He went off with it up the garden path and let himself into the house.

He walked quickly through into the kitchen and to the back door. He slid the bolts back softly, took the chain off and put the key, which Shirley had left in the door, into his pocket. Then he went back to the car.

"Did you find it?" asked Shirley.

He gave her back the front-door key. "Yes, on the kitchen table. Sorry to have kept you."

When he had deposited her at the Boar's Head he drove on to the police station but found that the sergeant was off duty. The same young constable who had received him when he brought the news of Dawson's murder said that he had no idea where the sergeant might be, but he could take a message. Mr. Amberley eyed him meditatively and said, after apparently profound consideration: "I don't think so. Thanks very much all the same."

The young constable informed a colleague two minutes later that that Amberley chap fair got his goat.

When he got back to Greythorne Mr. Amberley put

through a telephone call. Felicity came into the library in time to hear him say: "And let me know at once. Got that? Right. That's all."

"Sweet telephone manners," remarked Felicity. "Who were you ringing up so politely, if I may ask?"

"Only my man," said Amberley.

The dinner party, which Lady Matthews thought would be rather stuffy, passed off well, and to Sir Humphrey's satisfaction no one stayed very late. Sir Humphrey, like Mr. Woodhouse, was firmly of the opinion that "the sooner every party breaks up the better." When he had seen the last guest off the premises he said that that was done, anyway, and prepared to go up to bed. His nephew detained him for a moment. "By the way, Uncle, don't be surprised if you hear a car. I rather think I shall have to go out. I thought I'd better warn you. If you hear stealthy footsteps in the small hours it won't be a burglar, but me."

"Going out?" said Sir Humphrey, astonished. "At this hour? In the name of all that's unreasonable, why?"

"No, not at this hour. Later," said Frank imperturbably. "I'm expecting a telephone call first. I shall go when I've taken it. Don't let it distress you, sir."

"It distresses me very much to see you making such a fool of yourself," said Sir Humphrey austerely. "No, you needn't tell me. I am well aware that you are going on police business, and I should have a better opinion of you if you ceased to meddle in matters that don't in the least concern you." He followed his wife to the door and turned back when he reached it to add: "And don't step on the fifth stair when you come in, unless you wish to wake us all up."

"Not the fifth, dear. The fourth," corrected Lady Matthews.

"I won't step on either," promised Amberley.

Left alone downstairs he wandered into the library and went over to the bookshelves to choose some suitable literature. He presently retired to the chair by the desk armed with Burton's *Anatomy of Melancholy,* and sat reading for over an hour, the telephone at his elbow. Occasionally he glanced at his wrist watch and as the time wore on, he frowned.

Shortly after midnight the telephone bell rang shrilly. Amberley lifted the receiver off the hook and said: "Hullo?"

The conversation was a very short one and confined on Amberley's part to three words only. He listened to what the voice at the other end had to say, replied: "All right. Thanks," and hung up the receiver. Then he consulted his pocketbook and rang up a number in Upper Nettlefold. After a prolonged wait the man at the exchange informed him that there was no answer. Mr. Amberley suggested gently that the exchange could try again. There was another pause, then a slightly testy and very sleepy voice said: " '*Ullo!*" with undue emphasis.

Mr. Amberley grinned. "Good evening, Sergeant. How are you?"

The voice lost its testiness. "Is that you, Mr. Amberley? What is it, sir?"

"I just rang up to know whether you were asleep," said Mr. Amberley.

The voice became charged with indignation. "Look here, sir—!"

"And if you were, to wake you up. *Are* you asleep, Sergeant?"

"No, sir, I am not—thanks to you! And if this is one of your little jokes——"

"Are you feeling fit, Sergeant? Full of energy and enthusiasm?"

There was a sound of heavy breathing. "One of these days," said the voice with emotion, "something'll happen to you, sir."

"Well, let's hope so anyway," said Mr. Amberley.

"I do," said the voice grimly. "Keeping me standing here in my nightshirt while you ask me silly conundrums!"

"I don't want to keep you in your nightshirt," said Mr. Amberley. "I feel sure I should hate you in it. Go and dress."

"Go and—— Here, sir, what's this all about? What have I got to dress for?"

"Decency," said Mr. Amberley. "I'm coming to fetch you for a little run in my car. I shall be round in about fifteen minutes. So long!"

A quarter of an hour later he picked the sergeant up outside his house and drove him away through the town to Ivy Cottage. The sergeant was in a state of high expectation and demanded instantly to know what they were going to do. Mr. Amberley said that they were going to collect a little evidence. "I rather think, Sergeant, that you will watch a man break into Ivy Cottage."

"Will I?" said the sergeant. "If I was to see anything like that I wouldn't waste time goggling at it, sir. I'd arrest him."

"When we make an arrest it's going to be on a charge of murder, not of housebreaking," said Amberley briefly.

He ran the car up the lane about a hundred yards past Ivy Cottage, rounding the next bend, and there switched off all his lights. The sergeant had not known that Shirley Brown had moved to the Boar's Head until Amberley told him. He wanted to know whether she had given Amberley the key, and when Amberley replied that he had taken it without her knowledge, he said uneasily that he hoped he was not going to get into trouble over this.

The cottage was very silent, lit dimly by the moonlight that came in through the uncurtained windows. Amberley told the sergeant to close the kitchen shutters and went off himself to draw the curtains in the other rooms.

"*I* see," said the sergeant brightly. "Make it look as though the young lady was still here. Then what do we do?"

"I'll tell you in a minute," Amberley promised.

When he had made his tour of the cottage he rejoined the sergeant in the kitchen and set his torch on the table. "Now, Sergeant, if you'll attend to me for a minute," he said. "With any luck you may be able to make that arrest you're so keen about. What I want you to do is to go upstairs and get into bed. If you hear anyone coming up the stairs, pull the clothes well over you. I rather think we're going to have a visitor."

"Is that all I've got to do?" said the sergeant. "Because if it is I'd as soon be in my own bed."

"Not at all, Sergeant. You're going to play the part of the dummy. If our visitor tries to suffocate you or chloroform you, collar him."

"I will," said the sergeant with feeling. "Do you mean to tell me that Albert Collins is going to do in the young lady?"

"No, I do not," replied Amberley. "No one is going to do her in if I can help it." He held his wrist in the beam of torchlight and looked at his watch. "To be on the safe side you'd better go up now. Don't make any mistake, will you? Unless he attempts to murder you keep quiet, but try to get a look at him."

The sergeant prepared to go upstairs. "Well, I don't know," he said. "Seems funny to me. I'm trusting you, Mr. Amberley, but I don't half like it, and that's the truth."

He went heavily up, and in a few moments a prodigious creaking announced that he had got into bed.

Amberley, left alone in the kitchen, set the door ajar and sat down on one of the wooden chairs and switched off his torch. Only the ticking of the clock on the mantlepiece broke the stillness.

The minutes crawled by. Upstairs in Shirley's narrow bed the sergeant strained his ears to catch any sound and wondered why he had not suggested that Mr. Amberley should be the dummy. He did not think he was a nervous man, but waiting in the dark for someone to come and murder one was a bit thick. He made up his mind to speak about it to Mr. Amberley. As ten, fifteen, twenty minutes passed he grew impatient. A doubt shook him. Could this be a practical joke, and had that young devil gone off home? He wouldn't put it above him; he had a good mind to go downstairs and see whether Amberley was still there. On second thoughts he abandoned the idea. Even Amberley wouldn't do this for a joke.

The wardrobe creaked and gave him a bad fright. He felt a cold shiver run down his spine and hoped that Mr.

Amberley was keeping a sharp lookout. He had barely succeeded in convincing himself that the creak really had come from the wardrobe when a long, eerie cry made him start up, clutching at his revolver. The cry was repeated and the sergeant drew a shuddering sigh of relief. He remembered that when he was a lad he had once shot and stuffed an owl. He was very glad he had; he wished he'd shot a few more while he was about it.

He lay down again cautiously. Mr. Amberley was keeping very quiet downstairs. Cool as a cucumber, he wouldn't wonder. Perhaps he wouldn't be quite so cool if he was lying up here waiting for someone to come and try to murder him.

A mouse gnawing at the wainscoting gave the sergeant a moment's uneasiness. He hissed at it, and it stopped.

Then a different sound broke the silence; the sergeant could have sworn he heard the garden gate open. The hinge was rusty and it gave a faint squeak. He took a firm hold of the coverlet and listened.

In the kitchen Mr. Amberley had risen silently from his chair and moved behind the door. The cottage was in pitch darkness. The clock's ticking seemed to reverberate through it.

There was the sound of a tiny chink coming from the living-room window. The frame creaked as though something had been forced between the two sashes. Then there was a snap as the bolt securing the upper and lower half together was forced back. It was followed by a few moments' silence.

Mr. Amberley waited, standing close to the crack of the door.

The living-room window was being pushed gently up from the outside; it stuck a little, and Amberley heard a hand slip on the glass. The betraying sound was again followed by absolute stillness, but after a moment the window was thrust up farther and the curtains were parted, letting in the pale moonlight.

Mr. Amberley, watching through the crack, saw for a moment a gloved hand holding back the curtain; then it moved and grasped the window sill. Soundlessly the nocturnal visitor climbed into the room; for an instant as he stood in the shaft of moonlight Amberley was able to study him. He seemed to be wearing a long coat, and as he turned Amberley saw that there was something over his head, probably a sack with eyeholes cut in it. It gave him an oddly sinister look; Amberley wondered what the sergeant would think of it.

An electric torch flashed over to the kitchen door; the unknown man moved softly into the small passageway that separated the two rooms, and the torch-beam swept round to light the stairs.

The man stood still, darkly silhouetted against the moonlight beyond. Amberley watched him take something out of his pocket and make a movement with his hand as though shaking scent onto a handkerchief.

Then he stiffened suddenly, listening. The gate had squeaked.

Amberley drew back noiselessly, feeling his way, and came to the larder door and groped for the handle. He began to turn it. Whoever the newcomer might be, he was not expected by the man at the foot of the stairs.

Someone else was getting in at the window; a boot scraped on the wall, and the whole window shook as a head came into sharp contact with the frame. A voice said involuntarily: "Blast!"

The man at the foot of the stairs turned and was gone like a flash into the kitchen. Under cover of the noise made by the second man Amberley had opened the larder door. When the hooded man's torch swept the kitchen it was empty. The man was wearing rubber soles, and his feet made no sound on the stone floor. He reached the back door, twisted the key round in the lock and a moment later was gone.

Mr. Amberley came out of the larder and strode to meet the second man, who had scrambled in at the window and was making for the kitchen. "You blithering idiot!" he said in a voice of rage. "You fat-headed, blundering ass!"

"Good Lord!" gasped Anthony Corkran, blinking in

the glare of Mr. Amberley's torch. "You don't mean to say it was you? What the devil are you doing here?"

Amberley turned to call up the stairs. "You can come down, Sergeant. The game's up."

Corkran jumped. "What? Sergeant Gubbins up there? Where's Miss Brown? I say, you know! Tut-tut!"

"Anthony," said Mr. Amberley with dangerous calm, "you are very near death. Don't provoke me too far!"

The sergeant came clumping down the stairs. "What's happened, sir?" he demanded.

"Nothing," said Amberley bitterly. "My friend Mr. Corkran has seen to that."

The sergeant's torch discovered Anthony; he looked at him with a kindly eye. "Well, I don't know that I'm altogether sorry," he said.

"But, I say, look here!" began Anthony, and broke off. "What on earth's the stink?"

"Chloroform," said Amberley, moving into the living room and striking a match.

The sergeant began to feel real affection for Mr. Corkran.

"But dash it all, it can't have been you I followed all the way from the manor!" protested Anthony.

"It wasn't." Amberley lit the lamp and turned. "It may interest you to know that the sergeant and I were lying in wait for the man you followed. If you hadn't come barging your way into the house with enough row to wake the dead we'd have had him by now."

"Well, damn it, if you were here, why didn't you nab him?" said Anthony.

"Because I wanted to get him in the act, you fool."

"Act of what?"

Amberley gave a sudden laugh. "Chloroforming the sergeant. Well, it can't be helped. You'd better tell us your side." He moved across to the window and shut it and pushed the bolt back into place.

It seemed that Corkran had been doing a little detective work on his own account. He had gone to bed upon his return from Greythorne to Norton Manor earlier in the evening, but not to sleep. He had read for some time; he did not think he could have turned his light out until past midnight, and for some time after that he had lain awake. He was just getting drowsy when he heard a faint sound outside. His room looked out on the front of the house, and he had often noticed that the noise of anyone's approach was considerably magnified by the loose gravel which covered the drive.

He had thought it an odd hour for anyone to be out and had had the curiosity to get up and look out of the window. At first the drive had appeared to be deserted, but all at once he had caught a glimpse of a man's back view as he emerged from the shadow of a big rhododendron bush. He must have been about thirty yards from the house and he was going towards the gate, so that Corkran only saw his back, and that very imperfectly. He was walking on the narrow grass border and pushing a bicycle. It must have been the bicycle wheels on the gravel that Corkran had heard. He wore a long coat and a tweed cap pulled down over his head. Corkran could not recognize him at that distance, but his stealthy mode of progression, coupled with the lateness of the hour, aroused all his suspicions. He had very little doubt himself that it was Collins, and he made up his mind there and then to follow him in the hopes of discovering some valuable clue.

He had hastily pulled on a pair of trousers over his pajamas, thrust his feet into a pair of shoes and socks, grabbed a coat, and tiptoed downstairs to the front door. He did not want to run any risk of waking Joan and alarming her, and he wasn't particularly keen on waking Brother Basil either. He happened to know that there was an old bicycle Joan sometimes used in a shed near the house. He had got hold of this and set off in pursuit.

By the time he had reached the gates there was no sign of the mysterious cyclist. Corkran had chosen the Upper Nettlefold Road, thinking it the likeliest way for the man to have gone. The seat of the bicycle was too low for him, and one of the tires badly needed pumping. Altogether it was a fairly uncomfortable journey, but he had kept on and been rewarded, about a mile from the manor, by catching sight of his quarry. After that the chase had been very good fun. He had taken care to keep well behind, for even though there was no lamp on his machine the moonlight would have betrayed him had the man he was following chanced to look round.

He had very nearly been discovered at the end of the journey. The unknown man had passed the end of the lane to Ivy Cottage, and he, Corkran, had pedalled staunchly after him. But some yards on the first man had dismounted and pushed his bicycle into the ditch. Corkran was luckily in the shadow of a clump of trees at the time. He too had sought shelter in the ditch and waited to see what his quarry would do. The man had turned and come back on foot. Corkran did not mind admitting that he had got a bit of a shock then. The fellow was no longer wearing his cap, but had got a sack pulled over his head with eyeholes cut in it. In the moonlight, and before he had had time to see just what it was, it had looked perfectly beastly. Of course, this had made him certain that whoever was wearing the sack was not up to any good. He wished he had got a weapon at that moment, but since Brother Basil kept the gun room locked, and he wasn't himself in the habit of travelling with a revolver, he hadn't. However, it seemed pretty feeble to give up the stalk at this moment, so he had followed the man, and from behind the hedge surrounding the cottage had watched him force open the window and climb in. After that, of course, weapon or no weapon, he had had to go on. The rest they both knew.

The sergeant, who had listened admiringly to this tale, said handsomely that it did him credit. Mr. Amberley said that his friend's intentions might be good, but the result was disastrous. He supposed he would have to run Corkran back to the manor.

"You suppose right," said Anthony cheerfully. "Nothing would induce me to mount the velocipede again, I can tell you."

"I'll go and lock the back door again," Amberley said. "We can go out by the front." He went through into the kitchen, carrying his torch. The door still stood open as the fugitive had left it. Amberley was about to shut it when a slight sound caught his ears. He switched his torch on and swept its beam round. Something moved by the door of the woodshed; for a moment he saw Baker's face; then it vanished, and a twig cracked under a retreating footstep. Amberley stepped quickly out into the little kitchen-garden; at the same moment Corkran came up behind him and asked what he was up to now? Had he seen anyone?

Amberley did not answer for a moment. Then he switched off his torch and said slowly: "No. I don't think so. I'm just going to shut the back gate. You might open the kitchen shutters again, will you?"

He waited till Corkran had gone back into the cottage and then went softly towards the woodshed. There was no one there, nor did there seem to be anyone lurking in the garden. Mr. Amberley stood still listening intently. No sound betrayed the butler's presence. Mr. Amberley's brows rose a little; he turned and went back into the house.

The sergeant and Anthony Corkran were getting on very well together. They were agreed on two points: that the man was undoubtedly Albert Collins; that Mr. Amberley ought not to have let him get away. This much Amberley heard as he re-entered the kitchen. He locked and bolted the door and said over his shoulder: "When we make an arrest, my well-meaning but misguided friends, it will be on a charge of murder—and other things. Not of housebreaking. Further, I would like to draw your attention to one small but significant point. The man who broke into this place tonight did not know of the existence of Bill."

The sergeant cast an eloquent glance at Corkran. "And who," he inquired, "might Bill be, sir?"

"Bill," said Mr. Amberley, "is Miss Brown's bull-terrier. Think it over."

CHAPTER XI

ANTHONY CORKRAN'S account of his share in the night's happenings was carefully expurgated next morning when he told it over the breakfast table. He had been coached by Amberley during the drive back to the manor, and he quite realized that to disclose the other two men's presence in the cottage would be a very false step.

His own idea was to keep the whole adventure dark, but he admitted that he might be wrong when Amberley pointed out that complete silence on his part must inevitably warn the unknown housebreaker that he was suspected. The man had come from the manor; further, he must know who had followed him, since Anthony had sworn aloud at hitting his head against the window frame. If Anthony preserved a rigid silence it would only put the man on his guard.

Accordingly, Anthony told Fountain next morning when Joan had left the table that he had been up all night chasing masked men. Fountain looked at him as though he were a mild lunatic and went on with his breakfast. He was never in his best mood at this hour, and the only response he gave was a grunt.

Anthony buttered another slice of toast. "To be strictly accurate," he said, "not men, but man. One. Complete with sack."

Fountain looked up from the paper and said, with a hint of exasperation in his voice: "What the devil are you talking about?"

"If you don't believe me, take a look at the bicycle," said Anthony. "It wasn't good when I first mounted it. It's definitely on the sick-list now."

Fountain put the paper down. "What bicycle?" he said. "I do wish you wouldn't talk such rubbish!"

"Joan's. I rode it seven miles. And back."

Fountain gave a short laugh. "Yes, I can see you riding a bicycle seven miles. Do you mind explaining the joke?"

Anthony explained it. It was some time before he could make his host believe that he was not pulling his leg. When he had succeeded in convincing him of his seriousness Fountain at once demanded to know who the man was. Anthony said that he didn't know, though he had a strong suspicion.

"Collins?" Fountain said, lowering his voice. "Good Lord!"

"Mind you, I'm not sure," Corkran warned him. "I never saw his face."

Fountain took no trouble to disguise the fact that he was thoroughly annoyed. He said that it looked as though he would have to sack the man. Anthony heartily agreed, but was himself annoyed to discover that Fountain was still somewhat dubious about his story. He remarked that it seemed fantastic; he wished Anthony had caught the man and unmasked him. As far as he could see, it would be most unwise for him to accuse Collins without any sort of proof to go on. He must think the whole thing over and keep a strict watch. It was all most unfortunate, not to say infuriating. If the police came to question the servants again the housekeeper for one would leave. She had been thoroughly affronted and upset already by the inspector's tactless method of interrogation. "In fact," said Fountain crossly, "I wish to God you hadn't looked out of your window. At least I shouldn't have known anything about it then."

At that moment Joan came into the room, and the discussion at once ended. She and Corkran were going to play golf. A polite suggestion that Basil should come and make it a three-ball match was refused. He was not going to play gooseberry, he said; besides which that old footler, Matthews, had rung up to say that he was coming round to see him on a matter of business.

"Of course I know what that means," Fountain said. "He dropped a hint at dinner last night, but I wasn't having any. I've got quite enough to worry me without the delinquencies of my head-keeper being added to the list."

"Poachers?" Joan inquired. "I know; Felicity was talking about it. I suppose Hitchcock is fairly slack."

"Well, I'm not going to get rid of him to please old Matthews," said Fountain.

Sir Humphrey was driven over at twelve o'clock by his daughter in her runabout, Ludlow being smitten with influenza. Baker ushered them both into the library and left them there while he went to find his master.

Sir Humphrey, after the manner of book-lovers, began to wander round studying the closely packed shelves. He said severely that he wondered Fountain had not had the library catalogued and arranged in decent order.

Fron her seat in the window Felicity remarked that she didn't suppose he cared. "Not bookish, darling," she smiled.

"That is self-evident," said her father, putting on his glasses and studying the backs of a row of calf-bound classics.

"They all look fairly dull anyway," said Felicity airily.

Sir Humphrey, who had discovered a treasure, did not reply. She transferred her attention to the activities of a gardener who was sweeping up the fallen leaves on the lawn and left her parent to browse in peace. When Fountain came in apologizing for keeping his visitor waiting, he was turning over the pages of a dusty volume culled from the obscurity of a top shelf and said absently: "Not at all, not at all. I have been looking over your books. My dear sir, are you aware that they are all arranged according to size?"

Fountain looked a trifle bewildered and said that he was afraid he was not much of a reader. He was told that he should employ someone to put the library in order. It appeared that many rare editions were in his possession, and that De Quincey was rubbing shoulders with somebody's *Recollections of the Russian Court*. He gathered from Sir Humphrey's tone that this was a crime and said that he was very ignorant in these matters.

"I believe your grandfather was a great collector," said Sir Humphrey. He held up the book in his hand. "Here is an old friend whom I have not met, alas, for many years. I cannot think why it is missing from my own shelves. I wonder if I may borrow it? A pernicious habit, I am aware."

"Do by all means," said Fountain, hoping to get away from the subject of books. "Very glad if you'd borrow anything you want to."

"Thank you. I just have a fancy to dip into these pages again. I will take the first volume, if I may."

Fountain gave his noisy laugh. "First volume, eh? I don't mind admitting I shy at anything in more than one volume."

Sir Humphrey looked at him with much the same wonder as he would have displayed upon being confronted by a dinosaur.

"Dear me!" he said. "Yet this work—it is Disraeli's *Curiosities of Literature*—you would find well worth the—ah—labour of reading. But I did not come to talk about books. I must not waste your time."

Fountain murmured a polite disclaimer but made no attempt to dissuade Sir Humphrey from coming to his business. At the end of twenty minutes' earnest conversation he promised that he would speak to his keeper. It was pointed out to him that some suspicious-looking men had been seen on his estate; Sir Humphrey felt that it was the duty of every landowner to stamp out this poaching menace and was sure that Fountain would agree with him.

Fountain was ready to agree with anything. Certainly poachers must be got rid of; he would have a word with Hitchcock.

Felicity, perceiving his scarce-veiled impatience, got up and said that if they did not go they would not have time to visit Upper Nettlefold before lunch. Sir Humphrey said, to be sure they were encroaching upon Fountain's time; he would rely on him to see that something was done.

He shook hands and was about to go when the door opened softly and Collins came in.

The valet stopped and said at once: "I beg pardon, sir. I thought you were alone."

"That's all right; since you're here you can show Sir

Humphrey and Miss Matthews out," said Fountain. "Good-bye, sir; I'll see about it at once. Sure you won't take the other volumes? Well, don't hesitate to borrow any book you happen to want. Only too glad!"

The valet's eyes rested for a moment on the volume Sir Humphrey carried. Then he looked quickly towards the bookshelves. Some quiver of emotion flickered in his face. He said: "Should I wrap the book up for you, sir?"

"No, thank you, I prefer it as it is," replied Sir Humphrey, going towards the door.

"I fear it may be very dusty, sir. Shall I wipe it for you?"

"Wipe it? No, no, it is perfectly all right!" said Sir Humphrey testily. "Well, good-bye, Fountain. Come along, Felicity, or we shall be late."

As Felicity started the car she said: "Did you notice that man? The valet, I mean."

"Notice him, my dear? I naturally saw him. Why should I notice him particularly?"

"I thought he gave you—such an ugly look."

"You imagine things, my dear," said Sir Humphrey. "Why should he give me an ugly look?"

"I don't know. But he did."

She drove the car into Upper Nettlefold, being commissioned by Lady Matthews to call at the Boar's Head to find out if Shirley Brown was comfortable there and to offer to accompany her to the inquest next morning. The porter thought Miss Brown was in her room, and went up to find her while Felicity and Sir Humphrey waited in the lounge.

Shirley came downstairs in a few minutes; she seemed pleased to see Felicity, but rather shy. She wore a black arm-band over her tweed coat, but no other sign of mourning, and although she looked worried she had certainly not been crying. She said that she was quite comfortable at the Boar's Head and declined Lady Matthews's offer of escort to the inquest. It was very kind of Lady Matthews but quite unnecessary; she would not like to drag her to anything so unpleasant.

"My wife," said Sir Humphrey, eyeing her askance,

"thought that perhaps you would be glad of—ah— support—under such painful circumstances."

Shirley gave him back one of her surprising clear looks. "I shan't break down," she said. "It has been a shock to me, and I'm upset. But I don't want to pose as being heartbroken. You see, I'm not. I'm sorry if this shocks you."

It evidently did shock Sir Humphrey. He said that perhaps she had scarcely had time to realize what had happened. Her smile was a little scornful, but she did not argue the point. On the question of her return to London she was inclined to be vague; purposely, Felicity guessed. There appeared to be business connected with Ivy Cottage which she would be obliged to settle.

She made no effort to detain her visitors when Felicity rose to go. Felicity thought, privately, that whatever she might choose to say, she was suffering from considerable strain. Her eyes betrayed her.

Sir Humphrey, on the way home, took no pains to disguise the fact that he did not like Shirley. His sense of propriety was offended by her lack of hypocrisy; he could not forgive such plain-speaking, however unsatisfactory Mark Brown might have been. Decency had to be preserved. He thought that the absence of mourning-clothes showed a lack of respect towards the dead. Whatever a man's character had been in life, death, in Sir Humphrey's eyes, made him instantly respectable.

In the middle of these reflections he broke off to hunt on the seat beside him for something. Felicity slowed down. "What is it, Daddy?"

"I seem," said Sir Humphrey with annoyance, "to have left that book I borrowed at the Boar's Head. I can't think how I could have done such a thing. We shall have to go back."

Leaving things behind was a habit he had so often condemned in his wife and daughter that Felicity could not forbear a little crow of laughter as she turned the car.

Ten minutes' run brought them back to the Boar's Head. Sir Humphrey went into the lounge where he found Shirley sitting alone, the book on the small table before her. She was flushed, and when she looked up at his approach, he was surprised to see so much light in her dark eyes. Upon his soul, the girl looked as though she had come into a fortune instead of having lost her only brother.

She got up, lifting the book from the table. "You left this behind, didn't you?" she said. "I've been—dipping into it. Also dusting it, which it badly needed." She put it into his hands. "Here you are."

"And what did you think of it?" said Sir Humphrey.

A little smile hovered on her lips. "It seems to have some very interesting things in it," she said.

Amberley was not in to lunch, having gone over to Carchester to confer with the chief constable, but he put in an appearance at tea-time, not in the best of tempers. An effort on Sir Humphrey's part to read aloud to him an anecdote about the Abbé Marolles was firmly checked at the outset. "I've read it," said Mr. Amberley.

"Indeed?" said his uncle huffily. "I shall be surprised, nevertheless, if you can tell me what book it occurs in."

"*Curiosities of Literature*," said Amberley without hesitation. "I didn't know you had the book."

Sir Humphrey, pleased to find his nephew more widely read than he had imagined, unbent and said that he had borrowed the book from Fountain that morning. He presently made another attempt to read a passage aloud but was still more firmly checked. "Do you remember this bit, Frank?" he began.

"Yes," said Mr. Amberley.

Sir Humphrey informed him that his manners were intolerable. By way of working off his spleen he said acidly that he trusted Frank did not intend to wake the entire household up in the small hours that night as he had done last night.

Mr. Amberley, who had heard his uncle snoring as he had passed his door at four that morning, grinned and said meekly that there would be no disturbance tonight.

He was mistaken. At twenty minutes past two the silence

of the house was shattered by a crash that woke not only Sir Humphrey, but his wife and his nephew also.

The noise had seemed to come from the drawing room, and it was followed by complete stillness. Amberley came softly out of his room with a gun in one hand and a torch in the other, and stood for a moment listening intently.

A board creaked somewhere below; Amberley began to descend the stairs in the darkness, making no sound.

At that moment the door of Sir Humphrey's room was wrenched open and Sir Humphrey hurried out. "Who's there?" he demanded and switched on the light at the top of the stairs.

Amberley said something under his breath and reached the hall in a couple of bounds. He was too late; when he flashed his torch round the drawing room it was empty. The French window was swinging wide, and the curtain bellied into the room in the draught. Amberley tore it aside and looked out. The moonlight flooded the garden, but there were patches of shadow cast by the trees. No one was in sight, the torch-beam revealed no lurking form. Whoever had broken into the house was by now well on his way to the road, and to follow would be a futile task.

Mr. Amberley went back into the drawing room and inspected the window. Two small panes of glass had been neatly cut out, enabling the burglar to unbolt the window, top and bottom.

Sir Humphrey's voice was upraised. "What the devil are you up to, Frank?" it demanded wrathfully. "Are we never to have a night in peace?"

Amberley strolled back to the hall. "Just come down here, Uncle," he said.

"I've no wish to do anything of the kind! What are you playing at?"

"You've had a visitor," said Amberley, and wandered back to the drawing room and stood in the doorway surveying the chaos there.

Sir Humphrey joined him. "It wasn't you? Do you mean to say—— God bless my soul!"

The ejaculation was provoked by the sight that met his

eyes. To a tidy man it was certainly startling. Someone would seem to have been frenziedly searching for something. The room was turned upside down; cushions, books, papers were scattered higgledy-piggledy over the floor. The drawers of Lady Matthews's bureau were all open and the contents thrown out. In the tiled fireplace the broken pieces of a large vase added to the litter. Obviously the intruder had accidentally knocked it over, and it was the noise of the smash that had awakened the household.

The window next caught Sir Humphrey's dazed eye. He repeated rather feebly: "God bless my soul!" and stared at Amberley.

"We'd better have a look round," said Amberley, and led the way to the library.

Here the confusion was even worse, while the condition of Sir Humphrey's study drew a faint moan from its unfortunate owner. His desk had been ransacked, and all his papers had been cast recklessly onto the floor.

"God bless my soul!" said Sir Humphrey for the third time. "It's a burglary!"

His nephew looked at him with scant respect. "How do you think these things out so quickly?" he inquired. "Hullo, Aunt. Come to look at the wreckage?"

Lady Matthews, with her hair in curlers and cold cream on her face, stood in the doorway looking interestedly round. She was not in the least put-out. She said: "Dear me, how exciting! Such a muddle! Poor Jenkins! Why the study?"

Amberley nodded. "You have a way of hitting the nail on the head, Aunt Marion, though no one would ever think it. Do tell me why you're plastered with white stuff?"

"Face cream, my dear. At my age so necessary. Do I look odd?"

"Quite ghastly," Amberley assured her.

Sir Humphrey danced with impatience. "Good God, Frank, what has your aunt's face to do with it? Look at my desk! Look at my papers!"

"Much better look for the silver, dear," said his wife.

"Or does Jenkins take it upstairs? Murdered in his bed, perhaps. Someone had better go and find out."

But Jenkins had not been murdered. He appeared at that moment with a coat and trousers put on hastily over his pajamas. Sir Humphrey greeted him with relief and was not disappointed. Jenkins's feelings rivalled his own, and the two mourned together until Mr. Amberley intervened.

"Take a look at the valuables, Jenkins," he requested.

Jenkins went off at once. Sir Humphrey took his wife to see the damage done to the drawing room window, and Mr. Amberley stood in the middle of the litter in the study, frowning.

He was joined soon by his cousin, who was in high fettle but indignant that no one had seen fit to rouse her. Mr. Amberley evinced a mild interest in the methods usually employed by her maid when calling her in the morning.

Jenkins came back to report that so far as he could tell without making an inventory of the silver, nothing was missing. The dining room had not been touched, and the Georgian saltcellars were still reposing on the sideboard.

Mr. Amberley went in search of his uncle, whom he found raging over the damage done to his window. Lady Matthews was placidly agreeing with him.

"I want you to come and see whether anything is missing from your study, Uncle," said Amberley.

"How the devil am I to tell?" said Sir Humphrey. "It will take me hours to get my papers in order again! Upon my word, it sometimes seems to me there's no law left in England!"

"Did you keep anything of value in your desk?" interrupted Amberley.

"No, I did not. It is some slight comfort to me to know that this damned thief's labour was entirely fruitless!"

"No money? You're quite sure?"

"Of course I'm sure! Do you suppose I should be likely to leave any money about?"

"You, Aunt?"

"No, my dear. Only bills and things. So dull for him. What do you suppose he wanted?"

"I don't suppose anything. I'm in the dark at the moment." He looked round the room, his eyes narrowed and speculative. "The drawing room, the study, the library, but not the dining room. Queer. It would seem as though you've got something that someone else wants rather badly, Uncle. A document?"

"Certainly not! Any important papers are lodged at my bank. Not that they could be of the slightest interest to anyone but myself."

"Why throw books on the floor?" said Lady Matthews. "So unnecessary, I feel."

Amberley looked quickly across at her. "Books! Good God!"

"Go on, Frank, what?" squeaked Felicity. "I *do* call this fun!"

Amberley paid no heed to her. "Where's that book you borrowed from Fountain, sir?"

"In my room. I took it up to bed with me. What has——"

Amberley turned. "Get it, will you, Jenkins? *Curiosities of Literature.*"

Lady Matthews sat down. "How delightfully mysterious," she said. "Why the book, my dear?"

"I rather think that it was the book that was wanted," replied Amberley. "I hope so anyway."

Jenkins came back, the book in his hand, and gave it to him. Amberley flicked over the leaves, shook it, peered down the back, carefully felt the thickness of the boards.

"Too thrilling!" murmured Lady Matthews.

But Amberley was looking puzzled. "I seem to be wrong," he said. "Yet somehow—I don't think I am." He glanced thoughtfully at his uncle. "I wonder."

"What do you wonder?" said Sir Humphrey. "Pray don't be obscure!"

"Whether anyone entered your room tonight," said Amberley.

Sir Humphrey, who like many others had an entirely erroneous belief that he was a light sleeper, was indignant.

He was ready to swear that no one could possibly have entered his room without waking him.

His wife interposed. "Dear Frank, all most intriguing, but don't annoy your uncle."

"Sorry, Aunt. It's all rather disappointing. I'm going back to bed."

Sir Humphrey demanded to know what was to stop the burglar returning through the damaged window. Mr. Amberley professed complete unconcern. He was still holding the book, and he went out carrying it with him.

CHAPTER XII

MR. ANTHONY CORKRAN was about to answer the telephone, which was ringing shrilly in the lobby off the hall, when he was forestalled by the polite Baker.

The butler apologized with his usual deprecating air for being late and took the receiver off the hook. He said: "Hullo!" and Mr. Corkran, still standing in the hall, could have sworn a female voice answered. The butler gave a sidelong glance towards him and said primly: "I do not know whether it is convenient just now—miss."

The voice spoke again. Baker listened and said: "What name, please?"

Apparently no name was given. Corkran saw a curious expression come into the butler's face and wondered. Baker set the receiver down carefully and went away across the hall to the kitchen premises. His interest aroused, Corkran lingered in the doorway of the library to see who was being fetched. Not entirely to his surprise Collins came into the hall a few moments later and went towards the telephone lobby. Corkran drew back into the library and shut the door.

Collins went into the lobby and picked up the receiver. "What is it? Collins speaking."

"I think you know who I am," said a woman's voice.

The valet cast a quick look over his shoulder and spoke urgently into the mouthpiece. "It's no use your ringing me up here. It's not safe. I told you before."

"Then I think you'd better meet me," said the voice coolly. "I can make trouble, you know."

The man's lips curled back in a rather mirthless smile. "You'll get no good by it."

"If you refuse to meet me that won't deter me," said the voice. "Either you come to terms or I wreck the whole

143

thing. I mean that. I can do it, too. 'Half a loaf is better than no bread,' and I have got just half a loaf. Well?"

Collins's fingers tightened on the receiver as though it had been someone's throat. "All right. But don't ring me up here again. I'll meet you. I don't know when I can get off. I'll let you know."

"Thanks, you can let me know now," said the voice.

"I tell you I can't get off at a moment's notice. You ought to know that. I'll see you on my evening off—alone."

"You will see me today," said the voice, stating a fact. "Certainly, alone."

"It's not safe. I can't get away for so long."

"I don't mind coming to you," said the voice obligingly. "If you're wise you'll manage to slip out for half an hour."

The valet gave another quick look behind him. "All right. I'll do that on condition you don't ring up here again."

"If you're reasonable I shan't want to ring you up," promised the voice. "Where do we meet?"

The man thought for a moment. "It's risky, but do you know the pavilion in the wood?"

"No. I'm afraid I don't."

"There's a gate before you get to the lodge, leads to the gamekeeper's cottage. The pavilion is by the lake, just beyond. You can't miss it. I'll be there at six." He hung up the receiver abruptly and stepped out of the lobby.

Fountain came out of the library pulling the door to behind him. A heavy scowl was on his face; his eyes were fixed suspiciously on the valet. "Who rang you up?" he demanded. "Mr. Corkran has just been asking me if I am aware that my servants use the telephone for their own private affairs. Who was it?"

Collins stood still, his eyes lowered. There was an unpleasant look about his mouth, and for a moment he did not answer.

"Some woman, eh?" Fountain said, coming a step nearer. "Isn't that so?"

The eyes were raised for a brief instant; Collins said

smoothly: "Yes, sir." He gave a little cough. "Merely the young lady I am keeping company with, sir. I explained that she must not ring me up again."

"Keeping company? That's something new. Now see here, Collins! I'll put up with a lot, but there are some things I won't stand. Got that?"

The valet bowed. "Perfectly, sir. It shall not occur again."

"It had better not," Fountain said grimly. "It seems to me it is about time I got rid of you. All things considered."

The shadow of a smile crossed Collins's thin lips, but he said nothing. Corkran came out of the library at that moment, and Fountain turned to meet him. The valet went away soft-footed across the hall.

"You were quite right, my dear chap," Fountain said. "Ringing up his girl! Bloody cheek! Thanks for tipping me the wink."

Seven miles away Miss Shirley Brown came out of the telephone-box at the Boar's Head with a triumphant look in her eyes. She was met by the hall porter, who informed her that a gentleman of the name of Amberley had called to see her, and the look changed to one of guarded secrecy. She told the porter to inform Mr. Amberley that she had gone out, adding as an excuse that she must take her dog for a run and could not wait now.

She allowed her visitor ten minutes' grace and then came downstairs followed by Bill. Mr. Amberley had gone, leaving no message. With a sigh of relief not entirely unmixed with disappointment, Shirley went out, walking in the direction of Ivy Cottage where she had Mark's packing to do.

At five o'clock in the afternoon she shut Bill into her bedroom and went out, dressed in a long tweed coat and a felt hat pulled low over her head. She went directly to the Market Square, where the omnibuses that served the surrounding villages started. No. 9 bore the legend LOW-BOROUGH on its signboard, and she boarded it. After some minutes its driver, who also performed the functions of conductor, got in and started his engine. Shirley, who had chosen a seat immediately behind him, leaned forward and requested him to set her down at the turning that led to Norton.

It had been cloudy all day, and the omnibus had not gone very far when a fine rain began to fall, rather like a Scotch mist. The light was fading quickly, and the landscape seen on either side of the omnibus looked grey and dreary. Shirley gave a little shiver at the prospect of flat, wet fields and was impelled by some inward suspicion to glance round at the other occupants of the bus. She thought she must be suffering from nerves, a complaint she despised, for she had had an unaccountable feeling that she had been followed from the Boar's Head.

Her fellow-travellers seemed ordinary enough. There were two farmers discussing the weather in broad Sussex accents; a red-faced man who might have been a gamekeeper, who sat all over a seat meant for two perusing *Our Dogs;* and several women, who had been doing the week's shopping in the town. On the route several others were picked up and hailed by those already in the bus. Behind Shirley an Irishwoman poured into the ear of a credulous and apparently interested acquaintance every detail of some unknown person's operation for appendicitis.

At the first village of any size most of the people left the bus, and the driver got down to deliver a parcel at the inn. Shirley and the red-faced man were left alone. Still with the uncomfortable sensation of being followed she took a surreptitious look at him. He was absorbed in his paper and did not seem to be interested in her. A mile beyond the village the bus stopped to set him down outside a kennels for gun dogs. Shirley settled herself more comfortably and sneered at her own qualms.

The bus stopped several more times to pick up passengers and once to set down another parcel. Unaccustomed to the leisurely progress of country omnibuses Shirley began to get impatient and to look at her watch. There was very little daylight left, and the driver had switched on the electric lights. Raindrops glistened on the windows; an unpleasant draught swept over the floor of the omnibus.

The driver drew in to the side of the road and pulled on his brake. "Here you are, miss. Wet evening."

Shirley took out her purse. "Beastly," she agreed. "What time is the next bus back, please?"

"I shall be coming back in an hour," replied the driver, indicating that there was only one bus. "Will you have a return ticket, miss? A shilling, that'll be."

"No, I might miss it," Shirley said.

"Sixpence then, please, miss."

She handed over the money, and he leaned sideways to pull the lever that opened the door of the bus. She climbed down onto the road and stood for a moment watching the omnibus disappear round the bend.

She was provided with a torch, but there was still sufficient light for her to see her way. She was standing at a crossroads. A signpost above her head pointed the road to Norton, and pulling up the collar of her coat to keep the rain from trickling down her neck, she set off at a brisk pace down the lane.

It was apparently a second-class road but in quite good repair. It wound between straggling hedges, passing an occasional cottage or farmstead. Two or three cyclists overtook her, and one car, but the road seemed to be little used. Once she saw a pedestrian ahead and rapidly overhauled him. A bucolic voice bade her good evening in the friendly fashion of country folk. She returned the greeting and pressed on.

A mile from the main road a cluster of twinkling lights showed where a small hamlet lay in a slight hollow. Beyond that the habitations were few. There seemed to Shirley, peering through the dusk, to be nothing but fields stretching sombrely to a far horizon that still showed faintly grey in the distance. About half a mile past the hamlet some trees broke the monotonous landscape, and presently these grew more thickly. Shirley could smell pines and see in the waning light the silver-grey bark of birch trees. The leaves were sodden and dripped onto the tarred road. No life seemed to be stirring. Perhaps it was too wet, Shirley thought, for the rabbits that were usually to be seen at this hour scuttling across the road, to venture out of their burrows.

She had no means of measuring the distance she had walked, but she supposed that she must have covered nearly a couple of miles, and began to look out for a gate. Half in anger at herself, half in a kind of scornful amusement, she blamed the weather and the twilight for her nervousness. The rain fell softly, steadily; there was no wind to stir the leaves of the trees; there did not seem to be a soul abroad. Yet several times she had caught herself straining her ears to catch the sound of—she scarcely knew what. Footsteps, perhaps; perhaps the hush of tires on the wet road. Once she thought she heard a car purring in the distance, but nothing passed her, and she concluded that she had either been mistaken or that another road ran somewhere near at hand.

A gleam of white ahead of her attracted her attention. She went on and found a gate leading into the wood on her right. It stood half open on to a grass-ride cut through the trees. She hesitated and searched for a name on the cracked posts.

With a wry little smile she reflected that she had brought a suburban mind into the country. Of course there was no name; country people always knew who lived where; you never found names on any gateposts. It was a little tiresome for strangers, all the same.

She went on a few yards, feeling herself rather at a loss, but after five minutes' walking she saw big iron gates ahead and the lights of a lodge. These must certainly belong to the manor; she turned and went quickly back towards the first gate.

The wood looked dark and mysterious; there was a good deal of undergrowth, bracken standing three feet high turning brown with the fall of the year, and blackberry bushes. Under Shirley's feet the ground was slippery with wet; in the wheel-ruts of the ride there were muddy puddles.

She walked forward cautiously, peering through the gathering darkness for a cottage. A little way from the gate the ride forked; she saw a light at the end of the shorter fork and bore onwards, leaving it on her right.

She smelled pines again, and a few steps brought her to clearer ground. The earth grew more sandy under her feet; a carpet of pine needles deadened the sound of her footsteps. Fallen cones were scattered over the ride; the undergrowth had come to an end; slim tree-trunks, gleaming with wet, surrounded her, stretching away, line upon line of them, into the mist and the enveloping gloom.

The silence was almost eerie; the rain which was falling soundlessly and fast, seemed like a blanket, cutting off all the small, ordinary noises of the wood. Shirley gritted her teeth together and felt, in the big pocket of her coat, the reassuring butt of her automatic.

The ride took a turn, and immediately lights became visible in the distance. Shirley had come to the lake, an artificial sheet of water set at the end of a broad avenue that had been cut to the south of the manor. There were little glowing lights in the distance; she could just discern the outline of the manor against the sky and see the sweep of a lawn running to meet the edge of the wood.

On the opposite side of the lake from the manor, forming part of the view to be had from the south windows, was a white pavilion built in the classical style so much in favour during the eighteenth century. It stood like a ghost in the darkness, its windows blank and uncurtained.

Shirley was aware of a pulse that throbbed in her throat. The pavilion, waiting for her amongst the trees, looked deserted and strangely forbidding. She had an instinct to tiptoe away from it, and for several moments she stood in the shadow of the trees staring at the quiet building with a queer sense of foreboding hammering at her brain.

She stood so still that her very heartbeats seemed to thud in the silence. Somewhere not far distant the unmistakable cry of a pheasant broke the dead calm, and she heard the whirr of wings. She jumped uncontrollably and waited, listening. No other sound succeeded the startled bird's flight; she decided, but uneasily, that some prowling fox had disturbed the pheasant.

She drew the gun out of her pocket and cocked it. The snap of the breech sounded comfortingly in her ears; she thumbed the safety-catch up and walked quietly towards the pavilion.

The door was not locked; the handle squeaked rustily as she turned it. She pushed the door inwards, standing backed against the wall. After a moment, since not the tiniest sound came to betray the presence of any living creature, she pulled her torch out of her pocket and switched it on.

The pavilion was empty. Some garden furniture was placed in it, wicker chairs and a table, several gaily coloured boating cushions. Shirley's torch travelled slowly round it, lighting every corner. She went in, closing the door behind her, and forced herself to sit down in one of the chairs and to switch off the torch.

As her eyes grew accustomed to the dim light she was able to distinguish, vaguely, the various objects in the room. The warning instinct that had urged her not to approach the pavilion prompted her to draw her chair back to the wall. The windows, grey oblongs in the darkness, seemed to be all round her. She had to assure herself that no one could see her from outside without the aid of a lamp.

She could hear her watch ticking and pulled down her glove to look at it. The luminous hands stood at twenty minutes past six; Collins was late. A fear that he might be going to play her false dispelled for a moment her growing sense of foreboding. Her lips tightened; she began to listen for the sound of an approach-footstep.

She heard nothing, not so much as the snap of a twig, until the scrape of the door-handle made her heart give a frightened jump. She got up, pressing down the safety-catch of her gun.

A man stood in the doorway; she could not distinguish his features. She waited, hardly breathing.

"Are you there, miss?" The words were spoken so softly that she barely heard them. The voice was the valet's.

"Yes. You're very late," she said, and switched on her torch.

He seemed to leap towards her. "Put it out! Don't show a light!" he whispered urgently.

She obeyed him but said as coolly as she was able: "Take care. You're likely to get shot if you dash at me like that. What's the matter?" The torch-light had given her a brief glimpse of his face, unnaturally pallid, sweat glistening on his forehead. He sounded out of breath and seemed to be listening intently, his head a little bent.

He moved to her side and grasped her left wrist. "For God's sake, get away from here!" he whispered. "I shouldn't have let you come. I warned you it wasn't safe. Someone followed me. Get out quickly!"

Almost without meaning to she lowered her voice, trying to keep it steady. "You're trying to put me off. I'm not having any. We're here to talk business."

He spoke with a kind of suppressed venom. "You know what happened to your brother. Do you want to go the same road? I tell you I'm being watched. Come away from here quickly!"

He pulled her towards the door. Realizing that his agitation was not feigned she went with him and allowed him to hurry her back into the shelter of the trees. He stopped to listen again. She could hear nothing, but he drew her still farther into the shade.

He let her go. "I daren't stop. I swear I'm on the level. I'll meet you, but not here. It's getting too hot for me. You ought never to have rung me up." He broke off to listen again. "He's on to me," he whispered. "I'll have to go. For God's sake, miss, go back to London! You're in much worse danger than you know. I'll meet you—on my word, I will!"

"You'd better," she said. "You know what I'm holding."

He gave a soundless chuckle. "Half a loaf, miss. That's not enough."

"Enough to make things unpleasant for you," she said harshly.

"Do that and you'll never get your other half," he said.

His tone held a menace. "You were mad to come here. You're not safe. I can't be on the watch all the time. You're not safe a moment."

She said steadily: "I shall stay at Upper Nettlefold till I get what I came for."

His hand closed on her wrist again compellingly. With his lips almost touching her ear he breathed the one word: "Listen!"

The wood seemed all at once, to her overwrought nerves, to be alive with tiny, nameless sounds. The fallen leaves rustled, perhaps a rabbit stirred amongst them; a twig cracked; the shadow of a tree seemed to move.

The man's fear communicated itself to Shirley. She felt that hidden eyes watched her and suddenly wanted only to get away from this haunted spot. Her hand shook in the valet's hold. He let it go and gave her a little push. "Go! You mustn't be seen with me. For God's sake, go!"

He moved away softly as a ghost. The night seemed to close in on Shirley, full of unknown perils. For a moment she knew a feeling of sheer panic that held her as though by force where she stood, her knees shaking. She threw it off and managed to take a step forward on to the ride. It had grown so dark that nothing was clearly distinguishable any longer. Not daring to switch on her torch she began to walk quickly away from the pavilion, restraining an impulse to break into a run.

She was brought up short by a circle of light that suddenly appeared a little way to the left of the ride, moving uncannily over the ground. There was someone else in the wood, searching.

She turned and made for the cover of the trees, hardly caring what direction she took. A great beech tripped her with its long roots; she fell, and looking back, saw the light moving towards her. She scrambled up, thankful in the midst of her fright that the safety-catch on her Colt was up. She broke into a run, heading for the thickest part of the wood.

Brambles caught at her coat and slashed her ankles; she tore free and reached a clump of blackberry bushes growing between the slender stems of some silver birch trees. She crouched down behind them, watching the light waver through the undergrowth.

She could hear footsteps now, deliberate steps, coming closer. A slight sound behind her brought her head round with a jerk, but she could see nothing.

The footsteps passed the bush; she could just perceive the darker shadow of a man's form. He stopped and stood still, listening, she guessed. The light he carried began to describe a circle; she wondered how dense the bushes were, whether dense enough to conceal her.

The man moved; he was coming round the bush. Her thumb felt for the safety-catch; she stayed still, waiting.

Then the boding silence was broken by a sound so incongruous that it came as a shock to her. Someone not far away was whistling "The Blue Danube."

The light disappeared; a faint rustle, the brush of a body passing through high bracken came to Shirley's ears, followed by complete silence. The whistle died away, the shadow had gone.

It was minutes before she dared to move. She crept forward in the direction where she judged the ride to be, stopping every few paces to stand still and listen. The light was no longer visible; it had vanished altogether, scared away by the sound of a waltz tune whistled in the distance.

She walked on, thrusting her way through the undergrowth, still not daring to use the torch.

No light warned her that she was still being followed. Several times she thought that she could hear the sound of a panting breath not far behind; once a twig cracked ominously, but when she stood still, peering behind her, she could see nothing and hear nothing.

She moved forward again; again she heard the heavy breathing, closer at hand now.

She fled on and stumbled out onto the ride. With the close turf under her feet and the dim outlines of the trees on either side to guide her she broke into a run.

A light flashed full into her face; a tiny scream, instantly checked, broke from her. She stood still and levelled the gun.

A cool, faintly mocking voice spoke: "Whither away, Miss Brown?" it said.

Her pistol-hand fell to her side; she drew a long, sobbing breath. "You!" she gasped, dizzy with relief. "It's—only—you!"

"That," said Mr. Amberley strolling towards her, "is not particularly complimentary. You seem to be in a hurry."

She put her hand out, clasping the sleeve of his coat; there was something comforting about its very roughness. "Someone following me," she said. "Someone following me."

He took her hand in a strong clasp; she was aware, through her jumbled emotions, that she was no longer afraid. She held Mr. Amberley's hand gratefully and followed the beam of his torch as it swung round.

Then a sharp exclamation rose to her lips. The torch had lit up a face for one moment, a face that shone pale in the bright light and disappeared instantly behind a bush.

"Who is that man?" she gasped. "Over there—didn't you see? He was watching us. Oh, let's get away!"

"By all means," agreed Amberley. "It's not really much of a night for a country walk."

"Did you see?" she insisted. "A man by that bush. Who was he? He was following me. I heard him."

"Yes, I saw," replied Amberley. "It was Fountain's new butler."

She drew closer to him instinctively. "I didn't know. He was following me. I—I don't quite—please let us go!"

Mr. Amberley drew her hand through his arm and began to walk with her down the ride towards the gate. Once she glanced back, saying nervously: "You're sure he's not still following?"

"No, I'm not sure, but I'm not letting it worry me," said Amberley. "Probably he is seeing us off the premises. This happens to be private property, you know."

"You don't think that!" she said sharply. "He wasn't following for that reason."

"No?" said Amberley. "Well, suppose you tell me what the reason is?"

She was silent. After a few moments she pulled her hand away and said: "What are you doing here?"

"Getting back to your normal self, aren't you?" remarked Mr. Amberley. "I thought it was too good to last. What I should like to know is, what are *you* doing here?"

"I can't tell you," she said curtly.

"Won't tell me," he corrected.

"Perhaps. I notice you haven't answered me."

"Oh, there's no mystery about me," said Amberley cheerfully. "I was following you."

She stopped dead in her tracks. "You? You followed me? But how? How did you know where I was going?"

"Intuition," grinned Mr. Amberley. "Aren't I clever?"

"You can't have known. Where were you?"

"Outside the Boar's Head," he replied. "I came on in my car. I should have liked to offer you a lift, but I was afraid you might not take it."

She said hotly: "It's intolerable to be spied on like this!"

He laughed. "You didn't think it quite so intolerable a few minutes ago, did you?"

There was a pause. Shirley began to walk on, her hands in her pockets. Mr. Amberley kept pace beside her. After a moment a gruff voice said with difficulty: "I didn't mean to be ungrateful."

"You sound just like a little girl who has been well scolded," said Mr. Amberley. "All right, I forgive you."

The ghost of a chuckle escaped her. "Well, I *was* glad to see you," she admitted. "But all the same, it isn't fair of you to—to follow me. Was it you who whistled?"

"A habit of mine," said Mr. Amberley.

She looked up, trying to see his face. "You complain that I'm—mysterious, but are you being quite open with me?"

"Not in the least," he said.

She was slightly indignant. "Well, then—!"

"You can't have something for nothing, my girl," said Mr. Amberley. "When you decide to trust me I'll be as open as you please."

She said: "I do trust you. I didn't at first, but that's all done with. It isn't that I don't want to confide in you, but I daren't. *Please* believe me!"

"That a sample of your trust, is it? I don't think much of it."

She was strangely anxious to explain herself. "No, it isn't what you think. I'm not afraid that you'd—give me away, or anything, but I daren't tell a soul, because if I do—oh, I can't make you understand!"

"You're mistaken; I understand perfectly. You're afraid I might put my foot in it and queer your pitch. I said I didn't think much of your trust."

They had reached the gate and passed through it on to the road. A little way down it a red taillamp glowed; they walked towards it.

"Mr. Amberley, how much do you know already?" Shirley asked abruptly.

She knew that he was smiling. "Something for nothing, Miss Brown?"

"If I only knew—had some idea—I don't know what to do. Why should I trust you?"

"Feminine instinct," said Mr. Amberley.

"If you'd only tell me——"

"I shan't tell you anything. You shall come all the way. Didn't I say so?"

"You're quite unreasonable," she said crossly, and got into the car.

CHAPTER XIII

MR. AMBERLEY breakfasted early next morning, and had been to Upper Nettlefold and back before the rest of the family had risen from the table. He sauntered in to find Sir Humphrey fuming and Felicity just about to go out.

Sir Humphrey was declaiming against the dilatory methods of glaziers, but he stopped when he saw his nephew and requested him to listen to that fellow Fountain's behaviour. Felicity slipped from the room, making a grimace at her cousin.

"What's the matter?" inquired Amberley.

It appeared that Fountain had done something unmannerly, boorish and inexplicable. He had sent a servant over at nine in the morning to ask for the return of his book. Had Frank ever heard anything to equal it?

"Never," said Amberley, not visibly impressed. "Which servant?"

"I fail to see that it matters."

"Nevertheless, it does matter," said Amberley, and rang the bell. When Jenkins came in he put the question to him and learned that it was the valet who had come. "I thought so," said Amberley. "Getting desperate."

Sir Humphrey jabbed his glasses onto his bony nose. "Why did you think so? Are you going to tell me that all this business has something to do with your—your meddlesome investigations for the police?"

"Everything," said Amberley. "Didn't you guess?"

"Damn it, Frank, next time you come and stay in my house——"

"But I'm enjoying it all so much," interposed his wife, emerging from her correspondence. "Shall we be murdered, Frank? I thought these things didn't happen. So very enlightening."

"I hope not, Aunt. I might be, of course. You never know."

She glanced up at him shrewdly. "Not pleased, my dear?"

"Not so very," he admitted.

"Annoying," she said, "losing things. I once lost my engagement ring. It turned up. Better not say where, perhaps."

He took his pipe out of his mouth. "You're too acute, Aunt. I shall go and play golf with Anthony."

"I prefer that you should not mention this disagreeable occurrence to Fountain," said Sir Humphrey stiffly. "I myself intend to ignore it."

"I should," said Amberley. "It would surprise me very much if he knows anything about it."

He arrived at the manor to find Corkran practising approach-shots on the lawn. Corkran hailed him with enthusiasm. It appeared that Amberley was just the man he wanted to see. He announced that the manor had just about got his goat. Joan was right: there was something about the darned place that made everyone behave in an odd manner. He enumerated the various vagaries, starting with his prospective relative's moodiness, and passing on by way of the murder of Dawson to the night prowlings of Collins and the extraordinary conduct of Baker. He wanted to know what Amberley made of a butler who started to dust the library at ten o'clock at night.

"Damn it, butlers don't dust!" he said. "Have you ever seen one at it?"

"Dusting the library?" repeated Amberley.

"Absolutely. Those people from the grange—woman with a face like the back of a cab, and spouse—were here to dinner and we played bridge. I went to fetch my cigarette case, which I'd left in the library, and I'm dashed if that Baker fellow wasn't there dusting the books. Well, I mean to say! Told me he didn't like to see them so dusty and understood Fountain didn't allow the skivvies to touch 'em. A whole lot of eyewash about not having time—no, leisure—to do it in the daytime. Too jolly fishy by half. What do you think?"

"I think I'd like to see Mr. Baker."

"Well, if you stick around long enough you will. He's gone to fetch me some more golf balls," said Anthony morosely.

The butler came out of the house at that moment with three golf balls on a silver tray.

"Looks like an egg-and-spoon race," said Anthony. "Silly ass!"

Baker came sedately across the lawn; he did not look at Amberley, but went to Corkran and presented his tray. "Your golf balls, sir. I could only find three in your bag."

Anthony took them with a brief word of thanks. The butler turned to go, but halted as Mr. Amberley spoke.

"Just a moment."

Baker turned and stood waiting, his head deferentially inclined.

"Do you know if Mr. Fountain sent to Greythorne for a book that was borrowed the other day?"

Baker flashed a quick look up at him. "A book, sir?" He seemed to choose his words carefully. "I could not say, sir, I am sure. I do not think that Mr. Fountain gave any such order. Not to my knowledge."

Mr. Amberley's pipe had gone out. He struck a match and held it between his cupped hands; over it his eyes held Baker's. "It's not important. Sir Humphrey had finished with it." He threw the match away. "Interested in books, Baker?"

The butler gave his little cough. "I do not get much time for reading, sir."

"Only dusting," said Anthony.

The butler bowed. "Exactly so, sir. I do my best—with indifferent success, I fear. Mr. Fountain has a large library."

"Quite a valuable one," drawled Amberley. "To connoisseurs."

"So I believe, sir." Baker met his gaze limpidly. "I fear I know very little about such things."

"A book is just a book, eh?"

"Yes, sir. As you say."

"Well, what the devil should it be?" demanded Anthony, pausing in the act of taking a chip-shot onto the terrace.

The butler permitted himself a discreet smile. "Will there be anything else, sir?"

"Not at present," said Amberley, and transferred his attention to the golf enthusiast.

Anthony professed himself entirely at sea over the whole business. He complained that Amberley was as bad as the rest of them; prowling about and saying nothing. "And just what are you doing?" he said. "I'm damned if I know."

"I'm looking for lost property," said Amberley.

"Whose lost property?"

"I'm not sure."

Anthony blinked at him. "Look here, what the devil are you driving at?"

"I'm sure, of course," said Amberley maddeningly, "but I've no proof. Awkward, isn't it?"

Anthony shook his head. "I can't cope with it. I thought you were looking for Dawson's assassin, and now you say——"

"I've never had much interest in Dawson's murder," said Amberley.

Mr. Corkran raised his eyes to heaven. "Of course I shall end up in a looney-bin," he said. "I can feel it coming on."

In spite of what he had told Sir Humphrey Mr. Amberley did not invite Corkran to play golf, but drove away from the manor to Carchester, where the chief constable and Inspector Fraser were awaiting him.

They found him in a discouraging mood. Colonel Watson was dismayed, the inspector triumphant. The inspector was following up a trail of his own and held forth on its possibilities until he realized that Mr. Amberley was not listening to him.

Colonel Watson, more perceptive than the inspector, had been watching Amberley. He said: "You're on to something?"

"I thought I was," Amberley replied. "I still think it. But the only piece of evidence in the whole case has gone astray, and I tell you candidly I'm afraid it may have got into the wrong hands or been destroyed. Where it is I don't know. Until it's found neither you nor I can do anything. Once I get my hands on it you'll have your whole case cut and dried."

The inspector gave a superior smile. "Very fanciful, sir. I suppose it'll clear everything up—Dawson's murder and all? Pity you can't tell us anything now."

There was a glint in Mr. Amberley's eyes. "Since you're so keen on Dawson's murder—a somewhat unimportant link in the chain, as I believe I remarked once before—I'll tell you who did murder him."

The colonel jumped. "You know?"

"I've known since the night of the fancy-dress ball at the manor," said Mr. Amberley calmly. "Collins murdered him."

The colonel stuttered: "But—but——"

"Very nice, sir," said the inspector, still smiling. "A little thing like a good alibi doesn't count, I suppose?"

"You should always beware of alibis, Inspector. If you'd had rather more experience of crime you'd have learned that lesson."

The inspector grew purple in the face. "Perhaps you'll favour us with the proof, Mr. Amberley."

"None," said Amberley. "One person might shake the alibi, but he daren't do it. You may as well make up your mind to it; you won't get a conviction."

"That's very interesting," said the inspector sarcastically. "Useful too. No charge of murder at all, in fact."

"On the contrary," said Amberley.

"I see," said the inspector. "I've heard your opinion of Brown's death. Going to charge Collins with that, I daresay?"

"Collins," said Mr. Amberley, picking up his hat, "was the last man in the world to want Brown dead." He turned to Colonel Watson. "About the missing evidence, Colonel. If you can get a tactful man onto the job—not Fraser—send someone to interview Dawson's sister. It is just possible that he had it at the time of his death. I want all his effects carefully gone through and any papers brought to me. It's a slim chance, but worth trying. Particularly a torn paper, Colonel. Remember that."

On his way back to Greythorne he stopped in Upper Nettlefold to see Sergeant Gubbins. The sergeant was busy with a motor accident, but he left it for a moment to speak to Amberley.

"Done as I asked?" Amberley said briefly.

"Yes, sir. Tucker. He won't make a second mistake."

"That's all right then," said Amberley, and departed.

It was at nine o'clock that evening that a scared housemaid presented herself in the drawing room at Greythorne and said hysterically: "Oh, sir! Oh, my lady! Burglars!"

"What?" snapped Sir Humphrey, letting the evening paper fall. "Here?"

"Oh yes, sir! At least it does seem so. It's Mr. Amberley's bedroom, sir. It give me such a turn, I feel quite bad."

Amberley regarded her with unimpaired calm. "What happened?" he inquired.

Her story was somewhat involved, and embellished with a great deal of irrelevant detail, but it seemed that she had gone upstairs at nine o'clock to turn down the beds and found that Mr. Amberley's room had been ransacked. Every drawer was pulled out and the contents strewn on the floor; the little desk in the window had been burst open and the papers all scattered about; his suitcases wrenched open; and a leather attaché-case in which he might be supposed to keep private papers, with the lock torn off. Even the bed had been disarranged, while as for the suits in the wardrobe, never had she seen anything to equal it.

She paused for breath; and Sir Humphrey, fixing his nephew with a smouldering eye, said that he had had enough.

Lady Matthews murmured: "Better tidy it, Molly. Did he find anything, Frank?"

Amberley shook his head. "Quite bright of him to suspect me, but not so bright to think I should leave it lying about in my room. So he thinks I've got it. That's illuminating anyhow."

"How fortunate, dear! So glad. Why, by the way?"

"At least it means that it hasn't fallen into the wrong hands," said Amberley, smiling at her.

"Delightful, my dear. Don't fuss, Humphrey. Nothing to do with us."

This was too much for Sir Humphrey. If a couple of robberies in his own house were nothing to do with him he would like to know what was. And how did the burglar get in without anyone hearing? Really, it was too much of a good thing.

Lady Matthews glanced at the long window. "Not locked, you know. While we were at dinner. Don't you think so, Frank?"

He nodded. Sir Humphrey picked up the evening paper and said with acerbity that it was time Frank got married to some woman who would put a stop to his senseless conduct. Mr. Amberley looked at him rather sharply, a tinge of colour creeping into his lean cheeks.

Lady Matthews's calm voice changed the subject.

But all was not over for Sir Humphrey. At three in the morning he was awakened by the telephone ringing in the library, which was immediately beneath his bedroom. He got up, swearing under his breath, and stalked out onto the landing just as the door of his nephew's room opened. "Since," he said awfully, "I have little doubt that call is for you, I will leave you to answer it." With which utterance he went back into his room and shut the door with terrible quietness.

Amberley laughed and went down the stairs, tying the cord of his dressing gown.

The call was for him. Sergeant Gubbins was speaking from the police station. There were fresh developments which he thought Mr. Amberley should be told about at once. All the same, if it hadn't been for Mr. Amberley's instructions he would not have taken it upon himself to rouse him at this hour.

"Get on with it!" snarled Amberley.

The sergeant said apologetically: "When I think how you had me out that night it makes me smile, sir."

"Does it?" said Amberley grimly. "What's happened?"

"That there Albert Collins has done a bunk, sir."

Amberley's irritable frown left him. "What?"

"Or so it seems," said the sergeant cautiously. "Mr. Fountain's just been on the phone, and Constable Walker put him right through to me."

"Fountain rang up the police station at three in the morning?"

"That's right, sir. Some people seem to think the police like being rung up at all hours. I've met 'em before—not to mention any names. I have known people who'd get you out of your bed to go on a wild-goose chase where nothing happened, nor was likely to."

"If I took it into my head," said Mr. Amberley distinctly, "to murder anyone—mentioning no names—I should do it very neatly, Gubbins, and leave no clues behind me."

A fat chuckle sounded at the other end of the wire. "I believe you, sir. A master criminal, that's what you'd be."

"Don't waste time flattering me. Get on with your story."

"I told you all I know, sir. Mr. Fountain says when he went up to bed there wasn't anything got ready for him, and no sign of Collins. So he rung, and the butler came up and said he hadn't seen Collins since before dinner. Well, it isn't his evening off, so Mr. Fountain had Baker go and look in his room. He wasn't there. Mr. Fountain sat up to wait for him, and when it got near three o'clock he rung up the station, like I told you. He said he couldn't get it out of his head how we all suspected Collins of having shoved young Brown into the river, and that's why he thought he'd best let us know before the morning. That's all, sir."

Mr. Amberley was staring at the wall ahead of him, his eyes narrowed, considering. After a moment the sergeant's voice asked if he was there.

"Yes. Be quiet. I'm thinking."

"Not a doubt about it, sir; he's properly got the wind up," said the sergeant, disregarding the behest.

There was a pause. Then Amberley transferred his attention to the telephone. "You may be right, Sergeant.

Did you ask whether any clothes were missing from his rooms?"

"I did, sir. Mr. Fountain said he didn't think so, but couldn't say for certain."

"Any car or bicycle missing from the garage?"

"Yes, sir; his own push-bike. Mr. Fountain had that from the butler."

"I see. You'll have to notify Carchester, I suppose. Tell them from me to find out whether Collins took a ticket for town, or elsewhere, from any of the stations within, say, a ten-mile radius, after half-past eight this evening. If so, follow him up. Meanwhile—by the time you get here I shall be ready."

"By the time I do what, sir?" asked the sergeant, startled.

"Get here," repeated Mr. Amberley maliciously. "On your bicycle. Immediately."

"Me come out to Greythorne at this hour?" gasped the sergeant. "What would I do that for?"

"To pick me up. I'll have the car waiting."

"Yes, but, Mr. Amberley, sir, I don't want to go joy-riding at this hour of night!" objected the sergeant. "What's the idea?"

"Furthermore," said Amberley, "I want you to bring a couple of men with you."

"But what *for?*" insisted the sergeant.

"For the simple reason that I think it just possible that Collins has not bolted. We're going to try and find him. Are you coming?"

"Yes," said the sergeant gloomily. "I'm coming, but whatever I was thinking about when I begged you to take on this case fair beats me."

"You were thinking of promotion, Sergeant, and you'll probably get it," said Amberley encouragingly, and rang off.

For a moment he sat still at the desk, reaching out his hand mechanically for the cigarette box beside him. He lit a cigarette and got up and began to walk slowly up and down the room, his brain busy with this new problem. When the cigarette was finished he stubbed it out and went upstairs again. He did not go at once to his own room, but opened Sir Humphrey's door and inquired whether his uncle was awake.

A grunt came from the bed. Mr. Amberley switched on the light. "Sorry, sir, but I'm going out. So don't pay any attention to uncouth noises."

Sir Humphrey raised himself on his elbow. "God bless the boy, what next? Why are you going out? What has happened?"

"Fountain's valet is missing. The police think he has bolted."

"Well, why can't you let them look for him? It's their work, not yours."

"Quite. But on the other hand he may not have bolted. I'm going to find out."

"You may go to the devil!" said Sir Humphrey, and turned over on the other side.

Mr. Amberley thanked him and withdrew.

When the sergeant and two enthusiastic young constables arrived, they found Amberley waiting for them in his car; he made them leave their bicycles in the drive and get into the Bentley. The sergeant climbed in beside him, leaving hs subordinates to sit in the back, and said without much hope that he trusted Mr. Amberley wasn't going to travel at ninety miles an hour, because he was a married man.

He need have had no qualms. Mr. Amberley was driving very slowly indeed; so slowly, in fact, that the sergeant, suspicious of a leg-pull, asked whether it was a funeral. "And if it's all the same to you, sir, where are we going?"

"On the road to Norton Manor. Somewhere round about eight o'clock, Sergeant, Collins was at Greythorne. This is not to be repeated. He ransacked my room."

"Ransacked your room?" echoed the sergeant. "You saw him?"

"No. But I know it was he."

"Good Lord!" said the sergeant. "But what was he after?"

"Something he thought I had. We're going to look for him."

"But, Mr. Amberley, sir!" protested the sergeant. "If you say he was at Greythorne at eight o'clock he's had time to get back to the manor a dozen times over!"

"Yes—if he did go back," replied Amberley. "Just keep a look-out, will you? Take the spot-lamp."

The car crept on; the two constables, who had heard of Mr. Amberley's predilection for speed, were frankly disappointed.

The sergeant held the spot-lamp at the end of its cable and studied the side of the road. "Going to search the woods, sir?"

"Perhaps. But he was riding a bicycle. That looks like the road. All preserves, this?"

"Most of it," said the sergeant. "General Tomlinson's land, this is. Runs alongside Mr. Fountain's preserves. We took up a poacher today. The general's keeper got him."

The car swung round a bend. "Mr. Fountain's land starts hereabouts," said the sergeant. "Hitchcock's had bad luck with his pheasants this year, so he told me."

"Poachers?"

"Them, and the gapes—lost a lot of young birds, he has. Hullo, what's that?"

The headlights showed the road running straight ahead. Something lay at the side, half across the grass border.

One of the constables was standing up and peering ahead. "It's a bicycle!"

The car shot forward. "It's something more than a bicycle, my friend," said Amberley.

There was something dark beside the bicycle. As the car drew nearer the sergeant gave a sharp exclamation. The curious heap on the roadside was the body of a man lying in a crumpled attitude, half hidden by the uncut grass that grew beside the ditch.

Amberley pulled up. His face was very grim. "Take a look, Sergeant."

The sergeant was already out of the car and bending over the still body, his torch in his hand. He recoiled suddenly and turned rather white about the gills. "My Gawd!" he said.

Amberley got down onto the road and walked towards the huddled figure.

"It's not—very nice, sir," said the sergeant gruffly, and turned his torch on again.

Amberley stood looking down at what remained of Albert Collins. "The top of his head's been blown right off," the sergeant said in rather a hushed voice.

"Shotgun," said Amberley briefly. "Close range."

There was a slight sound behind him. One of the young constables had retired to the ditch. The other stood his ground, but he did not look very happy.

The sergeant switched off the torch. "Nasty sight," he said. "Come along now, Henson! Easy to see *you* wasn't in Flanders." He turned to Amberley. "This was what you were looking for, sir?"

Amberley nodded.

"Who did it, sir?"

"I wasn't here, Sergeant," said Amberley gently.

The sergeant looked at him. "Takes a lot to upset you, sir, don't it?"

Amberley glanced down at the dead man. "It would take more than the murder of that creature," he said. His voice grated. "I find this rather a comforting sight. I was afraid he'd escape the noose. I've no sympathy to waste on him."

The sergeant stared. "It's a nasty way to die, sir."

Amberley walked back to the car. "Very, Sergeant. And entirely appropriate," he said.

CHAPTER XIV

LEAVING one of the constables to stand guard over Collins's body, the sergeant requested Mr. Amberley to drive on to the manor. Mr. Amberley nodded and set his foot on the self-starter.

The manor was in darkness, but after they had rung the bell they had not long to wait before a light appeared in the fan-shaped glass over the front door.

"H'm!" said the sergeant. "Not hard to wake, are they, sir?"

The door was opened by the butler, who had a pair of trousers and a dressing gown pulled on over his pajamas. He did not appear to be very sleepy. On the contrary he looked rather alert and showed no surprise at perceiving a policeman. His shy brown eyes stole from the sergeant's face to Amberley's. He stood back, allowing them to enter.

"Were you expecting us?" said the sergeant sharply.

Baker shut the door. "Oh no, Sergeant! That is, I knew of course that Mr. Fountain had rung you up. Do you wish to see Mr. Fountain?"

The sergeant said he did and followed the butler into the library. When the man had withdrawn, he turned to Amberley and said: "What do you make of that chap, sir?"

"I'll tell you one day," replied Amberley.

"Well, I'd like a little talk with him," said the sergeant darkly.

"So should I," agreed Amberley.

Fountain soon came downstairs. He was surprised to see Amberley and asked quickly what had happened.

The sergeant told him. Fountain said blankly: *"Shot? Collins?"* His gaze shifted from the sergeant to Amberley.

"I don't understand. Who could have shot him? Where was he?"

"It might," said the sergeant judicially, "have been poachers. Or it might not. That'll be investigated. Meanwhile, sir, if you've no objection I should like to use your telephone."

"Yes, of course. I'll show you." Fountain led him out into the hall and left him talking to the constable on duty at the police station. He went back into the library and stared in a bewildered way at Amberley. "I can't make it out!" he said. "It seems fantastic! First my butler, now my valet. Amberley, I don't like it!"

"No. I don't suppose Dawson or Collins liked it either," said Amberley.

Fountain began to walk about the room. "Who found him? Where was he?"

When he heard that Collins had been shot not a mile from the manor he gave a gasp. "Good God! Do you think it was poachers, then?"

Mr. Amberley declined to give an opinion.

A fresh aspect of the case seemed to strike Fountain.

"What made you go to look for him? Don't tell me you were expecting this to happen."

"Oh no," said Amberley. "We were on our way to speak to you, that's all."

Fountain shook his head. "I can't get over it. It's a ghastly business. My God, it makes one wonder—who next?"

The sergeant came back into the room and asked Mr. Fountain to be good enough to answer a few questions. Fountain was quite ready to answer anything he could, but had little information to give. The valet had been in his room at half-past seven when he went up to dress for dinner. He had not seen him since then, nor thought about him until, on going up to bed shortly before midnight, he had found nothing prepared for him. He had rung the bell; Baker had answered it and had said that Collins had not been in the servants' hall at suppertime. He had gone to look in his room and found it empty.

Fountain admitted that he had felt suspicious. Ordinarily he would have merely supposed that the man had taken French leave and slightly overstepped the mark, but certain circumstances made him think there was more to it than that. He thought it significant that the valet's disappearance occurred on the very day he had received a month's notice.

Mr. Amberley, who had picked up the current number of *Punch* from the table and was idly perusing it, raised his eyes at that.

"You had given him notice?"

"Yes, I had. This morning. All things considered, I thought it best. The man's been presuming on his position. And then there was that business about young Brown. The more I thought over what you said, Amberley, the fishier the thing looked to me. Dawson, too. Once you start suspecting a man you don't know where to stop. And if you get into that frame of mind the only thing to do is to sack the servant."

"But Collins, if I remember rightly, had a sound alibi on the night of Dawson's murder."

"Yes, so I thought. Never bothered my head much till Brown fell in the river. Collins was pressing a suit for me at the time and I saw him. But it's extraordinary how you can pick holes in an alibi. I've been trying to calculate the time it would have taken him to reach the Pittingly Road, supposing he took the motor-bicycle. I shouldn't have said he could have done it, but I've got just a faint doubt. That's a beastly state of affairs between master and servant, you know. I gave him notice today. When he was missing tonight it flashed across my mind that he might have thought that I suspected him, got the wind up and bolted. The more I considered it the more certain I felt. When he hadn't come in by three o'clock I rang up the police station. But I never dreamed that anything like this had happened."

"No, sir, I don't suppose you did," said the sergeant. "And you didn't hear him go out or see anyone else go out?"

"No, but I might not have, you know. I was in this room most of the evening, writing letters. I should have

heard the front door open, but Collins wouldn't have left
by that door."

"Quite, sir. If it's convenient to you I should like to
have a word with that butler of yours."

"Certainly." Fountain walked to the fireplace and
pressed the bell.

The door opened almost immediately to admit not Baker, but Corkran, looking tousled and sleepy. He blinked at
the assembled company and shut his eyes tightly for a
moment. Then he opened them again and shook his head.
"I thought it was a mirage," he said. "But I see it really is
you, Sergeant. All is discovered, what? I'll go quietly,
'strewth, I will!"

The sergeant grinned, but Fountain said sharply: "It
isn't a joking matter. Collins has been shot."

Corkran gaped at him. Then he looked at Amberley
and requested him to explain.

It was Fountain who answered him. Anthony listened
in amazement and at the end said that he took a very poor
view of it. "I didn't like the man," he said. "In fact, I
hadn't any time for him at all. But this is a bit too thick. I
don't mind a spot of crime just to liven things up, but I
bar homicidal maniacs. Three deaths all on top of each
other! No, really, that's coming it too strong!"

Fountain swung round towards Amberley. "Good God,
do you think that's it?" he exclaimed. "Could it really be
what Tony suggests? These utterly inexplicable murders—
what do you think?"

"Some people," said Mr. Amberley carefully, "consider
that all murderers are maniacs."

"You rang for me, sir?"

The sergeant looked round. "I want to ask you a few
questions," he said. "You come inside and shut the door."

The butler obeyed. "Yes, Sergeant?"

Out came the notebook. "What time was it when you
saw Collins last?" asked the sergeant.

The butler answered promptly: "At twenty minutes past
seven."

"Oh! What makes you so sure?"

"Collins himself drew attention to the time, Sergeant,

and said he must go up to lay Mr. Fountain's dress clothes out."

From the other end of the room Amberley spoke. "You didn't see him leave the house?"

"I did not, sir. He must have gone during dinner while I was engaged in waiting."

"Why?" said the sergeant at once.

The butler's mouth twitched nervously. He said after an infinitesimal pause: "I think I should have seen him go had I been in the servants' quarters."

"You would, eh? Were you friendly with him?"

"I have not been in Mr. Fountain's employment for long, Sergeant. I have endeavoured to be on good terms with the rest of the staff."

The sergeant surveyed him closely. "Where were you before you came down here?"

A shade of discomfort crossed the butler's features. He replied, not quite so readily: "I was temporarily out of service, Sergeant."

"Why?"

"I was suffering from ill health."

"Address?"

"My—my home address is in Tooting," said the man reluctantly. "In Blackadder Road."

"Previous employer?"

"My late master has gone to America."

"He has, has he? Name?"

"Fanshawe," said Baker still more unwillingly.

"Address when in England?"

"He has no address in England, Sergeant."

The sergeant looked up. "Look here, my man, he had an address while you were in his service, hadn't he? What was it?"

Mr. Amberley's quiet voice interposed. "You were with Mr. Goeffrey Fanshawe, were you?"

The butler glanced towards him. "Yes, sir."

"Eaton Square, in fact?"

The butler swallowed. "Yes, sir."

"Then why make a mystery of it? No. 547, Sergeant."

"Do you know the gentleman, sir?"

"Slightly. He's a member of my club."

"Is it true that he's gone abroad?"

"I believe so. I could find out."

The sergeant addressed Fountain. "You had a reference, sir, I take it?"

"Yes, of course. But Baker gave it to me. I wasn't able to write to Mr. Fanshawe myself because he had gone—or was said to have gone—to New York. The chit was written on club notepaper."

"Trace him through the club," said the sergeant, writing laboriously in his notebook. "Or you will, sir?"

"Yes, I will," Amberley said. "I should like to know one thing, though." His hard eyes rested on Baker's face. "You say you would have heard Collins leave the house had you not been in the dining room at the time. Did you see or hear anyone else leave the house during the course of the evening?"

The butler said slowly: "Two of the maids were out, sir. None of the rest of the staff."

"You are sure of that?"

"Yes, sir."

"Were you in the servants' hall?"

"No, sir. I was in my pantry most of the evening. Before that I was in the dining room clearing things away."

"So that you would have known had anyone left the house by the front door?"

"No one opened the front door this evening, sir," said Baker, meeting his gaze squarely.

Mr. Amberley returned to the study of *Punch*. He appeared to take no further interest in the sergeant's examination of Baker, but as the butler was about to leave the room ten minutes later, he raised his eyes for a moment and said: "Did it appear to you, when you looked in Collins' room, that he had taken anything away, as though he were leaving for good?"

"No, sir," replied Baker. "Mr. Fountain told me to look particularly. I took the liberty of glancing in the cupboard and the chest of drawers. So far as I could judge nothing had been taken away."

"And you looked pretty thoroughly?"

"Yes, sir. There was nothing of a suspicious nature to be seen."

"Thank you," said Amberley.

The sergeant shut his notebook. "No more questions, sir?"

"No, thanks, Sergeant," said Amberley tranquilly.

"Then I'll be getting back to the station, sir. Sorry to have knocked you up, Mr. Fountain. I expect the inspector will want to see you tomorrow."

Fountain nodded somewhat gloomily. "Yes, I expect he will," he agreed. "I shall be in all the morning."

"Well, if that's all," said Anthony, "I'm going back to bed. And I'd like to take a gun with me. I should feel happier."

"I'm sure I'm not surprised, sir," said the sergeant cordially.

"You come with me, Sergeant," invited Anthony. "What we both need is a drink."

Fountain was roused to his duties as host. "Of course. What am I thinking about? You'll have a drink too, won't you, Amberley?"

Amberley declined it. The sergeant, eyeing him somewhat aggrievedly, murmured something about regulations, but allowed Mr. Corkran to persuade him. When he came back he was wiping his moustache and seemed to be on the best of terms with Anthony. As he drove away from the manor he informed Mr. Amberley that he didn't know when he had taken such a fancy to a young gentleman. "And what's more, sir," he said confidentially, "though I don't say he's right, there might be something in that idea of his about a homicidal maniac. After all, sir—three murders, without any rhyme or reason to them. What do you think?"

"I think you and Mr. Corkran were made for one another," said Amberley. "The murders were not all committed by the same man. Dawson was killed by Collins."

"Eh?" The sergeant was startled. "But you never seemed to make much of Collins, Mr. Amberley! I've suspected him all along, but you——"

"The trouble is, Sergeant, that you suspected him of the wrong crime."

"Oh!" said the sergeant, rather at sea. "I suppose you mean something, sir, but I'm blessed if I know what. Did you make anything of what we heard up there?" He jerked his thumb over his shoulder in the direction of the manor.

"There were one or two points," replied Amberley.

"That's what I thought, sir. I don't mind telling you I got my eye on that butler. I'd like to find out a bit about him. He'll bear watching. Crops up out of nowhere, so to speak, and knows more than what you'd expect. Not at all surprised to see us, he wasn't. Might have been expecting us. Well, I got a feeling about him, and when I get a feeling I'm not often wrong. That's your man, Mr. Amberley, you mark my words!"

Amberley glanced enigmatically towards him. "You've a marvellous intuition, Gubbins."

"Well, that's as may be, sir. But you wait and you'll see I'm right."

"I think, Sergeant," said Mr. Amberley, swinging round a sharp bend, "that you are nearer the truth than you know."

CHAPTER XV

FELICITY, upon hearing the news at breakfast, at once declared her intention of going over to see Joan that morning. Sir Humphrey accused her of a morbid love of horrors, which imputation she quite blithely admitted. Sir Humphrey himself was very much shocked by what had happened and forbore to rate Frank for disturbing him in the small hours. Although he had so frequently asseverated that he took no interest in crime when not seated in judgment upon it, crime in Upper Nettlefold was assuming so wholesale an aspect that he was induced to inquire into it. From his nephew he got no more than the bare facts, which he said (several times) were shocking.

Mr. Amberley left the breakfast table in the middle of Sir Humphrey's dissertation on hooliganism in These Modern Times, pausing only to recommend his uncle to send his views to one of the Sunday papers. He told Lady Matthews not to expect him to lunch and went out.

Sir Humphrey, cut short in this summary manner, spoke bitterly of the lack of manners of the younger generation. His wife heard him out patiently, merely saying when he had done: "Never mind, my dear. Poor Frank! So worried."

"Was he, Mummy?" Felicity looked up.

"Yes, darling. Of course. Such a lot on his hands. I shall come with you this morning."

Sir Humphrey demanded whether she too had become obsessed with a morbid mania for horrors. She replied placidly that she had not, but she wanted to be driven into Upper Nettlefold.

"Do you mind going to the manor on the way back, Mummy?"

"Not at all," said Lady Matthews. "Poor Ludlow. A hundred and two."

"A hundred and two what?" snapped Sir Humphrey.

"I forget, dear. Point three, I think. Temperature, you know."

Felicity was surprised to find, when she and her mother set out, that Lady Matthews's main objective was the Boar's Head. She was curious to know what she wanted to do there, but all Lady Matthews would say was that she wished Shirley Brown to come back to Greythorne.

Felicity had not imagined that her mother would feel so much interest in a stranger as reticent as Shirley. She looked rather sharply at her and accused her of having something up her sleeve.

Lady Matthews requested her to look where she was going. Felicity obeyed, but kept up the attack. She knew her mother very well and was aware that in spite of her vagueness Lady Matthews was often disconcertingly shrewd. She began to suspect that Frank had confided in her. It seemed unlike him, but she knew that he held her in considerable respect. Lady Matthews, however, denied that Frank had told her anything. Pressed further she became so inconsequent in her answers that Felicity gave it up.

Shirley was in the lounge when they arrived at the Boar's Head. It struck Felicity that she had a stunned look and that her smile of welcome was forced.

Lady Matthews said simply: "My dear, very uncomfortable for you here. Come back to Greythorne."

Shirley shook her head. "I can't. I—thank you very much, but I think I'm going back to town. I—I don't really know."

Lady Matthews turned to her daughter. "Darling, butter. Could you?"

"I could, and I will," said Felicity, rising. "No one shall say that I don't know how take a hint."

She went away and Lady Matthews, casting a speculative glance at a man reading the newspaper at the other side of the lounge, said gently: "My dear, better tell Frank. I expect he knows anyway."

Shirley looked at her in a frightened way. "What do you mean?"

"All about yourself. Silly not to, because he could help you. Much the cleverest of his family."

Shirley said hardly above a whisper: "He can't know. It isn't possible. What—what have you guessed about me, Lady Matthews?"

"Can't talk in a public lounge, dear child. So unwise. They always do it in bad thrillers, and it invariably leads to disaster. But of course I guessed at once. I can't imagine what you're doing, but much better tell Frank. Don't you think so?"

Shirley looked down at her clasped hands. "I don't know. If he weren't working for the police. But he is, and I—I think I've been compounding a felony." She gave a nervous little laugh.

"It sounds very exciting," said Lady Matthews. "I'm sure he'd like to help. How does one compound a felony?"

"I'm in a mess," Shirley said, her fingers working in her lap. "I suppose I managed it badly. But it was all so difficult, and my—my brother—wasn't much use. And now things have gone so hopelessly wrong that there doesn't seem anything left for me to do except go back to town. I have thought about telling your—your nephew, only I'm half afraid to, because I don't really know him, and he—he's rather an—uncompromising person, isn't he?"

"But so good to animals, my dear. I should tell him. Such a pity to give up now."

Shirley sat still for a moment, staring ahead of her. She drew a long breath. "Yes. I can't bear that, you know. Is Mr. Amberley—would he—could you ask him to come and see me, do you think?"

"Quite easily," said Lady Matthews, smiling. "But better come back to Greythorne with me."

"I—would rather not, please. You think I'm in danger, don't you?"

"No danger at Greythorne," said Lady Matthews. "Lots of burglars, but we can take care of you!"

"I'm quite safe, Lady Matthews. Did you see a flat-faced person hanging about outside this place?"

"There was a man," admitted Lady Matthews. "He reminded me of weddings. You know. The detective who guards the presents. So pathetic. Quite obvious, and they must feel very conspicuous."

Shirley smiled. "Yes. Well, I'm the present. He's watching me. Your nephew put him there."

"So like him!" sighed Lady Matthews. "Very disconcerting, but perhaps just as well. I'll tell him to come and see you. Does the poor man follow you all day? I feel I should be impelled to give him a bun or a penny or something."

"All day," said Shirley. "There's another one who relieves him. So you see I'm safe enough if—if somewhat impeded." She looked up; Felicity had come back into the lounge.

"Secrets all over?" inquired Felicity without rancour.

"No secrets, darling," Lady Matthews said, rising. "Shirley won't come to Greythorne. Dreadfully obstinate. Any time, my dear?"

Shirley managed to follow this cryptic utterance. "Yes. That is, I'm going to Ivy Cottage this afternoon, just to finish the packing and have everything ready to be fetched away. So if I'm not here I'll be there."

"Very well. I won't forget," said Lady Matthews. "Did you get the butter, darling? Whatever shall we do with it?" She drifted out, murmuring: "Toffee, or something. Why didn't I say oranges?"

At Norton Manor they found Joan looking white and frightened. Corkran, who was rather enjoying himself in the rôle of Protective Male, announced that he was taking her to stay with his people. Lady Matthews seemed to think it an excellent idea. The girl was obviously in a state of overwrought nerves, and even her step-brother, who was not usually perceptive, admitted that she looked ill, and would probably be better away from the manor for a bit. As soon as things had been cleared up he meant to take a holiday himself.

Joan did not want to return to the manor. It was as much as she could do to spend another night there, and so uncontrollable was her aversion from the place that she had said, a little hysterically, that she would rather not be married at all than be married from it.

Her betrothed seized the opportunity to suggest a quiet wedding in town and even advocated, though without much hope, a registrar's office.

Joan was ready to agree to anything, but Fountain put his foot down. He was quite willing to have the wedding in town, but it must be a function. After all, a great many guests had already been invited, and there was no justification for a hole-and-corner affair. Did not Lady Matthews agree?

Lady Matthews did. She thought Joan would feel quite different when she got away from the manor and heard no more talk of crime.

"All the same," said Felicity irrepressibly, "we've never had so much excitement here before. It'll be frightfully dull when it's over. I mean, just think of the past fortnight! We've had three deaths and two burglaries. I call that pretty good for a place like this."

"Burglaries? Who's been burgled?" said Fountain.

"We have, only nothing was taken. It was a real thrill."

"Time we were going," said Lady Matthews. "Humphrey won't like it if lunch is late."

"But I never heard about this!" Fountain said. "When did it happen?"

"Oh, the first was the day Daddy and I came to see you about poachers, and he borrowed that——" She caught her mother's eye and broke off, flushing.

"Borrowed the book?" Fountain said. "I remember. Is he ready for the other volumes yet? Didn't he say there were some more?"

Felicity stared at him. "I say," she said slowly, "*did* you send for it, or—or did Collins come on his own?"

There was a moment's silence. "Send for it?" Fountain repeated. "Collins?"

"I thought there was something odd about it!" Felicity cried. "Daddy's fearfully fed up. Collins came and said you'd told him to fetch it back. Didn't you?"

"No," said Fountain. "No. Of course I didn't! He said that, did he? And did your father give it to him?"

"Well, yes, naturally he did. Was there something hidden in it after all?"

"My dear, too ridiculous," said Lady Matthews. "I'm sure just a misunderstanding."

"But, Mummy, don't you see? It's important! Only I'm pretty sure there wasn't anything in it, because don't you remember we looked, after the burglary? And Daddy would have noticed before that, because he was reading it." She wrinkled her brow, puzzling over it.

The smile had been wiped from Fountain's face; his eyes were fixed on her. He said: "I can't—understand it at all. I'm most upset that such a message should have been given as coming from me. What on earth must your father have thought?"

"Well, he was slightly peeved," admitted Felicity. "Mr. Fountain, do you think we're on to a clue? Could there have been anything in the book?"

"If there was I've not the smallest idea what it could be," Fountain said. He turned aside and fumbled for a cigarette in the box on the table. "Sounds to me like a piece of damned officiousness."

Felicity was not satisfied. "Yes, but the burglary? The library and Daddy's study and the drawing room were all turned upside down, but not the dining room, and there was nothing taken. I believe Collins thought there was something, you know. He must have mistaken the book. What a sell for him! Daddy wouldn't have taken anything out of it, and it was never out of his hands, except for about ten minutes, when he left it behind at the Boar's Head when we went to call on Shirley."

Lady Matthews's mild voice broke into this speech. "Darling, such a lively imagination. But we really must go. Pray don't be upset, Mr. Fountain. All a misunderstanding. I'll tell my husband."

"I wish you would," he said. "I'm—most annoyed. Wouldn't have had such a thing happen for the world."

He seemed rather more put out than the occasion warranted and he relieved his feelings by turning on the butler, who had come in, and asking him roughly what he wanted.

Joan interposed. She had rung for Baker to show Lady Matthews out.

Lady Matthews was looking at Baker rather thoughtfully. It struck Felicity that the manor servants had an uncomfortable way of quietly entering the room whenever anything of importance was being said. When she was driving her mother home she remarked on this. "I think he heard, Mummy. Don't you?"

"I shouldn't be surprised," said Lady Matthews. "I'm afraid, darling, you were a little indiscreet. And Frank not in to lunch."

"Well, I didn't know they'd got another servant who crept about and listened at keyholes," protested Felicity.

Lady Matthews relapsed into silence. Her daughter was surprised to see something very like a frown on her face, but failed to get her to talk.

The frown was still there at lunch-time. Lady Matthews was unusually restless and twice murmured: "Why doesn't Frank come back? Tiresome!"

Shortly after two the telephone bell rang. Sir Humphrey, who was seated in the library, answered it and said a little hastily that Mr. Amberley was not in, and he didn't know where he could be found. Yes, of course a message would be delivered to him immediately he came in.

Lady Matthews, who had entered the room, wanted to know who was trying to get hold of Frank.

"Fountain," said Sir Humphrey. "Most odd message!"

"Well, dear?"

"I'm to tell Frank that he's gone up to London and won't be in till late. Did Frank want to see him?"

"I don't know. Quite possibly. Did he speak about the book?"

"It wasn't Fountain himself. The butler gave the message. Said Fountain was particularly anxious that Frank should know he'd gone to London and would be at his club all the afternoon."

Lady Matthews shut the door. "Very worrying," she said. "Must try and get Frank."

Her husband declared himself quite unable to see why

she should be worried, and once more settled himself with his book on the sofa. Lady Matthews sat down at the desk, sighing, and rang up Carchester police station. Sir Humphrey evinced a certain surprise, for only in moments of great stress could his wife be induced to use the telephone.

The sergeant on duty could give her no certain intelligence. Mr. Amberley had been in Carchester during the morning, but had gone out with the chief constable. Since then he had not been seen.

Lady Matthews, sighing more heavily still, rang up Colonel Watson's house. The colonel was out.

"Sometimes," said Lady Matthews pensively, "one can't help believing in a malign providence."

When Amberley had not come in by four o'clock, she said that he was just like his father. This pronouncement roused all Felicity's curiosity, for matters must indeed be serious if her mother said that. Lady Matthews refused to unburden her mind either to her or to Sir Humphrey. When she absently refused first a scone, then bread-and-butter, and lastly cakes, her relatives became quite worried and hailed the appearance of Amberley at a quarter past five with considerable relief.

"Thank goodness you've come!" exclaimed Felicity. "Wherever have you been?"

He glanced indifferently down at her. "Investigating last night's affair. Why this sudden desire for my company? Can I have some tea, Aunt Marion?"

His aunt chose two lumps of sugar from the bowl with extreme deliberation and spoke without looking up from this delicate task. "Two messages, dear Frank. Burdening my soul. That girl wants you. Either the Boar's Head or the cottage. Such a disagreeable place."

Amberley looked at her with a curious little smile in his eyes. "I wondered whether she would. All right."

Lady Matthews lifted the milk-jug. "That butler. At the manor."

The smile vanished; Mr. Amberley regarded her fixedly. "Yes?"

"A message from Basil Fountain. He has gone to town."

"When?"

"At about two o'clock, my dear."

"Who gave the message?"

"The butler. Didn't I say so? His club, all the afternoon."

Amberley seemed to consider, his eyes on the clock. "I see. I think, on the whole, I won't wait for tea."

"No, dear boy," agreed his aunt. "Much wiser not. Something interesting to tell you. So stupid of Humphrey! That book. You've been at sea over it."

"Entirely at sea. Well?"

"Humphrey left it at the Boar's Head by mistake. He and Felicity, you know. Calling on Shirley. Forgot it."

Amberley swung round to face his uncle. "You left it there?" he snapped. "'Did she have it?'"

"Now I come to think of it, I did leave it behind," said Sir Humphrey. "We went back for it immediately, however. Miss Brown gave it to me at once."

"Why the devil couldn't you say so before?" demanded Amberley. "When did this come out? Who knows about it?"

"Felicity, my dear. Told Basil Fountain. Lots of people know. Joan and that nice young man and me and the butler."

Felicity quailed before the look on her cousin's face. "I'm awfully sorry if I've put my foot into it, but how was I to know I wasn't to mention it?"

"You're a damned little fool!" said Mr. Amberley with distressing outspokenness, and was gone before she could think of a suitable retort.

A moment later they heard the whirr of the Bentley's self-starter. The car shot off under the window with something of a roar.

Sir Humphrey recovered from the shock of his nephew's rough usage of him. "God bless my soul!" he ejaculated. "Really, I had no notion it was so important. I began to be quite alarmed."

Lady Matthews looked round at the cake-stand. "Why has no one given me anything to eat?" she said plaintively. "I'm exceedingly hungry."

"You refused everything," Felicity reminded her.

"Nonsense, my dear. Give me a scone, please," said Lady Matthews, placid as ever.

CHAPTER XVI

WHEN LADY MATTHEWS had left her that morning, Shirley found herself torn by conflicting feelings. She was at once anxious to shift her burden of worry onto shoulders that seemed to her eminently capable of bearing it, and nervous of the result. She could never quite forget that painful grasp on her wrist beside the dead man's car on the Pittingly Road. It had left a bruise, and it had given her the impression that Mr. Amberley (however kind he might be to animals) would have little mercy on persons whom he detected in breaking the law. His association with the police had made her doubly wary. It was true that he did not seem to have mentioned her presence on the scene of the murder that night; equally true that he had not given her away at the fancy-dress ball. But this forbearance had always seemed to her to be due not so much to chivalry as to a desire to give her enough rope with which to hang herself. He had been watching her from the start and not, she felt, with a kindly eye. Certain words of his still rankled. He had said that he did not like her at all, and she thought that he spoke the truth. She could never discover in him any signs of liking. On the contrary, when he was not mocking her he was very rude and never lost an opportunity of telling her that she was callow and foolish. She set very little store by his unwonted gentleness on the night of Mark's death. After all he was not a cad, and only a cad would have been anything but kind on such an occasion. Moreover, she would not put it above him to have changed his tactics with the hope of inducing her to confide in him. He seemed to her a singularly ruthless individual.

Lady Matthews had guessed a part of her secret and had appeared to think that he also knew it. Shirley was not much surprised at Lady Matthews's perception, but failed to see how Amberley could know. At the same time, she had more than once had an uncomfortable feeling that he knew more about her than he pretended.

A sensation of lassitude had succeeded her first dismay on hearing of Collins's death. Success had, for the first time, been within her reach. Now the valet had been shot, and with him died her hopes. There did not seem to be anything left that she could do; if Mr. Amberley could help her, let him try; if he had her put into prison, what matter?

Her own words to Collins jigged in her brain. Half a loaf! Half a loaf! Better than no bread, was it? She thought bitterly that if the other half had gone it would be better by far had she never set eyes on that tantalizing half-loaf.

She realized with a start that she had wasted an hour in vain speculations, so that there was not time before lunch to visit Ivy Cottage. She went out instead to buy a packet of luggage labels and saw, with a wry smile, that her faithful attendant was following at a discreet distance. Had she not been so depressed she did not think that she could have resisted the temptation to lead him on a long cross-country walk over ploughed fields and through hedges. He did not look like a walker.

She meant to set out for the cottage immediately after lunch, but when she had buckled on Bill's collar in preparation for the walk she paused and glanced uncertainly towards her dressing case. Bill reproached her for the delay, but she shook her head. "Wait a bit, Bill. I think we'll be on the safe side," she said slowly.

Bill lay down with a sigh, his nose on his paws, whining softly. His mistress took a small key out of her handbag and unlocked the case and drew a torn piece of foolscap out of one of its pockets. She stood for a moment in uncertainty and then went across to the writing-table by the window and sat down. The letter she wrote was quite short, but took her some time to compose. She read it through, hesitated, and then with a shrug folded it. She carefully placed the torn foolscap into an envelope and sealed it, and inserted both it and her own note into another larger envelope. She addressed this and said to Bill, whose whines had become despairing: "All right, you shall go. I've a feeling I've done the right thing. What do you think, old boy?"

Bill thought that it was time they started for their walk and said so quite unmistakably.

Together they descended the stairs. To Bill's disgust their first objective was the post office, where Shirley registered and posted her letter. Then she set off towards Ivy Cottage, and Bill, released from his lead, bounded ahead of her joyfully. In the rear Constable Tucker plodded dutifully after them.

It was three o'clock by the time Shirley reached the cottage, and she found the charwoman whom she had appointed to meet her there at half-past two standing on the doorstep and looking aggrieved.

The cottage felt cold and smelled musty, of dry rot. Shirley flung open the windows and told the charwoman to put a kettle on for hot water. The kitchen floor had to be scrubbed, she said. The charwoman remarked that it wasn't everyone who was so particular how they left a place.

"Possibly not," said Shirley. "And while you're waiting for the water to boil please put those plates away in the cupboard and fold up that rug for me to pack."

There was a good deal to be done in the cottage. Shirley finished packing her own trunk and tied a label on it; and then, with rather a heavy heart she began to sort out Mark's possessions. She did not want to be obliged to go through them again, and she had made up her mind to send most of his clothes to an East End mission. She went down to hunt for brown paper and string and did up four large parcels.

The charwoman acted for the first time on her own initiative at four o'clock. Having found a tin of condensed milk in the larder she made some tea and brought it upstairs to Shirley. Shirley declined the tinned milk but was glad of the tea. Remembering Lady Matthews's parting words that morning, she told the charwoman to offer some to the man outside in the lane. Apparently it was accepted, for presently, looking out of the window, she saw Constable Tucker coming up the path behind the charwoman. He looked sheepish but grateful. When he had retired again to his post Shirley told the charwoman that she could go as soon as she had washed up the tea-things. She herself saw the end of her labours in view and hurried to get everything finished before the light went.

The charwoman came upstairs for her money, and while Shirley searched in her purse, volunteered the remark that she wasn't surprised miss had left the cottage. "Lonely, I call it," she said.

"I don't mind that," said Shirley.

"Well, everyone to 'er taste, miss. It 'ud give me the creeps after dark, this place would. Rats too, I shouldn't wonder."

"Mice," said Shirley.

"I don't know but what I 'ate them worse, miss. I 'ad an aunt once sat on a mouse what had run up under her skirts. It give her a regular turn."

"I should think it gave the mouse a turn too," said Shirley. "Here you are, and thank you. Go out by the front, will you? And shut the door, please."

The charwoman went off downstairs. Bill, lying at the foot of them in a bored attitude, left the house with her and went round to the back on a quest of his own. He shared her belief in the presence of rats.

Constable Tucker, who had left the lane for a rustic seat in the garden, sighed and lit a cigarette. A dull job, shadowing Miss Brown. He hoped she wasn't going to be much longer. Constable Westrupp was due to relieve him at six o'clock, but he'd be waiting outside the Boar's Head. He wondered whether the young lady was going to keep him hanging about here much longer, and sent out thoughts towards Mr. Frank Amberley that were by no means loving.

The autumn afternoons soon got chilly and damp, he found. He drew up his coat collar and sat for a while contemplating a solitary star. Bill came round the house and growled at him.

Shirley looked out of the window. "Who's that?" she said sharply.

Feeling a little foolish, Tucker said with a slight cough: "It's me, miss."

"Oh!" She sounded amused. "Shan't keep you many minutes. Shut up, Bill. You ought to know him by now."

Bill was sniffing suspiciously at Tucker's ankles. Tucker made propitiating noises and wondered why the young lady couldn't have had a nice little Pekingese. He advanced a nervous hand towards Bill, assuring him that he was a good dog. Bill was more interested in trying to ascertain whether he was a good man. He came to the conclusion that no steps need at the moment be taken to evict the constable and went off again to continue operations in the back garden.

Inside the cottage Shirley had lit a lamp and was burning a collection of old letters and bills in the kitchen grate. The trunks were all packed and labelled ready for the carrier to take away; she had counted the laundry and left it in the basket in the scullery. Having watched the last piece of paper burn away, she picked up the lamp and went to make a final tour of inspection and to shut and bolt the windows again. She was annoyed to find that she had forgotten to look inside the cupboard on the landing, where Mark had kept some odds and ends. Disposing of these took her some little time, and she was startled to see, on looking out of the window, that it had grown quite dark.

In the garden the tiny glow of a cigarette-end advertised the presence of Constable Tucker. For the first time since he had started to shadow her she was rather glad to feel him close at hand. The charwoman was right: it was lonely in the cottage. She went down to assure herself that the back door was properly secured and took the opportunity of calling Bill in again.

An occasional car could be heard passing down the main road at the bottom of the lane. As she put on her hat she distinctly heard the change of gear as one turned into the lane and came up the slight hill towards the cottage. Hoping that the car might be Mr. Amberley's she went to open the front door. When the car went on past the cottage and she realized that it must be going up to the farm, she was slightly annoyed at her feeling of disappointment and shut the door with a cross little bang.

The thought of Mark's tragic end came into her mind. She found herself listening rather intently and glancing over her shoulder. The uncurtained windows, framing darkness, made her nervous. She could not help expecting to see a face suddenly pressed up against the glass staring at her. The idea was absurd, of course, but once admitted would not be banished. To hearten herself she pulled the Colt automatic out of the pocket of her long coat before she put it on and laid it on the table beside her.

She buttoned the coat closer up to her neck and pulled on her gauntlets. Bill's leash was not to be found; it never was, she thought savagely. A short search brought it to light hanging on a peg on the back of the kitchen door. She unhooked it and went to the table to pick up her gun and to turn out the lamp.

Then she remembered that she had left the window open in the living room.

"Pull yourself together, you ass!" she said severely, and went to shut it.

In the small passageway between the two rooms a dark figure loomed up suddenly to meet her. Her breath caught on a startled gasp. She fell back a pace, peering. "Mr. Amberley?" she said, her voice trembling uncontrollably.

The figure was upon her before she could move. A vice-like arm encircled her; she tried to scream, and something soft, sickly with the fumes of chloroform, was pressed over her nose and mouth, stifling her.

She fought desperately and heard through the roaring in her ears Bill's snarl, coming as though from an immense distance away. Then the anæsthetic overpowered her; she felt her head growing lighter and lighter, and a numbness paralyzing her limbs, and slid into unconsciousness.

The man who held her had kicked the kitchen door to just in time to stop Bill's murderous rush. On the other side of it the dog was clawing frantically at the wooden panels, barking in a frenzy of rage.

The unknown man laid Shirley down roughly and forced a gag between her slack jaws and secured it with a scarf bound over her mouth. He drew a coil of thin rope from his pocket and quickly lashed her wrists and her ankles together. Then pulling her up, he flung her across his shoulder and went out with her, through the shadowed garden to the lane and up it, keeping close under the lee of the hedge until a closed car was reached. He thrust his burden into the back of it, on the floor, and threw a rug over the girl, completely concealing her. A moment later he was in the driving-seat and had switched on the lights. The car crept forward, gathering speed, reached the main road and swung round on to it.

In the cottage Bill turned from the unyielding door to the window and gathered his haunches under him for the spring. There was a smash, the tinkle of broken glass, and a big bull-terrier, his white coat flecked with blood, put his nose once to the ground, sniffing, and was off, following the scent of a man he meant to pull down.

CHAPTER XVII

THE BENTLEY swept into Upper Nettlefold and drew up at the Boar's Head. Miss Brown, the porter informed Amberley, had not yet come in. He was about to leave the place when he paused and said briefly that he wished to telephone. The porter led him to the box and left him there. Mr. Amberley opened the telephone book and swiftly found the number he sought. In three minutes he was speaking to the hall-porter of a certain London club.

Yes, Mr. Fountain had been in the club that afternoon, but he had left shortly before tea-time. No, the hall-porter could not say where he was going, but he would no doubt be found later at the Gaiety Theatre. He had reserved a seat there for Mr. Fountain over the telephone.

Amberley thanked the man and rang off. He strode out again to his car, beside which he found an indignant constable who proposed to take his name and address for dangerous driving in the town.

Amberley got into the car and started the engine. "Get out of the way," he said. "No doubt I shall see you later. I can't stop to chat with you now."

The constable jumped back just in time as the car shot forward. He was left standing speechless on the curbstone and had only just enough presence of mind to jot down the Bentley's number.

Amberley drove straight to Ivy Cottage and drew up outside the gate with less than his usual care. He saw that a light was burning in the house and drew a sharp sigh of relief. He was just getting out of the car when the bull-terrier came into sight in the lane, questing about to pick up the scent he had lost. Amberley stopped short and called to the dog. Bill came at once, recognizing the voice. He was whining with suppressed eagerness and dashed off again immediately. But Amberley had had time to notice the gashes on his muzzle and flanks. He made no attempt to catch Bill but strode into the garden, calling to Constable Tucker. There was no answer.

His foot scrunched on something brittle; he looked down and saw the gleam of broken glass. There was a hole in the kitchen window, and no need to speculate on what had caused it.

The front door was shut, but Amberley thrust in his arm through the broken window and unbolted it and flung up the lower sash. He climbed in and took in at a glance the lamp, still burning, Shirley's handbag lying on the table, and beside it the Colt automatic. Even at such a moment as this Mr. Amberley's thin lips twitched into a smile that was amused and rather scornful. He pocketed the gun, got out his torch and made a tour of the house.

A strong smell of chloroform assailed his nostrils as he opened the kitchen door; a scrap of cotton-wool, torn by Shirley from the pad in her struggle, lay at the foot of the stairs. Amberley picked it up and held it to his nose. The anæsthetic was still clinging to it; he judged that it could not have been lying there for more than a few minutes. The living-room window was open, and there was a cake of mud on the floor with the imprint of a rubber heel on it. Amberley gathered it up, taking care that it should not crumble, and laid it down on the table. There was no one in the house and no sign of Constable Tucker.

He went out into the garden again, and using his torch, made a tour of it. A groan led him to a lilac bush beside a rustic seat; Tucker was on the ground, as though he had fallen from the seat, trying to raise himself on his elbow.

Amberley's torch flashed full into his face; he blinked stupidly at the light, still groaning. Amberley dropped onto his knee beside him. "Come on, man, come on," he said impatiently. "What happened? Pull yourself together!"

Tucker's hand went up to his head. "My head!" he muttered. "Oh, Gawd, my head!"

"Yes, I've no doubt something hit you. Luckily your head's a hard one. Drink this!" He snapped back the lid of his brandy flask and put it to Tucker's mouth. The raw spirit revived the man; he managed to sit up, still clasping his head. "What happened?" he said dazedly. "Who hit me?"

"Don't ask me questions! Try to think!" snarled Amberley. "Did you see anyone?"

"No. I don't know what happened. I was sitting here waiting for the young lady. Somebody must have hit me."

"My God, you're a fine policeman!" Amberley said savagely. He got to his feet. "Do you mean to tell me you didn't hear anything? No footstep? No car?"

The unfortunate Tucker tried to concentrate his mind. "A car. Yes, I heard a car. But it went up to the farm. It didn't stop."

"What sort of a car? Did you see the number plate?"

"No. No, I only got a glimpse as it passed the gate. I think it was a closed car. It was a big one."

"Colour?"

"I couldn't see, sir. It was too dark to see."

"Listen to me!" Amberley said. "There's a cake of mud on the table in the living room. You've got to take that to the police station. There's an imprint on it. Understand?"

Tucker nodded and managed to get up. Mr. Amberley turned and strode towards the gate. Bill's desperate whines made him look over his shoulder. "Look after the dog. There's a leash in the kitchen."

He was gone. Tucker heard the car start and sat down on the seat to recover his equilibrium.

Amberley drove the car into Upper Nettlefold and through the High Street to the Market Square. There was a garage at the corner with petrol pumps displaying globes lit by electricity. He ran the car under one of these, said curtly to the man in attendance: "Fill her up!" and got out, slamming the door behind him.

The police station was on the opposite side of the square. Sergeant Gubbins was behind the door marked PRIVATE, and Mr. Amberley walked in without troubling the constable on duty to announce him.

The sergeant looked up austerely but broke into a smile

when he saw who was his visitor. " 'Evening, Mr. Amberley. Anything new?"

Amberley had no answering smile for him. "Sergeant, instruct that constable outside to ring up all surrounding police stations to stop and search a blue Vauxhall limousine, number P.V. 80496."

The sergeant knew his Mr. Amberley. He did not stop to ask questions, but got up and went to the door and repeated the order to the constable in the outer room. Then he turned and said: "What's happened, sir?"

"The girl's been kidnapped. Can you come with me at once?"

The sergeant stared. "Good Lord, sir!" he ejaculated. "Kidnapped? Where's Tucker?"

"At the cottage. Someone knocked him out. He saw nothing, heard nothing. My only consolation is that he's feeling something. Are you coming?"

"Half a moment, sir, and I'm with you," said the sergeant, and pushed through into the outer room and conferred briefly with the constable, who was already sending out the message. By the time he had finished and had got his helmet and a revolver, Amberley had left the station and re-crossed the square to the garage.

The sergeant followed him and climbed into the car while Amberley was paying for his petrol. As Amberley put his foot on the self-starter he asked where they were going.

"I don't know," replied Amberley, and swept round the square and out of it to the crossroads above the Boar's Head.

The constable on point duty, who had taken his number half an hour earlier, saw the Bentley coming and held up his hand to stop it. It drew up alongside him, and Amberley leaned out to speak to him.

"Has a dark blue Vauxhall, five-seater limousine passed during the last hour? Number P.V. 80496. Think, man!"

The constable said grimly: "I don't need to think for what I'm going to do. I'll trouble you for your name and address."

Amberley sat back. "Speak to the fool," he said.

The sergeant was already preparing to do so. He spoke a language the constable could easily understand and had heard before.

"But—but, Sergeant, I 'ad my hand up, and he went past me like a streak of lightning. He must 'ave seen it, but he never took no notice. He went——"

"The wonder to me is he could see what was behind it," said the sergeant unflatteringly. "You answer him and be quick about it. He's Mr. Frank Amberley, that's who he is."

"I didn't know who 'e was," said the constable resentfully. "All I know was he disregarded my signal to him to stop."

"Get on with it! You can charge me some other time," said Amberley. "A Vauxhall limousine, P.V. 80496."

The constable scratched his chin. "There was a Morris-Oxford went down the Lumsden Road," he said. "That wouldn't be it."

"Oh, my God!" said Amberley. "A large car, man! Bonnet with two scoops out of it."

"No, I haven't seen it," said the constable as though he were glad to be able to say so. "I seen Mr. Purvis' Daimler, but I haven't seen no other big car, not during the past hour I haven't."

Mr. Amberley's hand found the gear-lever. "Hold up that cart; I'm going to turn," he said.

"Don't stand there goggling, hold it up!" commanded the sergeant. "Lor' I never see such a fat-headed lout! Right away, Mr. Amberley, sir, and for Gawd's sake mind that perishing cyclist!"

The Bentley went round the constable with a growl and shot off down the High Street. The constable, still holding up the horse and cart like a man in a trance, heard the infinitesimal check of the gears changing, then the hum of a high-powered car travelling at speed away into the distance and came back to earth to hear himself being rudely addressed by the carter.

"Where's the nearest constable on point duty past Ivy Cottage, Sergeant?" asked Amberley.

"There ain't one. There's an A.A. man about a mile on,

at the Brighton Road crossing, but he won't be on duty now. It's too late."

"Damn. What are the turnings?"

"None, till you get to the Brighton crossing, if you don't count the lane leading to Furze Hall. I'll tell you what, sir! They're widening the bridge at Griffin's corner, just before you reach the crossing. There'll be a man there directing the traffic."

"Well, pray God he's not a fool," said Amberley, swerving to avoid a careless pedestrian.

The sergeant clutched the door and righted himself. He refrained from comment but said: "I dunno, sir, but if you ask me it ain't what you'd call a brainy job, turning a signboard round and waving a lantern. Look out, sir, there's a bend coming!"

"You leave me to drive this car my own way," said Mr. Amberley.

The sergeant held his breath as the car swung round the bend, and ventured to relax again. "I've been in this district some years now, sir," he said slowly.

"You won't be here much longer," said Amberley.

"Not if you're going to drive at this pace, I won't," retorted the sergeant. "But what I was going to say was, I know a good few of the cars about here."

"Bright of you."

The sergeant ignored this. "And I know who owns a blue Vauxhall limousine, Number P.V. 80496. And I can tell you this, Mr. Amberley, you've got me fair gasping. That's the bridge ahead, sir! Go easy!"

The youth on duty there was moodily swinging a green lamp, but Amberley pulled the car up. The sergeant was nearest the youth, and he leaned out and inquired whether the Vauxhall had passed over the bridge.

The youth turned out to be typical of his generation. Very few cars passed him which he did not closely inspect and appraise. He was not interested in number-plates, but he had held up a big Vauxhall about three quarters of an hour earlier to let a lorry come over the bridge from the other side. He began to enter into a detailed description of the horsepower and year of the car, but was cut short.

"I don't want to buy the car," said the sergeant. "Which way did it go?"

The youth was looking admiringly at the Bentley. His lips moved in a silent enumeration of her points, but being in awe of policemen, he dragged his gaze away from it and answered Sergeant Gubbins. "It went over the bridge, first, then I seen it turn off at the crossing."

Amberley spoke. "Who was in it?"

The youth shook his head. "I dunno, sir."

"I mean, a man, or a woman, more than one person?"

"I dunno, sir."

"It's no good talking to him, sir," said the sergeant. "I got a nephew like him. If a kangaroo happened to be driving the car he wouldn't notice. Sickening, I call it. Jabber about differentials all day long that sort do, but take a bit of interest in something that don't move on wheels, oh no! Not them!"

The Bentley moved forward. "The Brighton crossing," Amberley said. "Heading south. I think—I very much think—I've got you, my friend. Sergeant, we shall have to travel rather quickly."

"Of course we haven't been, have we?" said the sergeant. He waited until the car had turned on to the secondary road leading southwards, and then seeing no immediate danger in front of them, said: "Now, sir, if you don't mind, where are we, so to speak? It seems to me you know a sight more than what I do. We're chasing a certain Vauxhall limousine which has got three quarters of an hour's start of us. I got my own idea who's in that car, but how he had the nerve to come by it I don't know. I've often noticed the quiet ones is the worst. It looks to me like a nasty case. Has he done in the young lady, sir, do you think?"

There was a moment's silence, and the car seemed to leap forward, like a horse given the spur. The sergeant, looking round at Mr. Amberley's profile, saw it so grim that he confessed later it gave him a turn.

"If he has," said Amberley in a very level voice, "if he has, he won't trouble the hangman."

This sinister pronouncement, coupled with the look on

Amberley's face, led the sergeant to infer that he had discovered something interesting, though not of much value as a clue. Feeling that the occasion was one for a display of tact he made no comment on his discovery, but merely requested Mr. Amberley to go easy. "No use meeting trouble halfway, sir," he said. "If you was to go and do a murder, where'd I be?"

Amberley gave a mirthless laugh. "Making a sensational arrest, I expect."

"I'd be in a very awkward position, that's where I'd be," replied the sergeant. "If I thought you meant it I'd be obliged to take away that gun you've got sticking into my hip at this very moment."

"I'm more likely to choke the life out of the swine," Amberley said. "I don't think he's done it yet. I'm pinning my faith to that—keep a look-out for a constable. Another killing would be fatal to him. Mark Brown's death passed for an accident, but another accident would be suspicious, to say the least of it. Shirley is to disappear. No body, no conviction, Sergeant."

"I get you, sir. Taking her for a ride and bumping her off miles from Upper Nettlefold?"

"Not unless he's a fool. If he does that, and the body's found, it will be traced back to him. Miss Brown doesn't own a car. How did she get so far afield? Any jury would assume that she had been taken there by her murderer. Much too dangerous. The body must be disposed of. Put yourself in the murderer's place, Sergeant. How is that to be done?"

Various gruesome visions came before the sergeant's eyes, but he thought it wiser not to advance a suggestion. A gentleman who had fallen in love with a young lady wouldn't take kindly to the thought of dismembered corpses or charred fragments. "We don't want to start talking horrors, sir," he said severely.

"I see," said Amberley. "Quicklime. No. No."

"Of course not, sir. Whoever heard of such a thing?"

"You're wrong," Amberley said. "I know you're wrong. He's heading south. The sea, Sergeant, the sea!"

The sergeant considered the suggestion and came to the

conclusion it was probably correct. "Seems to me, sir, we'd better hurry up," he said gruffly. "Unless—— Anyway, we've got to catch him, and that's all there is to it."

The car roared through a hamlet; the needle of the speedometer was creeping up.

"He won't have killed her yet," Amberley said. The sergeant had the impression that he was trying to reassure himself. "He daren't run the risk. Supposing he had a slight accident? Supposing he was held up, and the car was searched? If the girl's alive they can't get him for murder. He'll think of that. He's bound to think of that."

The sergeant agreed, though he felt a little dubious. In his experience murderers seldom laid such careful plans. However, the killing of Mark had certainly been very cleverly planned, so perhaps Mr. Amberley might prove to be right.

The lights of a village twinkled ahead of them; the car slowed to a more respectable pace, and the sergeant espied a constable on point duty at a crossroad in the middle of the main street.

Amberley pulled up beside him, but let the sergeant do the talking. The constable, unlike the one they had left in Upper Nettlefold, was an alert young man. Not many cars had come by him during the last hour, and he was almost sure that the only one of any size had been a Vauxhall limousine. But the number was not P.V. 80496. That he could swear to. The Vauxhall he had seen bore the letters A.X. He was not prepared to state the number, but he thought it began with a nine.

The sergeant looked inquiringly at Amberley. "Don't quite fit, sir."

"False number-plate. Probably no such number exists. Which way did the car go, Constable?"

"It turned off to the right, sir," replied the policeman, pointing.

"I see. Where does that lead to?"

"Well, sir, it goes to Larkhurst, but there's a good many turnings off it."

"Can you get to the coast by it?"

"No, sir, not exactly you can't. You'd have to go 'cross country a bit."

"Turning off where?"

The constable thought for a moment. "Well, if you went by Six Ash Corner and Hillingdean, you'd want to turn off at the first pub you come to, past Ketley. On the other hand, sir, if you didn't mind a roundabout sort of way, you could cut down to Chingham and bear on to Freshfield and Trensham and reach the coast at Coldhaven."

Amberley nodded. "Thanks. Did you notice whether that Vauxhall was travelling fast?"

"Nothing out of the ordinary, sir."

Amberley let in the clutch. "My compliments; you're the brightest policeman I've met during the past fortnight."

The sergeant said with a cough as the car started: "Bright for a constable, sir."

Amberley smiled, but for once in his life forbore to retort caustically. His attention was all for the tricky road he was following; the sergeant got monosyllabic answers to his questions and wisely gave up all attempt at conversation.

The trail was a difficult one, often lost. The Vauxhall had left the main roads for a network of country lanes. From time to time Amberley stopped to ask whether it had been seen. Mostly a stolid headshake answered the question, but twice he got news of the car; once from a railway official in charge of a level-crossing, once from a night watchman huddled over a brazier in a wooden hut beside some road repairs. The Vauxhall seemed to be heading southwest and to be maintaining a steady but not extraordinary speed. Obviously the driver was taking no risks of meeting with an accident or a holdup; it seemed too as though he had no very great fear of being followed.

The sergeant, who, when they plunged into the second-class roads, pursuing an erratic course, privately thought there was little chance of catching a car bound for an unknown destination and bearing a false name-plate, began after a little time to realize that Amberley was pushing forward to some definite point. When they stopped at Hillingdean and the sergeant conferred with a constable on point duty there, he got out a road map and studied it intently.

The warning, sent out from Upper Nettlefold, had been received by all the southern stations but bore no fruit. No car of the stated number had anywhere been seen. Amberley cursed himself for having given the fatal number and wasted no more time in inquiring for it.

There were many circuitous byways that led to the coast, so that it was hardly surprising that the sergeant should consider the chase hopeless. For miles they had no intelligence of the Vauxhall, but Amberley never slackened speed except to read a signpost here and there, and never hesitated in his choice of direction. It became increasingly apparent to the sergeant that he had a fixed goal in his mind, for it could scarcely be due to chance that they picked the trail up again twice when it had seemed completely lost.

Once Amberley bade him take the map over a difficult piece of country and guide him to some village the sergeant had never heard of. The sergeant ventured to ask where they were going. He had to raise his voice to be heard above the roar of the engine. He saw Amberley give a shrug, and managed to catch the word, "Littlehaven." It conveyed nothing to the sergeant. As the Bentley rocked over a stretch of lane pitted with holes he said: "If you're sure where he's gone, sir, why don't you take the main road?"

"Because I'm not sure, damn you!" said Mr. Amberley. "It's the best I can do."

The sergeant relapsed into silence. Except for the discomfort of travelling at a shocking pace over bad roads he was not sure that he wasn't glad they had chosen deserted lanes. At least they ran less risk of an accident. He shuddered to think what might happen on a main road. As it was he spent most of his time clutching at the door to steady himself, and although his nerves were becoming dulled, he had several bad frights. Once, when a bicyclist wobbled into the middle of the road and the Bentley's wheels tore at the loose surface as it took a sudden swerve round the unwary cyclist, he was moved to shout:

"People like you, Mr. Amberley, didn't ought to be allowed anything more powerful than a Ford!"

He had thought it a still night, but the wind whistled past his ears and once nearly swept his helmet off. He jammed it on more firmly and thought Mr. Amberley must be fairly scared out of his senses to treat his car in this frightful fashion.

The moon had come up and was riding serenely overhead, occasionally obscured by a drifting cloud. The country through which they were travelling was unfamiliar to the sergeant. He retained ever afterwards the memory of untarred roads with puddles gleaming in the moonlight, of hedges flashing past, of villages where warm lamps glowed behind uncurtained windows, and of signposts stretching cracked arms to point the way to unknown hamlets; of hills up which the Bentley stormed, of sudden sickening lurches as the car took a bad corner, of the electric horn insistently blaring at slower-going vehicles, forcing them to draw in to the side; and above all of Mr. Amberley's face beside him, with the eyes never wavering from the road ahead and the mouth compressed in a hard, merciless line.

He ceased to peer nervously ahead in search of danger. Amberley never paid any attention to his warnings but drove on and on, very expertly, the sergeant had no doubt, but quite scandalously. The sergeant wondered in a detached way what his own position would be if they ran into or over something. Hurtling along at over fifty miles an hour, and him a police officer! Nice set-out it would be if they went and killed somebody.

At the level-crossing, where they halted for the gates to be opened, they picked the trail up again, and even the battered sergeant felt that the speed had been justified when he heard that the Vauxhall had passed over no more than twenty minutes earlier.

Mr. Amberley's bleak look lightened. As he drove over the lines and changed up, he said: "I was right. We're going to shift a bit now, Sergeant."

"Well, I'll thank you to remember that this ain't Daytona Beach, sir," said the long-suffering sergeant. "Far from it. Now be careful of the bus, for Gawd's sake, Mr. Amberley!"

A country bus was grumbling along ahead, on the crown of the road. Mr. Amberley kept his hand on the hooter, but the bus meandered along unheeding. The Bentley charged past, mounting the tufty grass that bordered the lane and clearing the omnibus by inches.

The sergeant, clinging to the door, hung out to hurl invectives at the bus-driver, already out of earshot. A swerve round a bend brought him round with a plump. He mopped his face with a large handkerchief and said that what they seemed to want was a blooming tank, not a motorcar.

CHAPTER XVIII

LITTLEHAVEN was a fishing village situated on the marshy alluviums where a small river emptied itself into the sea at the head of a creek, running about a mile inland. The village itself was old, with twisted streets smelling of seaweed and of tar. It had a small harbour, where the smacks rode at anchor, and over the beach were always to be found black nets, redolent of fish scales, spread out for mending. Westward along the coast, towards the mouth of the creek, a modern bungalow town had sprung up, for the place provided good boating and fishing, and in the season the sea was alive with small craft; and the one hotel, a gaunt structure towering above the one-storied houses, was so full that it could afford to charge extremely high prices for most inferior accommodation. Out of season half of it was shut up and the bungalows presented an equally deserted appearance. Most of them were owned by enterprising tradesmen who furnished them for the purpose of letting them at exorbitant rents for three months of the year and were content to allow them to stand empty for the remaining nine months.

Along the coast on the other side of the creek were a few better-built bungalows standing grandly apart. These were the privately owned houses, disdaining to rub shoulders with their humbler neighbours, even holding themselves discreetly aloof from each other. They boasted quite large gardens, and were served by a road from the town of Lowchester, some ten miles inland.

On the Littlehaven side of the creek the bungalows grew less and less pretentious till they petered out altogether; at the creek mouth a few fishermen's cottages huddled together round a Martello tower.

When the Bentley tore through Littlehaven Mr. Amberley did not stop to inquire for the Vauxhall, but jolted over the cobbled streets till he met the coast road. This had a tarred surface, and the car, badly hampered by the cobbles, leaped forward again and ran beside a depressing asphalt sea-walk, with the beach and the moonlit sea beyond, and a row of red and white bungalows on the other side of it.

From the level-crossing onwards Amberley had met with bad luck. Once the road was up and the signals had been against him; he had lost time waiting for a horse and wagon to crawl slowly over the narrow causeway; once, in a town of some size, he had been held up at every crossing and still further detained by the efforts of a blandly unconcerned female to turn a large Humber in a narrow road. She blocked the way for several precious minutes, twice stopping her engine, and looked stonily indignant when Amberley put his thumb on his electric hooter and kept it there. The sergeant's heart jumped into his mouth when, long before the female had completed her turn, the Bentley glided forward, mounted the pavement and almost brushed past the other car still, as it were, spread-eagled across the path.

But in spite of this ruthless manœuvre time had been lost, and glancing at his watch Amberley doubted whether he had lessened the distance between the Bentley and the Vauxhall.

The sergeant, when he saw the sea with the moonlight on the water, was moved to remark that it looked pretty. He got no answer. "Where are we going to, sir?" he inquired.

"There's a creek," Amberley replied briefly. "We're almost on to it. On the opposite side, set back about four or five hundred yards from the seacoast, there is a bungalow. That's where we're going."

"We are, are we?" said the sergeant. "I suppose we just drive across the creek. Or swim."

"We shall go across in a boat," replied Amberley.

"Well, I'd as soon have gone round by road, sir," said the sergeant. "I never was a good sailor, and I don't suppose I ever shall be. What's more, I haven't got any fancy to have you driving me about in a motorboat, and that's the truth. Besides," he added, as a thought struck him, "how are you going to come by a motorboat at this hour?"

"I've got one waiting."

The sergeant was beyond surprise. "The only wonder to me is you haven't got an aeroplane waiting," he said. "Pity you didn't think of that. How did you come to have this here boat?"

"I hired it. I've a man watching the bungalow from this side of the creek. He'll take us across. I daren't risk going round by road. Takes too long, though that's the way the Vauxhall went. There's a wooden landing-stage at the bottom of the bungalow garden."

"Know all about it, don't you, sir?"

"I ought to. I came down here this morning to investigate."

"Well, I'll be jiggered!" said the sergeant. "Whatever made you do that, sir? Did you find anything out?"

"I did. I found that a certain privately owned motorboat has been fetched from Morton's Yard, which we passed a little way back, and made fast to a mooring-buoy about a quarter of a mile up the creek. Not only has she recently been overhauled, but her tanks are full. I found that so interesting, Sergeant, that I'm paying a longshoreman who lives in one of the cottages this side of the creek to watch the boat and the bungalow and let me know what he sees."

The sergeant found that he could still feel surprise after all. He would very much have liked to ask why Mr. Amberley should suddenly dart off to Littlehaven unknown to anyone, and why the vicissitudes of a motorboat should interest him in the least, but he thought it unlikely that he would get a satisfactory answer just now. He merely said: "Well, sir, I'll say one thing for you; for one who ain't in the Force you're very thorough. Very thorough indeed, you are."

The road curved inland; the sergeant could see the sheen of water and knew that they must have reached the creek. The car was slowing down and stopped presently in front of a small cottage about five hundred yards from the

coast. The sergeant, peering, could just see the dark line of
the shore on the other side of the creek, and something
that might have been a house reared against the night sky.

Amberley had opened the door of the car and was
getting out when suddenly he checked and said sharply:
"Listen!"

Through the stillness of the evening the throb of a
motorboat's engines drifted over the water to their ears.

A figure came across the road towards the car and
shouted to Amberley, who looked quickly round.

"Is that you, sir? Well, I never! I was just a-going to get
off to telephone you, like you said I was to. Well, of all
the coincidences!" He caught sight of the sergeant's helmet
and added: "Lumme, is that a bobby?"

"You come here and tell us what you seen, my man,"
commanded the sergeant sternly.

It struck him that under his tan Mr. Amberley was very
pale. Amberley's eyes were fixed on the longshoreman's
face. "Be quick; let me have it."

"Well, there's someone gorn off in the motorboat," said
the man. "Gorn off this very minute. Ah, *and* he 'ad
something with 'im, wot he carried over 'is shoulder. Well,
I thought to myself, taking your luggage with you, are
you? It might ha' been a sack. Well, sir, 'e come down to
that there landing-stage and 'e chucks this 'ere sack, or
whatnot, into the dinghy wot's been tied up to the jetty,
like you saw when you was down 'ere; and 'e gets out 'is
oars and off 'e rows up the creek, me follering this side
unbeknownst, and 'e comes alongside 'is motorboat and
gets aboard with the luggage. Well, I thought, wot might
you be up to now?—me not being able to see clear-like.
Then I seen wot it was 'e was so busy with. Danged if 'e
weren't hitching the dinghy on to the motorboat. Then 'e
starts 'er up and off 'e goes, 'eading for the sea, the dinghy
bobbing be'ind 'im. And wot 'e wants to take it along for
fair beats me."

It beat the sergeant too, but he did not say so. He was
looking sympathetically at Amberley, whose hand, lying
on the door of the car, had gripped till the knuckles shone
white. The longshoreman's description had convinced the

sergeant that Shirley Brown had been done to death already. He did not wonder that Mr. Amberley stood there as though he'd been turned to stone. He wished he could have thought of something kind to say, but only managed to murmur gruffly: " 'Fraid we're too late, sir."

Amberley's eyes turned towards him; behind their blankness his brain was working desperately. "The dinghy," he said. "The dinghy. That means something. God, why can't I think?" He smote his hand down on the car in an impotent gesture.

"I must say, I don't see it myself, sir," said the sergeant. "What did he want it for when he had the motorboat?"

"To come back in!" Amberley said. "What other reason? Think, man, think!"

The sergeant did his best. "I don't hardly know, sir. He wouldn't hardly send the—the body out to sea in it, would he? He'll throw—— I *should* say, he'd be more likely to throw it over—— Well, what I mean is——" He broke off in embarrassment and was startled to find Amberley staring at him with a dreadful look in his face.

"My God, no, it's not possible!" Amberley said in a queer, strained voice.

" 'Ullo!" said the longshoreman suddenly. "Engine's stopped."

Amberley's head jerked up. The chug of the motorboat, which had been growing fainter, had suddenly stopped altogether.

"Well, 'e's a rum 'un if ever there was one!" said the longshoreman. " 'E can't 'ave got much beyond the mouth o' the creek. Wot's 'e want to stop for?"

Amberley gave a great start. He swung himself back into the car and switched on the engine. "Get out!" he snapped. "Get out, Sergeant. You, there—Peabody! Row the sergeant across the creek. You've got to get that man, Sergeant. Stand by that Vauxhall; he's coming back to it. God's teeth, will you get out?"

The sergeant found himself thrust into the road. The Bentley was already moving, but he ran beside it shouting: "Yes, but where are you going, sir?"

"After that motorboat," Amberley shouted back at him. "She's alive, you fool!"

The next moment he was gone, leaving two amazed creatures to stare at one another.

The longshoreman spat reflectively. " 'E's touched. Thought so all along."

The sergeant collected his wits. "You'll soon see whether he's touched or not," he said. "Come on now; I've got to get across the creek to that landing-stage I've heard so much about. Look lively!"

Back along the shore road tore the Bentley. The needle of the speedometer crept up to fifty, to sixty, to seventy. The creek was just a mile from Littlehaven, and Mr. Amberley reached Littlehaven harbour in one minute and a half and drew up beside one of the yards with a jerk that sent a shudder through the car.

There was a man in a blue jersey locking up. He looked round in mild surprise as Amberley sprang out of the car.

When it penetrated to his intelligence that the gentleman wanted to set out to sea at once in a motorboat he glanced instinctively round for protection. It seemed to him that a lunatic had broken loose from some asylum.

"I'm not mad," Amberley said. "I'm acting for the police. Is there any boat here ready to start?"

One had to humour lunatics; the sailor had often heard that. "Oh yes, sir, there's a motorboat all ready," he said, edging away.

His arm was grasped urgently. "Listen to me!" Amberley said. "A man has set out in a boat from the creek. I must catch that boat. There's ten pounds for you if you get me there in time."

The sailor hesitated, trying to loosen the grip on his arm. Ten pounds were ten pounds, but the gentleman was clearly insane.

"Do I *look* as though I were mad?" Amberley said fiercely. "Where's that fast boat you had moored here this morning?"

The sailor scanned him closely. "Lord love me, I do believe you're the Lunnon gentleman what come down here today arsting questions!" he exclaimed.

"I am. For God's sake, man, hurry! Any boat that's ready to start, the faster the better."

"Are you a plain-clothes man, sir?" inquired the sailor, awed.

"Yes," said Amberley without hesitation.

"Well, there's Mr. Benson's racing motorboat, and she's half full, I know. He had her out today, but I don't know as how——"

"Ten pounds!" Amberley snapped.

"Right you are, sir, and you takes the blame!" said the sailor, and let him into the yard.

The racing motorboat was moored some fifty yards out. The sailor, having taken the plunge, seemed to realize that the need for haste was desperate and led Amberley at a trot to the steps. In less than a minute both men were in the dinghy that was tied up there and the sailor had cast off and shipped the oars.

The motorboat was covered with a tarpaulin, which was quickly stripped off. The sailor climbed into the well and started the engine. "She's warm, sir," he said. "Lucky, ain't you?"

Amberley was at the wheel. "I hope so," he said curtly.

The boat forged ahead, threading her way between the craft moored in the harbour. The sailor, perceiving that his odd passenger knew how to steer, took heart and needed no urging, once clear of the harbour, to speed the boat up. White foam began to churn up under the bows, the engine took on a deeper note.

The sea looked silver in the moonlight, deserted. Amberley held a course to the southwest, steering for a point out at sea where he judged he would overhaul the slower boat. The minutes crept by; to Amberley they seemed like hours. The noise of the engine thundered in his ears; he made a sign to the other man to shut it down.

The sailor obeyed. The sudden silence was like a blanket for a moment. The boat glided on, began to roll. Then through the silence Amberley's ears caught the sound for which they were listening. In the distance another boat was ploughing out to sea. He put the wheel over and called to the sailor to start her up again. The boat cleaved forward in a slightly altered course.

Amberley held her on this course for another five minutes and again signed to the sailor to shut down the engine. This time the noise of the other boat sounded closer at hand.

"There she is! Go on!" Amberley said.

As he restarted the engine the sailor wondered who could be in the boat they were pursuing, and wished he had asked the gentleman. It was quite impossible to be heard above the noise of the engine, so he had to content himself with all manner of speculations, none of them, he felt, really probable. He kept an eye cocked in Amberley's direction, ready for another signal. It came very soon.

This time no sound broke the silence. The sailor, puzzled, said: "Thought we must have been right on her, the course we was steering! What's happened?"

Amberley pulled his torch from his pocket and sent its powerful beam out across the sea, sweeping a circle. It lit up the water for about two hundred yards but showed nothing but the silver ripples.

"Quickly! Start her!" Amberley jerked out. "Half speed!"

The boat began to cruise about, the torch-beam describing an arc of light ahead. The sailor heard Amberley say in a strangled voice: "Too late—God, I'm too late!"

Going round in a circle. I believe he's a looney after all, thought the sailor. Then he saw Amberley wrench the wheel hard over, staring out to where a dark object just showed above the water.

"Get on!" Amberley rapped out. "She's sinking fast!"

"Good Lord!" ejaculated the sailor, unprepared for this. "Sinking?"

"Get on, damn you!"

The boat gathered speed. They could see the other clearly now; she was down by the stern, half submerged.

The racing boat bore down upon her. "Easy!" Amberley ordered, and began to put the wheel over to come alongside. "Stop!"

The noise of the engine died, the racer glided on gently for a few feet and rocked beside the foundered boat.

The well was half full of water; Amberley had thrown his torch down to have both hands free, but the moonlight showed him all he wanted to see. Up against the side of the boat a white face was lifted just clear of the water, a scarf tied round the lower half of it.

"My Gawd in 'eaven!" gasped the sailor. "It's a woman!"

Amberley leaned over and grasped Shirley. She was strangely heavy; bound and weighted, he guessed. He said: "It's all right, my poor child, it's all right, Shirley," and shot over his shoulder: "A knife, quickly!"

The sailor, hanging on to the boat-hook with one hand, fished a clasp-knife out of his pocket and held it out. Amberley opened it and bent over the side, feeling under the water in the well of the other boat. His hand touched something hard about Shirley's waist; he could feel the links of an iron chain and the cord that tied them, and slashed through. In another moment he had her in his arms and had laid her down in the well of his own boat. She was deathly pale, but her eyes were wide open, fixed almost incredulously on his face. Her wrists and ankles were lashed together tightly; long shudders were running through her.

Amberley undid the scarf and took the gag out of her mouth; then he pulled the flask out of his hip pocket and put it to her blue lips, holding her against his shoulder. "Drink it, Shirley! Yes, I'll undo you, but drink this first. Good girl!—Take her in to shore as quick as you can, you—what's-your-name?"

"Aye, aye, sir. Leave it to me," said the sailor. "If you'll just steer her clear of this bit o' wreckage—— Thank you, Captain!" He took the wheel over from Amberley and set the boat's nose back to port.

Amberley knelt beside Shirley and cut the ropes that bound her. Her wrists were deeply scored by them, but a faint, indomitable smile quivered on her lips. "You—always—turn up," she said, through chattering teeth. "Th-thanks!"

CHAPTER XIX

THE EXPERIENCE she had gone through and the shock of her immersion had their inevitable result on Shirley. The brandy dispelled the blue shade from her mouth, but she lay in a state of semi-consciousness while the boat made its way back to port.

There was very little that Amberley could do for her. He stripped his overcoat off and wrapped it round her, but under it her own clothes were sodden, and her flesh felt very cold. He began to rub her limbs; her eyes were closed, the dark lashes lying wet on her cheek.

The sailor offered sympathetic advice and shouted once in Amberley's ear: "Who done it?" He got no answer and bent to bellow confidentially: "I thought you was off your rocker."

There was an inn on the quayside, and when the boat got back to the harbour Amberley carried Shirley there, led by the sailor. The landlady, a startling blonde of enormous proportions, came out of the bar and in spite of her appearance proved to be a capable person who took the situation in at a glance. The sailor, glad of a chance to unbosom himself, launched into a graphic description of the rescue while Amberley laid Shirley down on a horse-hair sofa in the parlour.

The landlady said: "Good sakes alive!" and sharply commanded Amberley to bring the young lady upstairs. She then screamed to someone apparently a mile away to take a scuttle up to the best bedroom, and waddled out, telling Amberley to follow her.

He carried Shirley upstairs and laid her, as directed, on a big mahogany bed in a bedroom smelling of must. The landlady then informed him that she didn't want him any longer, and he retired, feeling that Shirley was in good hands.

Downstairs he found the sailor regaling the occupants of the bar with his story, which was not losing anything in the telling. He did not wish to accept the two five-pound notes that Amberley drew out of his case, but allowed himself to be overruled after a short argument. Amberley left him treating everyone to drinks in the most liberal fashion. It seemed probable that before long he and his cronies would be cast forth into the street; he hoped the sailor would not end the night in the lockup.

The Bentley was standing where he had left it, outside the yard. He got into it and turned to drive back to the creek. It was now some time after eight o'clock and growing chilly. Amberley felt his overcoat, found it decidedly damp, and threw it onto the back seat.

He drove fast but decorously to the longshoreman's cottage, and had barely pulled on his brakes when the door opened and the sergeant bounced out.

"Is that you, Mr. Amberley?" he demanded. "Lor' sir, I've been getting nervous. It's almost an hour since you made off. Did you catch the boat? Where've you been, sir?"

"In a pub," said Amberley, himself again.

The sergeant shrugged with his emotions. "In a—in a—oh, you have, have you, sir? And very nice too, I daresay."

"Very," agreed Amberley. "Did you get him?"

"No," said the sergeant bitterly. "I didn't. And why? Because this perishing fool here hadn't thought to put any petrol in his motorboat." He realized suddenly that the bleak look had gone from Mr. Amberley's face. "Good Lord, sir, you're never going to tell me you've got her?"

"Oh yes, I've got her," Amberley replied. "She's at the pub I told you about."

"Alive, sir?" said the sergeant incredulously.

"Just. I'm waiting to hear her story."

The sergeant was moved to wring his hand. "Well, I don't know when I've been more glad of anything, Mr. Amberley. You're a wonder, sir, that's what you are—a blinking wonder!"

Amberley laughed. "Spare my blushes, Gubbins. What happened to you?"

An expression of disgust succeeded the sergeant's cheerful grin. "Yes, you may well ask, sir. A motorboat waiting! Oh, it was waiting all right—bone dry! When you went off sudden-like, I got hold of this here Peabody and told him to look lively. So off we sets, the two of us, up the creek to where he said he'd got this boat moored. Well, that was all right; he had. What's more, he'd got a little rowboat all handy to get out to it. I don't like them rickety little boats, they weren't made for men of my size, but I knows my duty and in I got. Well, Peabody rowed out to the motorboat, and a nice work he made of it, besides passing an uncalled-for remark about fat men which I'm not accustomed to and won't put up with. However, that's neither here nor there. We got out to the motorboat and come up alongside. And I'm bothered if that fat-headed chump didn't let me get into it before he remembered he hadn't filled up with petrol. Yes, you can laugh, sir. I've no doubt there's nothing you like better than clambering out of one boat into another, with the thing bobbing up and down and kind of slipping away from under your feet all on account of a born fool that can't keep it steady for half a minute."

"I'm afraid Peabody has been having a little game with you, Sergeant."

"If I thought that," said the sergeant, fulminating, "well, I don't hardly know what I'd do, though I'd be tempted, sir. Very tempted, I'd be. Well, he went and remembered about the petrol, like I said, and out I had to get again. I don't know which was the worst, getting out of that little cockle-shell or getting back into it. However, I done it, and I told this Peabody to look slippy and row for that landing-stage. Which was the best I could do, sir, seeing as the motorboat was no use and I'd got to get across the creek somehow. I won't repeat what that Peabody said, because it don't bear repeating, but——"

"I said," interrupted a voice with relish, "I said I 'adn't been 'ired to row an 'ippo across the creek, and no more I 'ad."

The sergeant swung round and perceived Mr. Peabody in the doorway. "That'll do!" he said. "We don't want you hanging about here. And let me tell you, if I have any more of your impudence it'll be the worse for you. Impeded the law, that's what you done."

Mr. Peabody withdrew, quelled by this dark implication. The sergeant turned back to Amberley. "Don't you pay any attention to him, sir."

"What I want to know," said Amberley, "is whether you saw anyone rowing back to that landing-stage."

"I'm coming to that," answered the sergeant. "I did and I didn't, in a manner of speaking. I got this Peabody to row for the other side of the creek, but the trouble was, we was so far up the blinking thing that it took him I don't know how long to get to the landing-stage. We'd just got in sight of it when I see a shadow climbing out of a rowboat like the one I was in and tying it up to one of the posts. Now, sir, perhaps you're going to blame me, because I'd got my torch in my pocket and it's a powerful one. But what I thought was: This cove hasn't seen our boat and consequent don't know he's being followed. If I was to switch the torch on to him so as to try and get a look at his face, he will know and he'll be off like a streak of lightning before I can get to land. No, I says to myself, the best thing for me to do is to keep quiet and get this chap Peabody to row for all he's worth. Which I done, sir. But we'd no sooner reached the landing-stage when I heard a car start up somewhere behind the bungalow, and a minute later I seen the headlights going off up the road that Peabody says leads to Lowchester."

"I see," Amberley said. "A pity. But on the whole, Sergeant, I think you were right."

"I'm sure that's a weight off my mind, sir," said the sergeant, relieved. "And if the young lady's alive, she'll be able to identify our man fast enough. Not but what we know who he is, eh, Mr. Amberley?"

"Do we, Sergeant?"

"Come, come, sir!" said the sergeant indulgently. "Don't you forget what I said to you when Albert Collins was shot!"

"No, I haven't forgotten. Anything else?"

"Yes, sir. One footprint, one tireprint. And the sooner I get to the police station here the better, because we want them taken. A large footprint it is, larger than what I'd have expected."

"Sergeant, you're invaluable," said Amberley. "You shall be taken to the police station at once. Hop in."

Much gratified, the sergeant climbed into the car. "Well, I done all I could, and I only hope it's going to mean an arrest."

"You'll make your arrest all right," promised Amberley. "I'm not sure you don't deserve promotion for this case. I wish I'd seen you getting into the motorboat."

"Yes, I've no doubt you do, sir. But p'r'aps instead of keeping on about me and the motorboat you'll tell me who I been chasing all this time?"

"But I thought you knew that," said Mr. Amberley, raising his brows.

"I got my doubts," confessed the sergeant. "When I said to you what I did say about that Baker—what I meant was——"

"Don't spoil it, Sergeant. You said he was my man."

The sergeant said cautiously: "Suppose I did?"

"You were quite right," said Mr. Amberley. "He is my man."

The sergeant swallowed hard, but recovered immediately and said brazenly: "That's what I was going to say—if you hadn't gone and interrupted me. Spotted it at once, I did."

Mr. Amberley grinned. "Yes? Just as you spotted the real criminal?"

"Look here, sir!" said the sergeant. "If it ain't Baker there's only one other man it can be, so far as I can see, and that's Mr. Fountain."

"At last!" said Amberley. "Of course it was Fountain."

"Yes, that's all very well," said the sergeant, "but why should he want to go and murder the young lady?"

"Because she's his cousin," replied Amberley.

"Oh!" said the sergeant. "Because she's his cousin. Of course that explains everything, don't it, sir?"

"It ought to," said Amberley, "if you can put two and two together."

The sergeant was still trying to work out this simple sum when the car drew up at the police station. Mr. Amberley set him down there and drove on to the inn on the quay.

The golden-haired landlady greeted him with comfortable tidings: the poor young lady was nicely warmed up and drinking a cup of hot soup. He might go upstairs to see her if he liked.

Shirley, looking very slight in the landlady's dressing gown and a great many shawls, was sitting on the floor in front of a huge fire sipping a cup of hot soup and drying her short, curly hair. She knew that decided knock and said, "Come in," rather shyly.

Mr. Amberley entered and shut the door behind him. He came towards the fire and stood looking down at Shirley with the hint of a smile in his eyes. "Well, Miss Shirley Brown," he said, "I do find you in awkward situations, don't I?"

She gave a small laugh but shuddered a little. "Please don't!" She glanced fleetingly up at him. "I must look an awful sight. Won't you sit down? I—I haven't thanked you yet."

He sat down in the plush-covered armchair she had vacated. "Oh yes, you have! Your manners are improving a lot. You thanked me at once."

"Did I?" She smiled at that. "I don't remember. I—when I heard the other boat—I had a feeling it was you. Did—did your policeman tell you what had happened?"

"Tucker? Oh no, he hadn't any idea. I apologize for having provided you with such a useless guardian. My own intuition brought me. By the way, Bill jumped through the kitchen window. I left him with Tucker."

"It was nice of you to think of him," said Shirley, feeling shyer than ever.

"I am nice," said Amberley coolly.

She laughed and coloured. "Yes. I—I know."

"I don't want to bother you," he said, "but there's just

one thing that's worrying me. What did you do with your half?"

She jumped and sat staring up at him. "My—my half?"

"Don't tell me you had it on you!"

"No," she said numbly, amazed at him.

"Well, where did you put it? Did you leave it about—as you left your gun about, by the way? Try and think; it's important. Your would-be assassin knew that you had it. Felicity let that out, damn her. That's why you had to be got rid of."

"Felicity?" she echoed. "How could she possibly have known?"

"She didn't. But she knew my uncle had left the book in your hands the day he borrowed it from Fountain and she said so."

She put her hand up to her head, pushing the hair off her face. "I can't grasp it. I can't make out how you knew about the book. Who can have told you?"

"No one told me. You must give me credit for some intelligence, my dear girl. Greythorne was twice burgled for that book. I naturally assumed it was the hiding-place Collins had chosen. Only it wasn't there. Owing to your absurd reticence I've been entirely at sea over that half. I only heard today that my uncle had left it behind for ten minutes at the Boar's Head. Where was it?"

She answered like one mesmerized: "In the back, pushed down behind the stitching. I found it quite by chance. But it's no good. Collins is dead, and he had the other half. It's all useless now."

"On the contrary," said Amberley. "That was Collins' half."

"Yes, I know, but he found Dawson's half."

"I hate to contradict you," said Amberley, "but he did no such thing. I've got Dawson's half."

"You?" she choked. "*You*'ve got it? But—but how did you know it existed? Where did you find it?"

He smiled. "I took it out of a drawer in a certain tall-boy. Didn't you guess?"

She shook her head hopelessly. "I thought Collins had it. I never thought of you. Did you *know* where it was?"

"No, but I followed you up from the hall when you first went to find it. When you were scared off by Collins, I went to investigate the drawer. Dawson's half of the will was in it. It confirmed all my suspicions."

"Where were you?" she demanded. "I never saw you! It seems unbelievable. I made sure Collins had got back to the tallboy before I could reach it!"

"I was behind the long curtains in the archway. When you and Collins came along the corridor together I beat a strategic retreat into the nearest bedroom. Very simple."

She blinked at him. "Was it? But how could you have known who I was? Lady Matthews hadn't set eyes on me, so it couldn't have been she who told you."

He was interested at that. "Aunt Marion? Do you mean to tell me she knows?" She nodded. "In fact, you confided in her rather than in me."

She found herself oddly anxious to refute this accusation. "No, indeed I didn't! She knew as soon as she saw me. She only told me today when I—when I asked her to send you to see me. I'm very like my father, you know. She recognized me."

"Did she?" Amberley gave a chuckle. "Ve-ry acute, is Aunt Marion. My suspicions were aroused by a certain portrait hanging on the corridor at the manor. A most striking resemblance. But all this isn't telling me what I want to know: what have you done with your half?"

"I put it in an envelope and posted it to Lady Matthews before I went to the cottage this afternoon," said Shirley. "I couldn't think of anything else to do with it."

"Thank God for that!" said Amberley. "It's the only sensible thing you've done yet." He glanced at his watch. "Now, my dear, at any moment my friend Sergeant Gubbins is likely to appear, and he'll want you to make a long statement. Before he comes I have a question to put to you. I should like a plain answer, please. Will you or will you not marry me?"

For a moment she felt that she could not have understood him. She sat looking up at him in sheer astonishment, and all she could find to say was: "But you don't like me!"

"There are times," said Mr. Amberley, "when I could happily choke the life out of you."

She had to laugh. "Oh, you're impossible! How can you want to marry me?"

"I don't know," said Mr. Amberley, "but I do."

"You told me ages ago that you didn't like me," she insisted.

"Why keep harping on that? I don't like you at all. You're obstinate and self-willed and abominably secretive. Your manners are atrocious, and you're a damned little nuisance. And I rather think I worship you." He leaned forward and possessed himself of her hands, drawing her towards him. "And I have a suspicion that I fell in love with you at first sight."

She made a half-hearted attempt to pull her hands away. "You didn't. You were loathsome to me."

"I may have been loathsome to you," said Mr. Amberley, "but if I wasn't already in love with you, why the hell didn't I inform the police about you?"

She found that she was on her feet, and that he was standing very close to her. She was not quite sure how she came to be there; she hadn't meant to let him pull her up. She studied the pattern of his tie with great intentness and said in a small gruff voice: "I don't know that I want to marry anyone who thinks I'm so objectionable."

Mr. Amberley caught her up in his arms. "My sweet, I think you're adorable!"

Miss Shirley Brown, who had just escaped death by drowning, found that a worse fate awaited her. It seemed probable that at least one of her ribs would crack, but she made no very noticeable effort to break free from a hug that was crushing all the breath out of her body.

The apologetic yet not altogether unreproving voice of the sergeant spoke from the doorway. "I beg pardon, I'm sure," it said, "but I knocked twice."

CHAPTER XX

IT was eleven o'clock when Lady Matthews, playing Patience, heard the unmistakable sound of the Bentley coming up the drive. Her husband and daughter, who had failed to induce her to tell them what was on her mind, heaved two separate sighs of relief.

Lady Matthews raised her eyes from the card-table. "Quite all right," she said. "It's come out three times running. I wonder if he's brought her here."

They heard the butler's tread in the hall and the opening of the front door. A moment later Shirley, an odd figure in garments that palpably did not belong to her, came in with Mr. Amberley behind her.

Lady Matthews got up. "I knew it was all right," she said placidly. "So glad, my dear. Did you tell Frank?"

Shirley caught her hands. "He knew," she said. "I suppose I've been very silly. He says so anyway."

Sir Humphrey, who had put on his glasses the better to survey her, looked in bewilderment at his nephew.

Amberley grinned. "Admiring Shirley's get-up? It is nice, isn't it? It belongs to the landlady of a pub at Littlehaven. Do you mind going to your study? I've pushed the sergeant in there; he wants a warrant to arrest Fountain."

"I never did like that man," said Lady Matthews.

"Arrest Fountain?" repeated Sir Humphrey. "God bless my soul, on what charge?"

"Attempted murder will do to start with. The sergeant will tell you all about it. Aunt Marion, is the last post in?"

"Certainly, Frank." She drew an envelope out of her work-bag and looked at Shirley. "Do I give it to him, my dear?"

"Yes, please," said Shirley with a sigh.

Amberley took the envelope and tore it open. Before he

drew out what was inside he looked curiously at his aunt and said: "What is this, Aunt Marion?"

Lady Matthews drew Shirley to the fire. "Probably Jasper Fountain's will," she replied.

"You ought to be burned at the stake," said Amberley. "It's a clear case of witchcraft. But only half of his will."

"Ah, that would account for it then," she said. "Better stick them together. There's some adhesive tape somewhere. My dear child, did he try to murder you? Do sit down!"

Amberley took the torn sheet of foolscap out of the envelope and laid it on the card-table. From his notecase he drew a similar sheet. "You seem to be quite sure I've got the other half," he remarked.

Lady Matthews put a log on the fire. "If you haven't, dear boy, I can't imagine what you've been doing all this time."

"I have." He went over to her writing-table. "Where is this tape? Can I look in the drawers?"

"Do by all means. Lots of bills. But I know there is some. Felicity, darling, tell Jenkins food for this poor child. And the Burgundy. He'll know."

Felicity found her tongue at last. "If one of you doesn't tell me what it's all about immediately I shall have hysterics!" she said. "I can feel it coming on. Who are you and why have you got those ghastly clothes on, and—oh, what is it all about?"

"Don't worry her now, darling. She is Jasper Fountain's granddaughter. She's going to marry Frank. So suitable. But I forgot to congratulate you. Or do I only congratulate Frank? I never know."

Amberley wheeled round, the tape in his hand. "Aunt Marion, you are a witch!"

"Not at all, Frank. Quite unmistakable. Engaged couples always look the same. Felicity, a tray and Burgundy."

Shirley interposed. "I'm very hungry, but not Burgundy, please, Lady Matthews. Mr. Am—I mean Frank—poured quarts of brandy down my throat when he rescued me. I really couldn't."

"Do as you're told," said Amberley. "That was two hours ago. And I think bed, Aunt Marion."

Felicity, who had come back into the room, went over to Shirley's chair and took her firmly by the hand. "Come on!" she said. "You're about my height. You can't possibly wear those clothes any longer. They give me a pain."

"She's going to bed," said Amberley.

Shirley rose gratefully. "I'm not going to do anything of the sort. I slept all the way home, and I'm not in the least tired. But I should like to get out of these garments."

"You may not think you're tired," said Amberley, "but ——"

"Oh, shut up, Frank!" interrupted his cousin. "Of course she isn't going to bed till all the excitement's over. Come on, don't pay any attention to him, Shirley. He's an ass."

Mr. Amberley retired, crushed, from the lists.

Ten minutes later another car drove up to the door, and Jenkins, patient resignation written all over him, admitted Inspector Fraser.

The inspector was torn between annoyance with Amberley for having kept him in the dark and delight at being about to make a sensational arrest. He assumed his curtest and most official manner, and took the opportunity to remark that the affair had been conducted in a most irregular manner. He then turned to Amberley, who was standing in front of the fire glancing through the evening paper, and asked him whether he wished to accompany the police to Norton Manor.

"Accompany you to Norton Manor?" repeated Amberley. "What the devil for?"

"Seeing that you've had so much to do with this case," said the inspector nastily, "I thought you might want to perform the actual arrest."

Mr. Amberley regarded him blandly. "I've no doubt you'll manage to make a mess of it," he said, "but there is a limit to the amount of work I'll do for you. I've given you your case; now get on with it."

The inspector choked, caught Sir Humphrey's austere eye, and stumped out of the room.

When the two girls came downstairs again an inviting supper had been spread on a table in the drawing room for Shirley. It was easy to see that Felicity had coaxed the whole story out of her, for she was round-eyed with wonderment. She had provided Shirley with her newest frock, so that it seemed that the engagement had her fullest approval.

It was three quarters of an hour later when they heard yet another car drive up to the front door, and Shirley had just finished her supper and declared herself able to talk of the events of the day with equanimity. Sir Humphrey was not unnaturally anxious to hear his nephew's explanation of all that had happened since the murder of Dawson. Even Lady Matthews was roused to request Frank to tell them about it. At the moment, she said, it was like a jig-saw puzzle. You saw what was on each piece, but you couldn't fit them together to make picture.

When he heard the car Sir Humphrey tut-tutted irritably. Were they never to be left in peace?

"I imagine it's the inspector," said Amberley. "He doesn't love me, but he knows better than to omit to notify me of the arrest."

It was not the inspector. It was Mr. Anthony Corkran followed by Sergeant Gubbins.

"Oh!" said Amberley. "Now what?"

Anthony was looking rather queer. "My God!" he said. "Sorry, Lady Matthews. I've had a bit of a shock. Look here, Amberley, this is pretty ghastly! I mean to say— Joan's all in. Perfectly frightful! I've left her with the housekeeper. I shall have to get back almost at once. Just brought the sergeant over to report. The fellow's blown his brains out!"

There was a moment of rather shocked silence. Then Amberley began to fill his pipe. "I thought Fraser would make a mess of it," he commented. "What happened, Sergeant?"

Lady Matthews said kindly: "Sit down, Sergeant. You must be worn out. Such a good thing, I feel. No scandal. Basil Fountain, I mean."

The sergeant thanked her and sat down on the edge of a

straight chair, clutching his helmet. Felicity took it away from him and laid it on the table. He thanked her too, but seemed uncertain what to do with his hands now that they had nothing to hold.

"Get on, what happened?" said Amberley impatiently.

"Just what Mr. Corkran told you, sir. Fair mucked it, the inspector did."

"I thought you were looking rather pleased. No one's going to run off with your helmet, so stop staring at it. What—happened?"

The sergeant drew a long breath. "Well, sir, we went off to the manor, me and the inspector and a couple of constables. We was admitted by the man calling himself Baker, who we know about!"

"What is his name, Frank?" inquired Lady Matthews. "I couldn't remember."

"Peterson. I didn't think you'd ever seen him, Aunt."

"Yes, dear, I called at your flat once when you were out. Never forget faces. I'm interrupting you, Sergeant."

"That's all right, my lady," the sergeant assured her. "We arrived like I said, and this here Peterson took us into the library, where we found Mr. Fountain and Mr. Corkran. Mr. Fountain wasn't looking himself, but he wasn't put out to see the inspector. Not he. The inspector showed him the warrant and said he was arresting him on a charge of attempting to murder Miss Shirley Fountain, otherwise known as Brown. Fountain sort of blinked, but he kept his head all right. I tipped the wink to the inspector to get the handcuffs on him sharp. Unfortunately the inspector wouldn't have it I knew better nor what he did, and instead of collaring Fountain and talking afterwards, he started in to tell him how the whole game was up, for all the world as though he'd discovered it himself. Regular windbag, he was. Of course when he let out about the young lady being rescued, Fountain could see the case was pretty hopeless. It's a queer thing, sir, but as soon as he heard that he give a sort of sigh like as if he was quite relieved. He said—which surprised me—that he was glad. 'I never meant to do any of it,' he says. 'It was forced on me. I've been through hell,' he says. Then he says: 'I'll go with you. I'm damned glad it's over,' he says—begging your pardon, my lady. Then he says: 'There's something I'd like to take with me,' and moves towards his desk. Of course I hadn't ought to have spoken, not with the inspector there, but I couldn't help myself. 'You stay where you are!' I tells him. 'We'll get whatever it is you want.' And I'm bothered if the inspector, just to give me a set-down, didn't tell him he could get it if it was in the room, and welcome. Told me to mind my own business and not teach him his. All in front of the two constables what's more, which he'll wish he hadn't done when it comes to the chief constable inquiring how it happened.

"Well, he lets Fountain go to his desk. Any fool could have told him what would happen. He opens a drawer and before you could say knife he'd whipped out a gun and blown his brains out."

"And Joan," said Corkran, "was standing in the doorway."

"I'm sorry," said Amberley.

"So am I," Shirley said. "I know Joan Fountain hadn't anything to do with it. I didn't want her to be hurt by it all."

"Well, as a matter of fact," said Anthony confidentially, "I don't think she will be, apart from this nasty little show tonight. I mean, he wasn't her full brother, and she never made any bones about the fact that they didn't get on. Bad shock, of course, and all that sort of thing, but you wait till I get her away from the manor." A thought occurred to him. "I say, I suppose the manor belongs to you now, doesn't it?"

Shirley said uncomfortably that she supposed it did. Mr. Corkran brightened considerably. "Well, that's something anyway," he said. "Never could stand the place myself. Altogether rather a good show. But I don't grasp it yet. Why were Dawson and Collins popped off? What had they got to do with it? Come on, Sergeant! You seem to know all about it. Spill the beans!"

The sergeant said that it would come better from Mr. Amberley. Mr. Amberley, with unwonted politeness, begged him not to be so modest.

The sergeant coughed and shot him a reproachful look. "I'm no hand at talking, sir," he said. "And I wouldn't wonder but what there's a point here and there didn't happen to come my way."

"Frank shall tell us about it," stated Lady Matthews. "Someone give Mr. Corkran something to drink. The sergeant too. Or mayn't you?"

The sergeant thought that he might stretch a point seeing as how he was, strictly speaking, off duty, and had been since six o'clock.

Amberley leaned his shoulders against the mantelpiece and glanced down at Shirley, seated on the sofa beside Lady Matthews. "I don't think I can tell you the whole story," he said. "There are one or two things it wouldn't do for the sergeant to hear about. Or my uncle, for that matter!"

"My dear Frank, pray don't be absurd!" said Sir Humphrey testily. "Why should we not hear the whole story? It is bound to come out!"

"Not unless I choose," replied Amberley. "To make it clear to you I should have to divulge certain illegal proceedings which might conceivably induce the sergeant to make two more arrests."

The sergeant smiled. "You will have your joke, sir. I don't know what you done, though I always did say and I always will, that you'd make a holy terror of a criminal."

"H'm!" said Mr. Amberley.

The sergeant, who by this time would have compounded a felony sooner than be left in the dark, reminded him that he was off duty. "Anything you say to me now won't go no farther, sir," he assured him.

"Very well," said Amberley. He puffed for a moment at his pipe. "To go back to the start." He drew the crumpled will from his pocket and read the date—"which was on 11th January, two and a half years ago, when Jasper Fountain made a new will. This is it. It was drawn up by himself on a sheet of foolscap and witnessed by his butler, Dawson, and his valet, Collins, in favour of his grandson Mark, or failing him, of his granddaughter Shirley. From which I infer that he had only just learned of their existence. Or he may have had a change of heart. It's quite immaterial. He left the bulk of his property to Mark Fountain and the sum of ten thousand pounds to his nephew Basil, who, under the previous will, inherited the entire estate. I find that he died five days later, which would account for the fact that no lawyer drew up this document. Jasper Fountain obviously feared he was very near death. What was done with the will I don't know, but that the two witnesses obtained possession of it at Fountain's demise is positive. Whether they tore it in half then or later, again I don't know. At some time or other this was done, the valet keeping one half and the butler having the other. Basil Fountain inherited the estate under the terms of the old will, and these two blackguards instituted a form of blackmail, holding the later will over his head." He paused and again looked down at Shirley. "You shall tell us why Dawson approached you," he said.

"I think he was afraid of Collins," she replied. "Collins wanted to get back his half. Dawson struck me as a timid sort of creature, not really cut out to be a blackmailer. I don't know how he discovered us." She flushed. "You see—my father was—not a particularly estimable person. When he died my mother moved from Johannesburg and called herself Brown. Mark and I kept that name after her death, and when we returned to England. I wasn't proud of our own name. Mark didn't care much either way. However, Dawson found us and wrote to Mark. It was a most mysterious letter, hinting at the existence of a will in his favour and warning him of all sorts of danger. It's at my bank now. I thought I'd better keep it. Mark thought it was a hoax. I didn't. I came down to Upper Nettlefold to inquire for rooms. Ivy Cottage was to let, and I took that. It suited me better really, because of—because of Mark's —habits. I made Mark write to Dawson, telling him he'd meet him. That frightened Dawson; he didn't want us here, it was too dangerous. He came once to the cottage, but he was terrified of being seen there, and he wouldn't come again. He told us very much what you've heard from Frank. He wanted to get out—I don't think he was afraid of the police so much as of Collins. He offered to sell us his half." She broke off and looked towards the sergeant. "Of course I knew I was going against the law in negotiating with him, but I couldn't put the matter into the hands of the police, because not only was the will torn in half, but if Collins got wind of the fact that the police were on to him he'd immediately destroy his half."

"Very awkward, miss," agreed the sergeant, who had been listening spellbound.

"The trouble was," Shirley continued, "he wanted a ridiculous sum for it, and naturally we couldn't possibly raise anything like the money until we came into possession of my grandfather's estate. It was rather a deadlock, but in the end we reached a compromise, and Dawson—principally, I think, because he was afraid if he held out we should make trouble with the police—agreed to trust us. He was to meet Mark on the Pittingly Road on his evening out and hand over his half of the will—which seemed to me better than nothing. In return Mark was to give him a plain I.O.U. for five thousand pounds."

"Hold on a moment, miss! Was your brother present when he was done in?" demanded the sergeant.

"You're off duty, Sergeant," Mr. Amberley reminded him. "We now come to my own nefarious conduct. You remember that I told you I wasn't sure that I was on your side?"

"I do, sir," said the sergeant, regarding him round-eyed.

"I informed you," proceeded Amberley, "that I had discovered the body of a murdered man in an Austin Seven saloon on the Pittingly Road. What I did not tell you was that standing in the road beside that car I found Miss Shirley Fountain."

The sergeant's jaw dropped. "Suppressing valuable evidence, Mr. Amberley, sir!"

"Exactly. But Fraser would probably have got her hanged for the murder if I'd spoken. Now you begin to understand why this very dull crime interested me so much. Dawson was alive when you found him, wasn't he, Shirley?"

"Just alive. He knew me. He hadn't brought his half of

the will. I don't know why not. Probably because he wanted to squeeze us for more money. Anyway he managed to tell me where it was. Then you came."

"You mean to tell me, sir," said the sergeant, "that you knew about this will, and all the rest, right from the start and never let on to us?"

"Not at all. I knew nothing. But I was interested. The only thing I knew was that the murder had been committed for the purpose of robbery. When I learned Dawson's identity I assumed that as it could hardly be money that he had, and as nothing of value was missing from the manor, it was in all probability a document. I made the acquaintance of Basil Fountain. It was on the occasion of my first visit to the manor that my suspicions were roused against Collins. He was rather too anxious to overhear what I had to say. What the connection between him and Fountain was I had no idea, but that there was one I was fairly certain. Fountain knew he was listening at the door, and he didn't want us to guess that. It seemed to me a point worth remembering, too, that Collins' alibi rested on Fountain's word alone. I was sufficiently interested to make a few casual inquiries about Fountain. Before I connected him with the crime at all, you, Aunt Marion, had divulged that you did not like him. I have a great respect for your instinct. You, Felicity, said that he was always grumbling about money. He kicked up a fuss about the cost of Joan's fancy dress. When I made his acquaintance that didn't fit in with his obviously generous, rather extravagant nature. He was the type of man who likes spending money. On the face of it, it looked as though he were hard up. Why? His fortune was considerable, and you, Anthony, informed me that he didn't go in for excesses. You described him quite accurately as a bonhomous sportsman. You also informed me that although he and Joan had never hit if off life had gone more or less smoothly until he came into possession of his uncle's estate."

"I seem to have told you the hell of a lot," remarked Anthony.

"You did. It was to you that I owed my knowledge of

his fondness for the sea. You described his bungalow at Littlehaven to me and the super motorboat he had, which was capable of crossing the Channel. At the time that conveyed nothing particular to me. It came in useful later. You also told me that he had asked you to remain on at the manor, actuated, you thought, by funk. He did not want to be left alone there. That might have arisen from his undoubtedly gregarious nature. On the other hand it looked very much as though the presence of guests in the house was a protection. So it was. While you and Joan were there Collins had to walk warily. Fountain was beginning to be afraid of him. He knew that Collins had murdered Dawson, but he dared not give him away for fear Collins should counter with the real will—which Fountain undoubtedly thought he possessed in its entirety. That he didn't eliminate Collins then was due, I feel sure, to his perfectly sincere horror of death. If you remember, Anthony, Miss Fountain mentioned that on the occasion of my first meeting with her. He could not bear the thought of a dead body—even a puppy's.

"After the inquest you, Sergeant, told me of Dawson's money. It puzzled you. You could find no explanation for it. It was then that the thought that he might have been blackmailing Fountain crossed my mind. But what you, Shirley, had to do with any of this I had no idea until the night of the fancy-dress ball at the manor. You attended that ball, quite uninvited, in the costume of an Italian peasant-girl."

"Good Lord, was it you?" cried Felicity. "Joan and I wondered who on earth it could be, because you weren't there at the unmasking. I say, how perfectly thrilling of you!"

"Restrain your ardours, my love," requested Mr. Amberley. "When I discovered the contadina's identity I thought it worth while to keep an eye on her. It did not seem to me probable that she had gate-crashed the ball from a mere desire to be at an amusing party. Putting two and two together I inferred that she had seized the opportunity to get into the manor for some very definite purpose. Then I saw the Reynolds on the passage."

"Beg pardon, sir?"

"A portrait, Sergeant. The portrait of a lady of the late eighteenth century. The resemblance is most striking, Shirley. Fountain came upon me while I was studying this portrait, and from what he said I knew that he was unaware of your presence in the district. He was not much interested in the picture but remarked, with perfect truth, that the lady had the family beetle brows. He thought she was probably a great-grandmother but recommended me to ask the housekeeper.

"The main facts in my possession then were, briefly, these: that Fountain's butler had been shot with robbery as the motive; that a mysterious lady bearing a startling resemblance to the family had been present on that occasion and was now masquerading in the house in disguise; and that Jasper Fountain had had a son, then deceased, whom he had disinherited on account of his predilection for drink—and other things. It proved nothing, but was an interesting coincidence that Mark Brown also drank." He paused and pressed the tobacco down in the bowl of his pipe with his thumb. "We now come to the extremely reprehensible proceedings of Miss Shirley Fountain. Dawson having informed her that his half of the will was hidden in a certain tallboy, she went to find it. She was interrupted by the appearance of Collins, who was watching her with great interest. Both he and she left the tallboy, which was in the passage leading to the picture gallery, and went downstairs. A bad moment, wasn't it, Shirley?"

"Thanks to you!" she retorted.

He laughed. "All your own fault, my dear. Well, when the two of them had gone I had a look in the tallboy myself and found the torn half of a will. Part of Jasper Fountain's signature was on it, and most of the signatures of the two witnesses. The names of the legatees were upon the other half, but the thing seemed fairly obvious in spite of that.

"In due course Shirley came back to the tallboy. Finding the will gone she leaped to the conclusion that Collins had been before her. Right?"

"Of course," she said. "What else could I think?"

"I'll tell you later," he said. "Collins, who came a few minutes later to secure the missing half, naturally assumed that Shirley had outwitted him. An engaging state of mind on both sides."

Shirley interrupted. "Yes, I've no doubt, but why couldn't you have told me you had it?"

"My good child, once I had that torn paper in my possession there was very little you could tell me that I didn't already know. It was, in fact, infinitely better that neither you nor Collins should know who really had the will. Your combined antics were far more helpful to me than your confidence would have been. There was another reason too, which concerns you and me alone. To continue: On the following day I sustained a visit from Colonel Watson and agreed to take on the case. I now held most of the strings of it. I knew that there was a later will in existence which at least two people were painfully anxious to get hold of. Your anxiety, Shirley, led me to suppose that it was in your favour; Collins' anxiety confirmed my previous suspicion that he was blackmailing Fountain with it. It seemed probable that he held the missing half. The first thing to be proved was your identity, and the main problem was how to get hold of the rest of the will, which obviously existed. It was no case for the police, who wouldn't have acted on an entirely valueless half. I went up to London. I instructed my man Peterson to apply for the vacant post of butler at the manor and provided him with a faked reference, which reminds me that you gave him a bad moment over that, Sergeant."

"Ah!" said the sergeant deeply.

"Quite. I thought it possible that he might manage to get hold of a clue to the will's hiding-place, but my chief object in putting him at the manor was to have someone watching Fountain's movements. It seemed to me that it could only be a matter of time before Fountain discovered who was living at Ivy Cottage, and when he knew that, anything might happen. On this same visit to town I visited the *Times* office to look through the back numbers for a notice of your father's death, Shirley. That represents the only occasion in my memory when you've let me down, Aunt Marion. Your recollection of dates is lamentable. He died five years ago, not three."

"Tiresome for you, dear boy," agreed Lady Matthews.

"It was. However, I found the notice at last and took down the address in Johannesburg. Then I sent a cable to a firm of inquiry agents there to ascertain whether he left any issue, and if so what became of the issue. To speed things up a little I also employed a private detective agency in London to trace the records of Mark and Shirley Brown.

"When I got back to Greythorne I found you there, Anthony. You gave me, though reluctantly, a valuble piece of information. You divulged that Fountain had received a letter from a firm of private detectives and that it had very much upset him. That could only mean one thing: he too was trying to discover what offspring his cousin had left and where they were. The fact that he was upset seemed to point to him knowing that both Mark and Shirley Fountain were actually at his gates. You told me next day that he had had a row with Collins. I imagine he had jumped to the conclusion that Collins was double-crossing him. Things were beginning to move rather quickly, and the devil was in it that while Collins still held that vital portion of the will it was extraordinarily hard to take any sort of action.

"Putting in a little detective work on my own I came to call on you, Shirley. That was a lucky coincidence. You, believing that Collins now possessed the entire will, had determined to try and buy him over and had sent for him to come and see you. He came because he thought that you held Dawson's half and might destroy his little game. I saw him leave Ivy Cottage. I imagine you must both have fenced very skilfully on that occasion, since neither of you was aware at the end of the interview that the other was not, after all, in possession of the missing half."

She smiled ruefully. "We did. We didn't even mention the word will."

"I should have loved to hear you," he remarked. "When Collins had left the cottage I entered it. You may possibly recall that I told you I had come for a piece of information which I managed to get. I ascertained that you had been in South Africa. Your kaross of King Jackal skins and your brother's artless conversation told me that. It was not proof, but good enough to go on with.

"The next move in the game was made by Fountain, who rang up to ask me to go over to see him. He had all along been keeping a weather-eye cocked in my direction. He was nervous, and like most people in that condition he couldn't leave well alone. He had to try and put me off the scent. Between them he and Collins hatched up an extremely improbable story about Dawson to account for the butler's inexplicable wealth. It had its uses: I was able to hand it to the inspector to investigate. He liked it very much, and it gave him a little harmless occupation.

"While I was at the manor a disturbance occurred. Mark Fountain, under the influence of drink, came to the house with a hazy idea of forcing Collins to disgorge the will by threatening to shoot him. It was very awkward for Collins."

"Good Lord, was that why he kept on urging Basil to let the kid go?" demanded Corkran.

"Yes, that was why. And since Fountain, who didn't know Mark from Adam, had every intention of sending for the police, Collins was compelled to divulge his identity. If you remember, he used the words: 'The young gentleman from Ivy Cottage,' which instantly enlightened Fountain. That incident looked as though I was right in my theory about his letter from the detective agency. In fact, it was all fitting in very nicely. But Mark's idiotic conduct was a serious complication. I can't say that I actually expected Fountain to make an attempt on his life: I had no reason to suppose that he was the type to commit a murder; but it was a possibility one couldn't ignore. I had him watched, not in the least unobtrusively. I regret to say that I thought the mere knowledge that the boy was being shadowed would be enough to choke Fountain off. He certainly wasn't pleased about it, but he wasn't as easily baulked as I'd expected him to be. I paid a visit to the manor just to let him know that I had put a man on to

Mark. Incidentally I saw that Peterson was safely installed.

"That evening I received the answer to my cable to Johannesburg. There was now no longer any doubt about your identity, Shirley, and I thought it well to pay a visit to Sergeant Gubbins to get him to tighten up the watch on Mark. Unfortunately I was too late. While I was at the police station the news of Mark's death came through." He paused and looked down at Shirley. "I'm sorry if this distresses you. I have something to say about it."

"Go on," she replied curtly.

"Mark," said Amberley, "did not fall into the river because he was drunk. He was drunk, of course—very drunk—but he was pushed in. Being drunk, he drowned. It was a murder planned so cleverly that I doubt whether it could ever have been brought home to Fountain. Mark's habits were a byword in Upper Nettlefold; several persons had wondered aloud how it was that he hadn't stumbled into the river long since. It is also a well-known fact that at this season of the year the mist that lies over the Weald after dark is nearly always pretty thick in that hollow where the road runs beside the Nettle. Fountain trusted to luck—or perhaps knew—that Tucker would not be following Mark particularly closely. For Mark's death Inspector Fraser was indirectly responsible. He gave Tucker to understand that he was being put on to that job merely to humour a whim of mine."

The sergeant coughed. "Be making a report, I expect, sir?"

"I shall, Sergeant, but don't interrupt. Fountain gave out that he was going to London that afternoon. He probably did go. If he hadn't had any luck in what he meant to do I have no doubt that he would have repeated the manœuvre next day. But he had luck. It all turned out as he had expected. He left his car probably in one of the lanes leading on to the main road and lay in wait for Mark beside the river where the fog was thickest. When Mark appeared he had only to push him over the bank. I don't suppose it required much strength, and in any case Fountain was a very powerful man. The river is fairly deep; Mark drowned, being too drunk to make any effort to save himself."

"Yes, but supposing he hadn't drowned?" objected Anthony.

"That would have been annoying for Fountain, of course, but not dangerous. If the boy had said that some-one pushed him in, who would have believed him?"

"You would," said Anthony.

"Possibly, but although Fountain was suspicious of me he never knew how much I'd found out. No, the thing was safe enough—and it worked. Had the mist been less thick, had Collins not lost sight, temporarily, of Mark, it would not have worked. But Collins was too late to save the boy's life, though there is no doubt that he put forth superhuman efforts to do so. From the moment that Fountain learned of his cousins' presence in Upper Nettlefold Collins was on the watch. He knew Fountain better than I did. His story about the cigarette case, Sergeant, was quite untrue, but I daresay Miss Fountain would have confirmed it, wouldn't you, Shirley?"

She nodded. "I was completely in his power. If he had the will I dared not give him away. That was partly why I didn't confide in you. He suspected you from the start of knowing much more than the police."

"And therefore it was unsafe to confide in me lest I should betray my knowledge? Many thanks. Now on the day following the murder Fountain came to call on me at Greythorne. Ostensibly his object was to inquire into Collins' presence on the scene. Actually he came to discover, if he could, what I was thinking and whether you, Shirley, were remaining at Ivy Cottage. I gave him to understand that I suspected Collins and also that you were remaining at the cottage. Since he had eliminated Mark I expected him to make an attempt on you next, and my plan was to catch him in the act and arrest both him and Collins on two separate charges. I should have been able to do that very successfully had it not been for the well-meaning but disastrous zeal of Corkran. When I took you to the cottage to collect your things, Shirley, I unbolted the back door and appropriated the key. Having desposited you at the

Boar's Head I motored back to Greythorne and rang up
Peterson, telling him to keep an eye on Fountain and let
me know if he left the house that night. You came into the
room in the middle of that conversation, Felicity, and
remarked that I had sweet telephone manners. Do you
remember? Peterson rang me up just after midnight to say
that Fountain had left the house and gone off on a push-
bike. I then got on to you, Sergeant, and we drove to Ivy
Cottage to await his arrival. Then, when things were
panning out almost miraculously well, Corkran gave the
alarm and Fountain escaped by the back door. You were
rather fed up with me for letting him go, weren't you? To
have stopped him would have been sheer folly. I couldn't
prove a thing against him except that he had broken into a
strange house. It had its amusing side, of course. Not only
did you follow him, but Peterson, having caught sight of
you pedalling down the drive, followed you both. Unnecessary but equally zealous. He didn't recognize you, and
fearing that I might be surprised by two criminals instead
of one, came along to lend a hand. I saw him when I went
to bolt the back door, and he was just going to come and
speak to me when he caught sight of you, Anthony, and
tactfully beat a retreat.

"That was Fountain's first attempt to murder Shirley. It
is my belief that he meant it to look like suicide—the
reason being Mark's death. Not a bad idea. But I gave
you a clue, Sergeant, and I think—I really think you
ought to have guessed a little more than you did. I pointed
out to you that whoever broke into the cottage evidently
did not know that Miss Fountain owned a bull-terrier.
Collins did know that, for he had been to the place
before. I am sad, Sergeant; sad and disillusioned."

"Yes, it was a nice clue, wasn't it, sir?" said the sergeant bitterly. "There might have been half a hundred
people that didn't know that."

"But Collins did know," said Mr. Amberley.

"Yes, sir, and I don't mind telling you now that that's
why I ruled him out," said the sergeant, fixing him with
what he hoped was a hypnotic stare.

"Ananias," said Amberley. "You take my breath

away." He put his pipe down on the mantelpiece and pushed his hands into the pockets of his trousers. "Then," he proceeded, "Uncle Humphrey took a turn."

"What?" said Sir Humphrey.

Amberley glanced down at him in some amusement. "You did, sir. You went to talk to Fountain about poachers, and you walked off with the missing half of the will."

"What the devil are you talking about, Frank?"

"Which," continued Amberley imperturbably, "Collins had concealed in the back of the book you borrowed. I should like to know whether Collins saw you take that book away."

"Yes!" Felicity said. "He did, and now I come to think of it he tried hard to get it out of Daddy's hands. He offered to dust it, and to wrap it up, but Daddy refused."

"So there was nothing left to do but to burgle this house," said Amberley. "But as my uncle took the book up to bed with him the attempt to regain possession of it failed. When I observed the very curious nature of the burglary it gave me furiously to think. It was Aunt Marion who supplied the clue. She wondered why the books had been strewn about. I really thought I was on to it at last, but when *Curiosities of Literature* was brought to me there was no sign of the missing will in it. Nor did either you or Felicity, sir, call to mind that you had left the book for a few minutes in Shirley's keeping. I shall find that very hard to forgive.

"On the following morning Peterson rang me up to tell me that a woman, he thought Shirley Fountain, had telephoned to Collins."

"Yes, I remember that," interposed Corkran. "I told Basil, and he was jolly annoyed."

"I've no doubt he was. It would account for his following Collins that evening, just as I followed Shirley. She had an assignation with Collins at the pavilion by the lake. I spent a very boring day keeping an eye on her. The assignation was kept, but Fountain kept it too, and so did Peterson, whose job was to watch him all the time. Had Fountain managed to catch Shirley I think he would have killed her there and then. Happily he didn't find her. I did instead.

"But that assignation drove Fountain to desperate measures. If Collins was double-crossing him Collins also must be got rid of. And providentially my uncle had shown him a fairly good way of doing that."

Sir Humphrey bounced in his chair. "I?"

"Yes, you, sir. All your talk of poachers. I'm not blaming you. I even think it was a very good thing, for there is no doubt that Collins murdered Dawson and equally no doubt that we should have had great difficulty in proving it. But before Fountain could accomplish this design Collins made another attempt to get the fatal book back. Rather a bold attempt, but a successful one. Meanwhile Peterson was searching diligently through the rest of the books in the library without any success at all. It was an unnerving period. The will had evidently gone astray, and if by some malign chance it fell into Fountain's hands it would of course be immediately destroyed. When Collins, on discovering that it was no longer where he had put it, leaped to the conclusion that I had got it, and ransacked my room here, I was most relieved. It showed me that at least Fountain hadn't got it. If he had he would have taken good care to let Collins know he had burned it. On his way back to the manor from this house Collins was shot by Fountain, who, if you remember, Sergeant, had spent most of the evening conveniently writing letters in the library.

"Again Fountain was a little too careful. He could not resist ringing up the police the same night. The reason he gave for doing that was rather too plausible. I never trust a plausible explanation. As soon as Peterson knew, he searched Collins' room for the half of the will but didn't find it. I expect you noticed, Sergeant, that he told me he'd found nothing when you had him in to interrogate him."

"That's right, sir," said the sergeant. "Noticed it at once, I did."

"You're wasted in Upper Nettlefold, Sergeant," said Amberley.

"Well, sir, p'r'aps I wouldn't mind a change," replied the sergeant visibly gratified.

"Try the stage," recommended Amberley. He left the sergeant to think this out and continued: "Fountain now began to give himself away. Instead of saying as little as possible and leaving Fraser to make a muddle of the case, he had to try and improve it. No sooner had he got rid of Collins than he proceeded to knock the bottom out of the valet's alibi for the night of Dawson's murder. That was overdoing things. Up till that moment he had refused to believe that Collins could have done anything he shouldn't; similarly he had refused to sack the man in spite of his evident dislike of him. But when Collins was safely out of the way we were told that he had been sacked that very morning. Let me remind you, Sergeant, that you asked me when we left the manor what I made of it all. I told you that there were one or two significant points. Those were the points."

The sergeant, who was becoming reckless, said: "I wondered whether you'd seen them too, Mr. Amberley, sir."

"Fortunately," said Amberley dryly, "I had. It appeared to me that Fountain was getting into a tight corner and knew it. It was on the day after Collins' murder—this morning, in fact—that I took the precaution of paying a visit to Littlehaven."

"I was told you were investigating the murder," remarked Lady Matthews.

"Officially I was. I had no desire to let Fountain get wind of my real whereabouts."

"But, Frank, what made you go to Littlehaven?" asked Felicity.

"That motorboat," answered Amberley. "I hadn't forgotten the existence of a boat capable of crossing the Channel. I'm not going to pretend that I foresaw the use it would be put to. I didn't. What I did suspect was that Fountain, realizing in what danger he stood, would have arranged a getaway in case things started to go wrong. The motorboat seemed the obvious way of escape. When I got to Littlehaven I made inquiries and discovered that she had been taken from Morton's Yard and moored to a buoy a little way up the creek, past Fountain's bungalow. She had been overhauled, and when I rowed out to take a look at her I found her all ready for sea. It looked as though my surmise was right, so I employed our friend the longshoreman to watch her and notify me by telephone the moment anyone took her out. This would have enabled the police to get on to the French ports and stop Fountain there. I still think that Fountain's original reason for having the motorboat in readiness was to provide himself with a way of escape. Once Collins was dead he hadn't the smallest desire to hurt Shirley. Without the will she could do nothing. Not one of his murders did he want to commit. I can quite believe that he spoke the truth when he said he had lived through hell. If he had never inherited his uncle's estate he would have remained what I think he was at heart—a cheery, kindly natured chap who only wanted a comfortable life and enough money to indulge his highly commendable tastes. The trouble was that he had regarded himself as Jasper Fountain's heir for so many years that when he found that he had been disinherited it was unthinkable for him to relinquish everything but ten thousand pounds. He had practically no private means, but had always received a large allowance from his uncle. He struck me as cunning when hard pressed, but by no means a profound thinker. I am certain that he never visualized the possible consequences of his initial, and comparatively mild, crime. The two servants could be kept quiet by a little money, and although it wasn't by any means the sporting thing to do, no doubt he argued that Shirley and Mark couldn't miss what they had never known. He had been brought up to regard the manor as his, and I expect he felt that he was more or less justified in suppressing the later will. Once he had taken the one false step everything else was, as he said, forced on him. And I believe that he hated it and would have chucked up the sponge if he could have done so without landing himself in gaol." He paused. His audience sat silently waiting for him to go on. "But Fountain's mental processes, though interesting, are rather off the point. I said that once Collins was dead nothing was meditated against Shirley. That, I am convinced, is true. But fate, in the person of my misguided cousin, dealt Fountain a blow. He learned from her of the adventures his book, *Curiosities of Literature,* had been through. She told him how interested I was in that book and how there was nothing in it, and although she had not remembered to inform me that Shirley had had it in her possession long enough to find the half of the will hidden in it, she had no difficulty in remembering it for Fountain's benefit."

"That'll do," said Shirley, quite in her old manner.

"It precious nearly did for you," retorted Amberley. "Fountain knew then where Collins had kept the will, and he knew that you'd got it. Having gone so far he had to finish the job or be caught himself. You know what happened next. Had it not been for my never-to-be-too-highly commended aunt, you might now be at the bottom of the sea. As it was, she passed on the information to me together with Peterson's telephone message, and I just managed to get to Littlehaven in time. Guessing all the way too."

Corkran found his tongue. "Guessing! Is that what you call it?"

"It is," said Amberley. "I'd no certainty. Once I found he'd struck south it was the best I could do. Luckily it turned up trumps."

"Just a minute," said Shirley. "Can you—*guess*—why he chose that way of killing me, and didn't take the motorboat out and just drop me overboard? It's been puzzling me."

"Yes, I think so," he replied. "For one thing it would have taken too long, and he wanted to get away from Littlehaven as quickly as possible. For another, I believe he was horrified at what he was doing. Remember, he had that curious complex about dead bodies. Because of that he didn't kill you before he sent you out to sea. You told me that he never spoke to you nor looked at you. I can quite believe that. The man was in hell, scarcely sane." He strolled over to the table and took a cigarette out of the box and lit it. His eyes travelled from one shocked, enthralled face to another. "I think that pretty well covers the ground," he said. "An interesting little case."

"Covers the ground!" ejaculated Anthony. "Well, I don't know what anybody else thinks, but in my opinion you're a blinking wonder! And don't you tell me you knew all about it, dear old Sergeant, because I'll bet you didn't!"

The sergeant replied without hesitation. "No, sir, I did not. But what I do say is that if Mr. Amberley hadn't gone suppressing valuable clues, like what he did when he never let on about the young lady being beside Dawson's body, it would have been a sight better for everyone. Why, if I'd have known *that,* we'd have had the whole case solved in a jiffy!" He met Mr. Amberley's eyes and repeated doggedly: "In a jiffy, Mr. Amberley. I don't say you haven't done well for an amatoor, but what you wanted, sir, was a trained mind on to it. That's what you wanted."